MW00439393

This book is dedicated to my beautiful wife, Tiffanie and my little bugbear, Lorelei. You both inspire me to be so much more than I could ever have imagined. To my mother, who always had faith I'd succeed. I'm still working on it, mom. To my friends and family who've always been there for me; I love you all. To Whitneye, for everything.

To Cookie Corrigan for supporting me and giving me a place to hide. To Josie, Jodale, and all my other early readers, thank you for wading through my slop. To the ladies of my writing group, Kim and Michele, thanks for keeping me on track. To Ben and Isaac for all the support and encouragement. To Mike, Art, Michelle, Liz, Jackie, and Adam for making two years of misery fun. Esydra!

Acknowledgements:

To Jessy Lucero for the amazing art.

The Enemy of My Enemy

There was a time when being related to Lucifer was enough to keep the proverbial wolves from the door. Judging by the snarling bastard who stood over me, his meaty fist dotted with my blood, those days were gone.

"Well, good morning to you too," I mumbled, looking up through watering eyes. My nose throbbed something awful.

The big bruiser—Marcus D'anatello—just smiled. While a pretty big guy myself, certainly not lacking in the muscle department, I had nothing on Marcus. Built like a silverback gorilla on steroids, he hovered over me enjoying the moment. His Armani-suited bulk blocked out what little light filtered between the buildings. Fortunately for me, his bald head and pearly white teeth provided enough to see by. I didn't like what I saw.

He gestured for me to get up, taking a short step back to give me room. I did so, hesitantly, expecting to be hit again. He surprised me.

Marcus and I had a history. It wasn't so long ago I took a 2x4 to that gleaming dome of his. I dented it up pretty damn good. Turns out, he's not the most forgiving of fellows.

"What can I do for you, Marcus?" I asked, not really expecting an answer that didn't involve his fists.

"It's not what you can do for him, Mr. Trigg, but what you can do for Baalth," a reserved, measured voice answered from behind Marcus.

I peered around D'anatello's hulking shoulder to see an older man striding toward us. My stomach tightened into a hard knot as I recognized him; Alexander Poe, Baalth's psychic enforcer. Dressed conservatively in an understated gray suit, a look of solemn determination etched into his face. I knew then it was business, not personal. Something was going down.

"Where's the bitch?" Marcus asked, the smile gone, his eyes feral.

As a modern man, relatively speaking, I've known many women who would have stood up and declared themselves the bitch he was looking for. However, I knew the instant he asked he could only be looking for one woman; Scarlett. Only she would be so willfully spiteful as to rattle the cage of a demon as powerful as Baalth.

"Why, you looking to get lucky?" It wasn't like I felt the need to protect Scarlett, she could take care of herself—being an angel tended to help in that department—it just went against my nature to give in to bullies.

The blur of Marcus's fist smashed into my

forehead before I even saw it. There was a meaty thunk, which I heard rather than felt, as my head collided with the brick wall. A whirl of stars filled my vision as the pain caught up to me. I slid to the ground and dropped unceremoniously onto my ass. Immediately, I felt the knot growing in the center of my forehead, easily the size of a golf ball already. I imagined I looked like a retarded unicorn.

"Once more, where's the bitch?"

I looked up at Marcus, or at least tried to; my eyes wouldn't uncross. I rubbed them to quell their revolt and through the blur, I saw the bruiser pull his fist back again.

"All right, all right." I chose the better part of valor. I may not like bullies, but I'm no martyr. You gotta choose your battles. This wasn't one I was willing to take on. Besides, it's not like I knew anything. "I don't know where she is."

It wasn't like Scarlett and I were friends. Cousins? Yes, but friends was a stretch. In my book, she wasn't a whole hell of a lot better than the big ape in front of me, but she served her purpose. Had I known where she was, I probably would have given her up.

Not liking my answer, Marcus reared back to hit me again. Normally, I would have just shot him and saved us both the grief; me from having to take a beating and him from having to live with all that anger rattling around inside. I'd have been doing him a favor, but I promised Abraham I'd play nice with Baalth. My shooting his goon would violate the old guy's trust no matter how good it would feel. So, I tucked my chin and waited for the hammer to fall. Abraham would be so proud. Yay me.

"Leave him be," Poe interrupted. "He's telling the truth."

As a mentalist whose power few humans could match, Poe knew I wasn't lying. Though he wasn't able to read my mind, my devilish genetics distorting his readings, he could still pull off a surface scan, which told him all he needed to know. It worked better than any lie detector I'd ever seen.

Marcus growled like a dog who didn't want to relinquish a bone. I could almost see the rusty wheels in his head spinning as he mulled over his options. None of them were good for me.

Poe's icy eyes narrowed. "We're done here, Mr. D'anatello." He laid a narrow hand on Marcus's shaking arm when the big man didn't respond. "Now is not the time for your personal vendetta." There was a finality in his voice, which was hard to ignore.

Marcus huffed and lowered his fist with reluctance. He glared at me, straightening his tie unconsciously. It looked more like he was strangling it. "You'll be seeing me again, Trigg."

"Always a pleasure." I tried to give him a welcoming smile, but judging from the look on his face

I missed my mark. I probably should have kept my tongue in my mouth.

He backed up about ten feet, his cold eyes on me the whole time, then turned and stormed out of the alley. Poe cast one last piercing glance in my direction before he strolled off after Marcus.

Once they were gone, I pulled myself to my feet, grunting. My head still throbbed on both sides. I ran my hand across the back of my shaved scalp and felt a small cut dribbling with blood, but nothing major. I touched the knot on my forehead and hissed. That was a good one. The bastard hit like a freight train. The things I do for people.

"You better be happy, Abraham," I shouted, my voice echoing down the alley.

"I'm sure he is, Frank."

I jumped when I heard the voice, and whirled about drawing my chromed .45 from the small of my back. I lowered it as soon as I saw the golden mane and grinning face of the angel it framed. "Goddamn it, Scarlett! Don't do that."

"Wow, a gun. That would have come in handy a minute ago." She smirked, clearly having witnessed Marcus's assault. The one I'd taken on her behalf. I could feel my anger welling up as I stared at her.

She leaned casually against the wall, her lithe figure defined by the skin-tight leather outfit she wore. Cousin or not, I couldn't help but follow the swollen trail of her V-neck blouse, her breasts a sight to behold. I have to give it to God, He knew how to make 'em. How could I be mad at those?

I slipped my gun back into my waistband and pulled my shirt out to cover it. It helped to cover everything else, as well. What can I say? I'm easily aroused.

"Oh, and don't use the Lord's name in vain. He doesn't like it," she warned, her palm absentmindedly fondling the hilt of her sword, Everto Trucido, loosely translated as Demon Slayer. I looked away from the mesmerizing sight of her hand sliding up and down the pommel, trying to keep my thoughts in check. Having seen the blade in action, I didn't want to be on the receiving end of it. It lived up to its name.

I couldn't, however, pass up an opportunity to give her grief. "What's He gonna do, strike me down?" I raised my arms and looked up to the heavens, chuckling.

Her eyes narrowed and the smile dropped from her face. I stifled my laughter and lowered my arms, not wanting to upset her more than I already had. The last thing I needed was to add a pissed off angel to my list of enemies. I might not get along with her all that well, but barring what I'd do if I found her gagged and tied to a bed, I sure didn't want to go to war with her. I think the worst part was she knew I could say whatever I wanted and God wouldn't do anything. He wasn't around *to* do anything.

You see, about fifty years ago, the Almighty and Lucifer had a sit down. Weary of the battle for the hearts and souls of humanity, they decided they'd had enough. They wanted an end to the war. Rather than raze existence and start fresh, they decided humanity had, for the most part, come into its own and had too much history and character to simply be wiped away. I guess they felt pity for the chess board pieces they battled over for so long. So instead, they chose to abandon it, letting it evolve as it would. An instant after they made their decision, they disappeared into the void, leaving the whole of creation behind.

The consequences of which were devastating. Connected to God in a way no other creature could claim, the angels were hit the hardest. It was as if the most important part of them had been ripped away, a festering black abyss left rotting in its place. Many went insane. As for the rest, well, let's just say there are varying degrees of insanity.

I could see the strain in Scarlett's eyes, their perfect green suffering from the loss of her Lord; herself. Her hand shook as it clutched the pommel of her sword, her knuckles white. I could see the tenseness in her shoulders, the quivering of her lip. Under the circumstances, I did what any gentleman would do for a woman whose whole world, whose life, whose very existence was crumbling down around her.

I changed the subject.

"So, what'd you do to piss off Baalth?"

She glowered at me, putting her hands on her hips. I could tell she wasn't sad anymore. The snarl on her face kind of gave that away. Mission accomplished.

"I meted out some divine retribution," she replied, her voice tinged with frost.

"Can you be more specific?"

She huffed. "I intercepted a shipment of guns last night."

I shook my head. "So, are we talking about the five-alarm fire at the railyard that wiped out at least twenty warehouses as well as destroyed two cargo trains and caused a handful of deaths?"

She shrugged. "What was I supposed to do? Let them deliver the guns so Baalth's men can use them to kill innocent people?"

"I didn't say all *that*." Subtlety was a foreign concept to Scarlett. "I just don't think it makes a lot of sense for you to go burning down the city. You're drawing attention to yourself and that's not good."

"Why not?" She puffed her ample chest out. "The humans need to know."

I tore my eyes from her cleavage and gathered my thoughts, yanking them from out of the gutter. Puppies and kittens, puppies and kittens. "What do they need to know? That God and the Devil have gone on permanent vacation? That they've left humanity to the mercy of a bunch of crazed angels and bloodthirsty demons who want nothing more than to bring about Armageddon?"

"Yes, exactly."

I rubbed my temples. "We've been over this a thousand times, Scarlett. If the humans knew what was really going on there'd be wholesale panic, chaos. They'd start killing each other in the streets, destroying everything they could get their hands on. You'd be helping the
pro-Armageddon forces bring about the end. Is that what you really want?"

"Would it be so bad?" I could see the weariness, the loneliness wearing on her, the emptiness welling up to moisten her eyes.

"You're starting to sound like Gabriel."

She wrinkled her nose at me. "I'm not suggesting we help bring it about like he wants, but maybe oblivion isn't such a bad alternative."

"How can nothingness be cruel?" I quoted the immortal words of Bayou poet, Dax Riggs.

She gave me a gentle smile. It made my crotch tingle.

"The truth is I'm not ready to not exist yet." I didn't think she was either. "Besides, it's not our place to make these kinds of decisions. It's way above my pay grade, for sure. God should be the one to say whether or not to pull the plug on existence. He willed this mess into existence so it's His job to clean it up."

She threw her arms up. "He's not around to make that decision."

I played my ace. "Don't you think He'd have wiped it all out before He left if that was what was in His heart?" I danced on the inside when I saw her resistance crumble.

"I guess you're right." She had a hard time admitting that, her voice slow to mouth the words.

I resisted the urge to rub it in. "Yeah, so how about we try to minimize the collateral damage and only burn down five warehouses next time, huh?" I tried to look compassionate. She probably just thought I had gas. "Oh, and maybe lay off Baalth a little bit too. I don't need his goons pounding my head in every time you decide to go vigilante."

"Get over it." She poked my forehead, the knot already gone. "It's not like they can hurt you."

That wasn't entirely accurate. I could be hurt just like anyone else. I still felt pain. I could bleed, break a limb, have my head cracked open, jaw busted; I just healed fast. That, and I can't be killed by any weapon forged by human hands. I guessed that was what she was talking about. She was still wrong though.

"I just don't appreciate it."

She rolled her eyes. "Well, I'm off to do some good for the world. Are you on your way to visit the Super Friends at the Halls of Justice?"

"The fact you know who the Super Friends are

frightens me." I shook my head. "And it's called work. You should try it sometime."

Scarlett laughed. "To each their own." She spun around and gave me a lazy wave as she strutted down the alley.

I can't say I was sad to see her leave, but I sure liked watching her go, or however that song went. Leather does a body good.

After she was gone, I gave myself a minute to get everything composed, then went off in search of some hot coffee. If my early morning encounters were any indication as to how the rest of my day would go, I was gonna need some caffeine.

DRAC

Certain I wasn't followed, I slipped into the alley behind the abandoned Plaza Theater, a cup of steaming, frothy goodness clutched in my mitts. I stayed close to the building to avoid being seen by anyone in the nearby low-rent apartments that faced the alley and made my way to the rear stage door. Once there, I grabbed the rusted handle and felt the familiar tingle of sensory wards, followed by the quiet click of the door unlocking. After another quick glance about, I whipped the door open and went inside. The instant it closed behind me I felt a gentle wave of mystical energy prickle the hair on my arms as the portal hummed to life. A gentle tickle danced along the nape of my neck as the humming intensified. A second later, the teleportation spell took hold, whisking me away. Less than a heartbeat later, I arrived in the receiving room at DRAC headquarters.

DRAC, or Demonic Resistance and Containment, was an organization that sprung up in response to the growing demonic threat after God's disappearance. Though it was later realized the pro-Armageddon forces weren't limited to demons, the name stuck. Founded by Abraham Solano, a psychic savant whose visions foretold of God's disappearance, the group had since gathered to their cause the most powerful wizards, psychics, and mystics the human race had to offer. Abraham would soon learn how big a mistake that was.

Only eighteen at the time of DRAC's formation, Abraham had little practical leadership experience. Without thought to the consequences, he set about gathering the world's magic and rallying its practitioners. For twenty years, he scoured the planet amassing the largest collection of magical resources and manpower ever compiled, in a single location. He would live to regret the last.

Not fully realizing the scope of what he'd envisioned, Abraham was caught off guard when the pro-Armageddon forces took note of DRAC's existence. Drawn to the shining beacon of power, which was the organization's mystical cache, demons raided the compound, laying waste to it. Few survived the attack. Most of the knowledge and artifacts gathered were stolen or destroyed. The organization shattered.

Wounded and ridden with guilt, Abraham would take another ten years to recover and muster the courage to reform DRAC. Nearing his seventies, he had learned the lesson of his past failure. The location I appeared at, just one of many secret facilities, was a testament to that.

Accessible only by teleportation, the receiving room was designed to contain intruders, both supernatural and human, who might make it past the initial portal security. On the floor was inscribed a large silver pentagram, its five points surrounded by the empowered summoning circle in which I appeared. Set upon the walls were an array of defensive wards, each designed to handle a defined instance of magical threat. The specifics were lost on me. Alongside them were small jets that could fill the room with poisonous gas. Above me, the thirty-ton steel roof was held in place by high-pressure hydraulics, which could be lowered to crush everything in the room. That part always made me nervous.

I stood there staring at the ceiling as I was assessed by DRAC security, my skin tingling from the scans. After what felt like forever, the circle powered down and a seamless door slid open in front of me. I waited for my escort, standard operating procedure, and looked to the door when a shadow blocked the light. My heart skipped a beat when I saw who it was. I took a sip of my coffee to hide my nervousness.

Katon De Peña was DRAC's muscle, their enforcer, their assassin. He didn't do grunt work, so I knew something was up. I felt a chill run down my spine as I speculated the reasons for his appearance. None of what I imagined was good. I had to admit, I wasn't looking forward to being killed. That would seriously ruin my day.

He could do it too. He was damn good at his job.

Though born human, Katon had long since become something else. Struck down by a vampire, he was rescued by Rahim Alakha, a powerful wizard on DRAC's High Council. Unable to save Katon's mortal life, Rahim evicted the vampire's spirit and corralled Katon's dying essence, installing it in place of the vampire's. Grateful for the rescue, Katon pledged his services to Rahim and DRAC. He'd worked with them ever since.

Dressed in black; jeans, T-shirt, calf-high boots, all topped off with a classic biker jacket with studded forearms and shoulders, he looked every bit the heavy metal badass. The hint of a smile etched his dark face. I could just see the points of his eyeteeth peeking out from under his top lip.

At his waist hung a short sword less than two feet long, its blade a deep crimson. Forged from the tip of the Spear of Longinus, the Holy Lance, which pierced the side of Jesus Christ, the sword was fearsome. It was said Christ's blood stained the blade, and having met Longinus, I could vouch for that fact. I could feel the power emanating from it.

"And to what do I owe this unexpected pleasure?" I asked, keeping my tone neutral, or at least attempting to. I took another sip of coffee.

He waved me through the door into the wide,

well-lighted corridor beyond. "I heard you had a run-in with Baalth's men."

"News travels fast."

Katon shrugged, his feral eyes peering at me. "Any particular reason why?"

"They were looking for Scarlett. It seems she made a bit of a mess at the railyards. I'm sure you saw all that on the news."

He nodded. "No other reason?"

I stopped and tossed my cup into a nearby trash can, its taste suddenly bitter, then turned to face him. "Why the twenty questions?" I didn't like challenging the guy, but I didn't appreciate the attitude.

He turned to me, his face cold, emotionless. "There's a lot of chatter about Asmoday ramping up to take a shot at Baalth. I was just wondering if his men brought it up."

"Why would they?"

"You and Baalth have a history," he stated bluntly, staring at me the whole time. "I thought he might be looking to cash in some old favors, what with him saving your life and all."

I felt my anger boil up to color my cheeks. "He may have saved my life an eternity ago, but I sure as shit don't owe him anything." I took a step closer against my better judgment. "Are you questioning my loyalty?"

"You are part devil."

He had me there"But to answer your question, no, I'm not. I'm just passing on a warning. Keep an eye out for a play by Asmoday. The info I have says he's got a surprise in store that'll shake up the status quo." He took a step back and waved me down the hall. "The last thing we need is another major player on the block gunning to be the next Lucifer. At least with Baalth, it's the devil we know, so to speak."

I started walking, only slightly mollified. "So, what's the plan?"

"Abraham will fill you in on the specifics, but the goal is always the same. Support the anti-Armageddon factions against the pro and keep DRAC out of the spotlight as much as possible."

I nodded, my anger still buzzed at the back of my mind. We walked the rest of the way to Abraham's office in silence. At the door, Katon turned to me.

"I've got a lead to hunt down. If I find anything, I'll make sure you hear about it." He patted me on the shoulder. I flinched. "Don't take it personally, Frank." With a wink and a sharp-toothed smile, he turned and left.

I took a moment to compose myself. Despite having lived for almost five hundred years, surrounded by death, I never once gave it much thought. But having Katon escort me in got me to thinking. In the old days, when God and Lucifer were in their places, death only meant I'd be recalled to Hell. No big deal in the grand scheme of things. I'd spend some time puttering around the Circles before getting back in line to be returned to Earth. Nowadays though, death was the end, even for me. There'd be no recall. No second, fifth, or tenth chance. I felt a cold chill run down my spine at the thought. I didn't like the feeling.

I derailed my morbid train of thought before it could run off the tracks and entered Abraham's office. The subtle scent of aged books hit me as I opened the door. I drew it in with a deep breath. I'd always loved the smell, so I took a few seconds to savor it.

A devoted collector of the written word, Abraham had more than his fair share of great books. The entire back wall of the large room was covered with shelves of rare books, magical tomes, and various dictionaries and encyclopedias, in a multitude of languages. Even more impressive was they were all hardcover, not a paperback to be seen.

Unlike the bookshelves, neatly ordered and pristine, the rest of the office was homey and cluttered. The oversized chairs and couch were upholstered in soft leather, dyed a deep burgundy. They were covered in a mismatched array of small pillows. Abraham's oak desk was a disaster zone of epic proportions. Its face was buried under a mountain of files and papers, which encircled his computer monitor.

Abraham looked up from his desk and saw me standing at the door. He waved me over with a subdued smile.

While old in human years, Abraham had a vitality about him, which defied his age. His bright green eyes flashed with intelligence through his glasses, his balding scalp just flashed. He gestured for me to sit.

"Have a seat, Frank. How are you?" He peered at me over the mounds of paperwork as he gestured to one of the chairs in front of the desk. I moved a multicolored pillow that only a grandmother would think attractive, and tossed it onto the couch before I dropped down. It was a day for leather, it seemed.

"Other than a mild heart attack at being greeted by your assassin, I guess I'm doing all right."

Abraham chuckled. "You should know by now, Frank, if we wanted you dead, we wouldn't dance around the issue. It would just be so."

He had a point, frightening as it might be. I took what little comfort in it I could and let it go. "So, what's the deal with Asmoday?"

He pulled off his glasses, setting them on the desk as he leaned back. "Word has it he's looking to take out Baalth and has figured out a way to do so."

Baalth was one of Lucifer's chief lieutenants until the powers that be went splitsville. Rather than giving in to the chaos caused by Lucifer's departure, Baalth took advantage. It's what demons do best. He left the Circles behind to set up his own little Hell on Earth. Entrenched in the mortal world, answerable to no one but himself, Baalth was in no great hurry to usher in the end of existence. As such, he often worked behind the scenes to thwart the pro-Armageddon forces while openly working against the Angelic Choir. That earned him enemies on both sides. Most recently, it had been Asmoday he'd pissed off.

"Any idea how?"

Abraham shook his head. "Not so far. We have Katon hunting down information, but Asmoday has been careful not to let anything useful slip." He raised a finger as if suddenly remembering something. "We also have Rachelle out testing the integrity of the gates. She'll be able to determine if anything big has come through recently."

Rachelle Knight was the third of the triumvirate who made up the High Council of DRAC. Though human, Rachelle could only be described as otherworldly. Her tall, thin frame moved without effort. She seemed to glide, her head somewhere in the clouds. She always seemed disconnected from reality. Her powers as a mystic though, rivaled those of the angels. She was not a woman to be trifled with.

"What do you need me to do?"

"For starters, we need to do something about Scarlett." His look made it clear that by "we" he meant "me".

"It's not like she's gonna listen to me. She's a grown angel who does what she wants."

"I'm not asking you to put a leash on her. I'm asking you to give her another focus." His words set my mind off on a tangent. I reined it in.

"Like an angelic hand grenade, you want me to pull the pin and toss her at Asmoday?"

"Crudely put, but yes. We do not need Baalth distracted by her misguided holy crusade while Asmoday waits in the wings. It also wouldn't hurt for her to cause Asmoday a little grief."

"Fair enough. What else?"

"I want you to pass this on to Baalth." He slid a folder across the desk. "This is all the intelligence we have regarding Asmoday's attempted coup. Make sure Baalth understands the precariousness of his situation."

I picked up the folder and shook my head as I flipped through it. "I'm all for leveling the playing field a bit, but don't you think we're going a bit too far by providing him with firsthand information?" I met Abraham's eyes. "We're playing with fire just by tolerating Baalth. We sure don't need to be hopping in bed with him."

"Our options are limited, Frank." I could see the frustration on his lined face. "We don't stand much of a chance against Asmoday as things are now. If he manages to usurp Baalth's place, there'll be no stopping him. Our best bet is to play the factions against each other in the hopes they weaken themselves, giving us an opportunity to take advantage. As it stands, Baalth is our safest bet."

I hated when the old man was right. It happened a lot.

"I guess I'm playing errand boy."

Abraham gave a crooked smile, celebrating his victory behind a mask of professional composure. "Be sure you're fully equipped. If Asmoday realizes you're playing Baalth against him, you could be in for some trouble."

And the Understatement of the Year Award goes to...

I stood up, the leather of the seat peeling away from my skin with a perverse sound. I couldn't help but grin. "I'm already in trouble. You've got little old me walking into the wolf's lair to let him know the jackals are outside." I threw my hands in the air. "This sheep is screwed."

"Always the optimist," Abraham chided.

"I don't need to be psychic to see my future." I rubbed my ass as I headed toward the door.

"One more thing, Frank," Abraham called out

before I left. "There's a rumor Veronica is back in town."

His statement hit me like a brick. I looked back at Abraham hoping to see a sparkle in his eyes, some indication he was joking. There was none. I hung my head and left the office, my skin clammy and cold, hands shaking.

As I headed off to face certain doom, caught between the two most powerful demons ever to walk the earth, all I could think about was that my ex-wife was in town.

Death couldn't come soon enough.

Keep Your Enemies Close

A couple of phone calls later and I had a meeting with Baalth set up. Lucky me.

He agreed to meet at a rundown strip mall in Old Town, at the edge of downtown El Paseo. Even in this one horse town with a bum hoof, Old Town stood out, though not in a good way. The entire neighborhood was one short step from being condemned. The only thing keeping it from being leveled were the healthy bribes that flowed from Baalth's coffers to the City Council. These under the table transactions also bought Baalth a healthy dose of freedom when it came to law enforcement in Old Town. The only time the police showed up was when Baalth requested their presence or the national news got whiff of something big and it couldn't be swept under the rug. Even then, the residents of Old Town understood in the end, no matter what, Baalth was pulling the strings behind the scene. He was the law: judge, jury, and willing executioner.

To paraphrase the Vegas commercial, what goes on in Old Town, stays in Old Town, usually in a shallow grave or hastily converted BBQ pit.

Full of rat-infested tenements, immigrant clothing shops, low-end car dealerships, and bustling pawn shops, Old Town was a haven for criminal activity.

Those who frequented the area were either crooks or victims, all too poor to escape.

I parked at a seedy pay-by-the-hour lot downtown and walked the rest of the way to Old Town, grumbling about the price. While the car belonged to DRAC and I really didn't care whether some lowlife snatched it or not, I didn't want to hear the endless diatribe about my carelessness. I'd heard it way too often.

Once on the strip, I pulled the hood of my dirty sweat jacket over my head and tried to appear inconspicuous, stuffing the folder Abraham had given me into my back pocket. Face toward the sidewalk, I peeked out of the corner of my eyes as I strolled down the walk. Harangued by the scads of shopkeepers trying to sell me everything from velvet Elvis paintings to generic prescription drugs, I pushed my way past them. I could smell the stinging aroma of green chili peppers being roasted nearby. It did nothing to hide the biting stench of the trash cans, which overflowed with rotting meat and decayed vegetables. Worse than either of those, I could smell the desperation of the Old Town residents, thick in the air. The cloying scent, like a losing high school locker room after a big game, stuck with me as I walked. Combined, it all smelled like Hell. I felt a little homesick.

As I neared the dilapidated electronics store where our meet had been set, the tinny sound of Black

Metal being blasted from an inferior car stereo drew my attention. I glanced over my shoulder and saw a beat up gray Chevy van driving slowly down the street, its windows down. I caught the gaze of the passenger as the van approached, his long black hair bouncing up and down as he mouthed the words to Emperor's "Inno A Satana."

He stopped singing when he saw me. His eyes turned cold and locked on mine. As the van rolled by, his gaze shifted to the mirror, watching me in the reflection until they rounded the corner. You gotta love the bravery of today's wannabe Satanists. They still think they're going to Hell.

"Forever will I bleed for thee, forever will I praise thy dreaded name," I muttered, catching the rhythm of the vocal line as it faded away. I laughed as I wondered what those kids would think if they knew Satan had made up with God and moved on, leaving them behind. That'd ruin their whole world view.

At the shop, I put on my serious face. I had work to do. I pulled the door to the electronics store open and the sound of ringing bells cleared the song from my head. That was fine with me, I much prefer Venom anyway.

I glanced about and spotted a handful of tables and wobbly shelves covered with ragtag blenders and low-watt microwaves. There were a few old TVs and FM radios scattered about the shop, along with a couple of turntables, but nothing I could see was worth a damn. To top it off, a thick layer of gray dust covered everything. For a front, this one was real obvious. I guessed they didn't have to try all that hard with Baalth's money lining the local constabulary's pockets. Corruption breeds apathy.

I looked to the counter and a short, fat guy wearing coveralls glared back at me. The sweat on his bald head reflected the sickly glimmer of the fluorescent lights. His hands were out of sight behind the counter, his arms wiggling. I was hoping it was a gun he was fiddling with down there and nothing else. Deep inside my head, I heard banjos playing. It brought a smile to my lips.

I stood there a minute before I realized he didn't intend to say anything. "I'm here to see Ba—" I caught myself. "I'm here to see Mr. Smith." That was the name they'd given me, seriously.

The fat guy gestured with a meaty thumb toward a curtained alcove at the back of the store. I gestured back. I don't think he appreciated it.

Without waiting for the limbed bowling ball to decide whether he was offended enough to get up, I slipped past the curtain. Beyond it stretched a narrow hallway that led to a closed door. I knocked and heard a muffled, "Come in." I turned the handle and stepped through.

Inside the cramped room full of battered

merchandise set on rickety shelves, a round wooden table sat in an opening near the back. Behind it sat Baalth. His flunkies D'anatello and Poe stood on either side of the door. I winced as Marcus pressed the barrel of his 9mm Browning against my temple.

"Make a move, I dare you," Marcus growled. His attitude hadn't improved any since the last time I'd seen him.

I could see his trigger finger quivering. "No, I think I'm good. Thanks." I stood as rigidly as I could. Even though Marcus's shot wouldn't kill me, it sure as hell would hurt more than just my feelings.

Disappointed, he pressed harder.

"You'll have to forgive our rudeness, one can never be sure these days," Baalth commented, sounding almost sincere.

The grin on his tanned face told a different story, however. Dressed in a high-dollar suit with a fancy tie, Baalth looked every bit the Wall Street financier. Most demons did.

You see, contrary to popular perception, demons and devils don't have horns and tails and run around wielding pitchforks. Well, maybe farmer demons have pitchforks, but it's not the norm. We look like humans, as do angels. We were all made in His image, after all. Some of us just pull it off better than others. Take Baalth for instance. His sculptured hair and perfectly trimmed goatee lent him a look of professionalism.

His manicured hands and perfectly shined shoes just screamed out confidence. His eyes, on the other hand, said volumes about the cruelty that lurked beneath his innocuous appearance.

I kept quiet, letting things play out.

Poe patted me down, starting at my legs and working his way up to my crotch.

"Easy there, Crocodile Dundee, that gun's attached."

The mentalist snickered in a way that made me think he was unimpressed as he went about his business. He slipped my .45 out of the small of my back and snatched the extra ammo strap I had picked up at DRAC headquarters. Done with the search, he set my gear on Baalth's desk and posted up beside his boss. Marcus just stood there pressing his gun to my head. He looked fit to blow a gasket, as usual. Baalth coughed and D'anatello reluctantly stepped back to the desk. He didn't lower his gun, though.

"You said you had some information for me," Baalth said, getting straight to the point.

I passed the folder to Poe, who handed it to Baalth. After a minute of reviewing its contents, he set it on the desk and raised his eyes to meet mine.

"What exactly do you stand to gain by giving me this?" Baalth gestured to the folder.

"Me personally? Not a damn thing." I saw Marcus tense up, just waiting for an excuse to shoot me. "But, as sick as it makes me to admit it, the world is better off with you than it is with Asmoday."

Baalth smiled so wide I could count his teeth. I stopped at five. I get bored easy.

"So, what do I get out of taking on Asmoday?"

I stood there shellshocked. "What do you mean?" My mind ran in circles, the hamsters trying their best to keep up.

"What's in it for me?" he repeated.

"Your ass is what's in it for you. Maybe you no speakie engrish, but I didn't think it was all that hard a concept to grasp."

Marcus growled and stepped forward. Baalth waved him back.

"Oh, I understand all right," he countered. "I just don't see anything in it for me. Asmoday is just one demon amongst thousands gunning for me." He tapped the folder. "You haven't given me anything I didn't already know. So, why should I step up and fight Asmoday when I can step aside and let you do all the work then clean up the mess afterwards?"

I have to admit, he had me stumped. Despite all the time I'd spent around demons, it never ceased to amaze me just how low they'd stoop to come out on top. "I'll keep Scarlett off your ass," I blurted out, my brain finally engaging.

Baalth just laughed. "You plan to do that already. You can't have her waging war on me because you need me at full strength to fight Asmoday."

I muttered a few unkind words under my breath. It only made Baalth smile wider and Marcus turn a deeper shade of red. "What's it gonna take to get you onboard, you know, considering it's your life on the line and all?"

"It's all of our lives, Frank," Baalth corrected. "You keep forgetting I'm a demon. I have no problem with Armageddon coming to pass. It's a minor inconvenience, all things considered."

Even though I knew he was lying, it wasn't in my best interest to call him on it. "Fine. So, what do you want?"

"I'm thinking a favor, to be collected at a later date."

Damn demons. It's always about the favors. Spend enough time around these guys and you'll owe them your nuts, if you're lucky. "I don't think that's gonna work. I guess we're done." I turned and stormed toward the door.

"Such theatrics. I'm sure we can work something out, Triggaltheron."

I hated when demons used my given name. It made me feel all icky inside, like I had a bad case of worms. I turned back and glared at Baalth.

"Come now, it'll be a minor favor. I won't ask you to betray your comrades or anything of that nature," Baalth cooed. "Imagine how disappointed Abraham will be when you return to DRAC empty-handed."

I could. "You're a bastard." I stuck my hand out for the contract.

As clichéd as it seemed, contracts were what brought order to the chaos of the Demonarch, the demon world. Signed in blood, a contract between demons or devils was as binding as they came. Fail to meet the terms of the deal and your soul was forfeit, its energy devoured and added to that of the contract holder.

To a demon the level of Baalth, these little deals were more of a formality than a means to gaining true power. My soul to him was like a drop in a bucket when it came to magical energy. But for the little guys like me, these deals were like playing the lottery. While the offer was always stacked in the favor of the dealmaker, the contract worked both ways. If the contract holder defaulted, the signatory had every right to claim the holder's soul and all the power that came with it. That was the hope that burgeoned every time I signed one of these damn things. With that kind of energy, I'd finally be able to cast magic just like the rest of the big boys.

Baalth pulled a sheaf of papers from a desk drawer and passed them to Poe. He in turn handed them to me. I sighed as I looked them over, the text as obscure and legally confusing as any written by the most sadistic of human lawyers. Fortunately, I'd seen my fair share of demonic contracts. While far from ideal—they never were—the terms of the agreement were just what Baalth had laid out. I could live with them.

I growled, then bit the palm of my hand until it bled. Once I had a little pool going, I bent my wrist to let it run down across my fingers. I flipped my hand over and pressed it down on the contract, making sure I left a clear mark. Once I was done, Poe took the signed contract and handed me a small towel. I used it to clean off the remaining blood, the wound already closing.

"Then we are agreed," Baalth said as he took possession of the contract.

I nodded. At least I got what I came for, no matter how much I'll likely regret it later. "Pleasure gettin' fucked by you." Ready to go, I pointed to my gear. "Mind passing me my piece?"

Marcus laughed. I noticed he did that a lot when he had the upper hand. It was kind of petty.

Baalth picked my gun up and examined it. "No, I think I'm going to hang onto it, just to be on the safe side." He winked at me.

"You motherfu—" The word caught in my throat as Baalth pointed my gun at me.

I hadn't wanted to get shot by Marcus because it'd hurt, plain and simple. But I'd survive it. That wouldn't be the case if Baalth shot me. Unlike Marcus's bullets, mine weren't made by humans. Crafted by a lesser angel and demon pair in the employ of DRAC, each was empowered with a drop of holy and unholy blood. Blessed and cursed, this made the bullets anathematic to angels, demons, and devil alike. In layman's terms, they'd blast a big hole in me that I couldn't heal without magical assistance. As it stood, I was perfectly content with the holes I already had.

"No need for violence. You can keep it." I raised my hands and took a step back. I did my best to smile and look gracious. I doubt I was very successful. I could picture myself looking like Johnny Depp in those pirate movies of his, only not quite so swishy.

Now don't get me wrong, I've nothing against effeminate men, but seriously, a pretty little fellow like that has got to be careful. One minute it's *Pirates of the Caribbean*, the next it's Sodomy on the Bounty, know what I mean? Besides, how are you gonna swing a sword effectively with wrists like that?

"How generous of you," Marcus barked, snapping me back to reality as he pointed to the door. "Time to go, Trigg."

I looked to Baalth who just nodded. So, with no reason to hang around and risk making things worse, I headed for the exit. At the door, I pulled it open and started through. Baalth called to me as I did.

"Any word from your uncle?"

I couldn't help but laugh. "Why? You worried I'm gonna tell on you?"

"Hardly. I'm just curious to know if he's been in touch."

"Have no doubt, if Lucifer were to return, you'd be one of the very first to know. I'd make sure of that." I left it at that and slammed the door behind me.

I walked swiftly down the hall and slipped past the curtain. The fat shopkeeper glared at me as I made my way out the front door. I ignored him. Once outside, I let loose a whistling sigh. I hadn't realized I'd been holding my breath.

Wanting to put some distance between Baalth and myself, I crossed the street and headed a couple of blocks over. I wanted to avoid the shopkeepers as well. Alone on a deserted side street, I finally relaxed a bit as I headed toward downtown to retrieve my car. That's when I heard the muffled sound of a vehicle coming up from behind, moving too slow to be passing traffic. I spun around to see a gray van idling a short distance down the street, a long-haired guy at the wheel. The side door had been pulled open and two more longhairs crouched inside and though the music had been turned down, I could still hear the muffled thunder of metal. It was Deicide this time. How ironic.

I met the gazes of the crouching Black Metallers as they neared. There was mischief in their gaunt faces. I shook my head and slowed my pace. If they were here to play, I was in the mood to oblige them.

Blast from the Past

I stopped as the van pulled up on my left side. I turned to face the longhairs with a smile.

"Something I can do for you boys?"

The two in the back hopped out as the driver put the van in park and stepped out, moving around the hood to join his friends. They all looked the same, with their black biker jackets covered in spikes and satanic patches. Each had on a different concert T-shirt proudly proclaiming their lack of Christian ethics, and each wore too tight black jeans with steel-toed stomper boots. They also wore the same slightly pointed goatee and narrow mustache. It was hard to tell them apart. Individualism gone astray.

"Eenie, Meenie, and Meinie." I counted them out. "Where's Moe?"

Their only response was to smile; a trinity of yellowed grins, which would have made any self-respecting dentist cringe. Before I could say anything else, the driver pulled a boot knife out and took a step toward me, waving the blade. His friends retrieved their weapons from inside the back of the van. The first pulled out a short sword, the second a small spear. They joined the first in his advance.

It was my turn to laugh. "C'mon guys, you really want to do this? Trust me when I say Satan isn't going to be impressed."

Eenie, the driver, responded with violence. He lunged in and slashed at my chest. Instinct took over. I whipped my arm up to block the shot, catching the blade flush on my forearm as I prepared my counter. I felt the blade bite into my flesh. I had expected that. What I didn't expect was how much it hurt. I heard a sizzle as the knife cut into me. A searing pain shot up the length of my arm, all the way to my shoulder. Flashes of light danced before my eyes.

I stumbled back, clutching my arm as the driver stood there laughing. I hadn't paid any mind to the weapon when he'd waved it in my face, but now all of my attention was focused on it. It was no ordinary knife. Carved down the length of the blade were runes, symbols of power. I looked at the other weapons and they too, had runes set into them. I realized this wasn't just some random act of violence. It was a hit.

"Who sent you?" I asked, stalling for time. It sure would have been nice to have my gun. Fucking Baalth.

Eenie took a step closer, ignoring the question. He waved Meenie and Meinie forward. "Kill him!"

Shit! I pushed away the pain and moved into the street toward the back of the van, hoping to put its bulk between us to slow their advance. I reached it just as Meinie thrust his spear at me. I sucked my stomach in and the point just missed hitting home, tearing a gash in my hoodie. In response, I pinned its shaft to the hood, then threw a right hook. Meinie turned his head just in time to avoid getting hit on the chin, but I caught him hard on the ear.

He fell into his buddies, blocking their approach, though he managed to pull his spear free. As it slid past, the blade caught my hand, slicing deep into the palm. I cried out as I felt its magic burning its way through my veins.

I fought back the urge to vomit and stumbled around the back of the van. Meinie sat in the street shaking his head to clear it while Eenie circled around the hood of the van to approach me from the driver's side. Meanwhile, Meenie timed his advance so he and Eenie could come at me from both sides at the same time. Unarmed and wounded, things didn't look good for me. I looked down the deserted business street, but there was no way I could make it around the corner before they were on me.

The two longhairs closed in as my mind scrambled to think of a way out. I stared straight at the van's double doors as I watched the two in my peripheral vision. Just then, an idea sprang to mind. As they reached the back of the van, I leaned forward and grabbed the latch of the back door. Fortunately for me, it was unlocked. I popped it open and swung it to my left with all my might. The door slammed into Eenie with a resounding thud. He crumpled. One down.

I spun to face Meenie, but he was faster. I heard the whistle of the short sword right before it struck me. I bit back my scream as the blade cut a quarter-inch deep groove down the length of my spine. I was lucky. Had Meenie been an experienced swordsman instead of just some Dungeons and Dragons wannabe, I'd have been dead.

Not interested in giving him another chance to get it right, I spun on him. I locked up his sword arm and used my weight to swing him around and slam him into the closed back door of the van. In tight, I managed to get one of my hands on his neck, my fingers locking around his throat. I kicked his feet out from underneath him and rode his skull into the bumper, putting all two hundred fifty pounds of my weight into it. It hit with a sickening thump. I saw his eyes roll back in his head as his body went limp.

Before I had a chance to grab the sword, Meinie charged at me. I stepped out of the way and matadored him past me, using his own momentum against him. He tumbled into a roll and got to his feet. I chose the better part of valor as I heard Eenie moaning behind me as he crept to his feet. I bolted around the open back door, past the slow-rising Eenie, and ran to the front of the van. Meinie realized what I intended and let out a string of creative curses as he raced after me.

Not waiting for him to catch up, I slipped into

the driver's seat and let out a hysterical laugh when I found the keys still in the ignition. I turned it over and the van roared to life. I popped it into gear and stomped the gas. The wheels dug in with a squeal and the van shot down the road. It just wasn't quick enough for a clean getaway.

Meinie caught the edge of the sliding door and managed to get his feet onto the small step below it, coming along for the ride. I could see his deranged grin in the passenger side mirror, his feral eyes locked on the reflection of mine.

I swerved the van back and forth, making him focus on hanging on rather than climbing inside. I kept my foot on the gas and hurtled down the street getting as far away from the other two as I could. Once I felt confident they couldn't catch up, I swung the van around a corner as sharply as I dared. The wheels screeched in complaint and the van shuddered, but I'd accomplished what I wanted. The side door slid shut, catching Meinie's hands in between it and the frame. He shrieked in agony as the door locked with a metallic click, crushing his fingers. His feet slipped from the step and bounced along the asphalt as I dragged him along. After a few spiteful seconds, I slowed the van and turned into an alley. I rode alongside a dumpster and turned the van into it, pressing Meinie into its metal side, wedging him between it and the van. I could hear his ribs snap inside his chest. He gurgled in complaint, nearly unconscious. That's when I stopped.

Ignoring my own pain, my wounds still burning, I climbed out and walked around to have a chat with Meinie, his head angled toward the front of the van.

I lifted his chin so we could see eye to eye. "Who sent you?"

His eyes rolled around in their sockets, not quite coherent. I growled and asked him again, digging my fingers into the soft spots under his chin. His eyes came into focus, but just barely. I could see him debating whether or not to tell me. Self-preservation won out.

"Veronica. It was Veronica," he gasped, his voice giving out at the end.

Her name hit me like a gunshot to the gut. I stumbled back, the urge to vomit rearing up once again. I steadied myself against the hood. "Are you serious?"

He nodded as best he could.

I hadn't expected that. I figured Baalth had set me up with his taking my gun and all. I would never have suspected Veronica, seeing how I hadn't heard from her in twenty years. I know we'd split on some pretty acrimonious terms, but I certainly didn't think she'd try to kill me. I guess you never truly know a person until they come gunning for you.

This was really turning out to be a shitty day.

Numb, I turned to leave.

"Wait," Meinie choked. "You can't leave me here."

I didn't even turn to look at him. "You made your bed…now wallow in the wet spot." I stormed out of the alley, my thoughts whirling a million miles a minute.

Around the corner, I looked to make sure Eenie and Meenie hadn't found me before hurrying as fast as I could toward downtown. I made it there in decent time, despite my oozing, aching wounds. At the car, I dug my keys from my pocket and unlocked the door. I slipped, inside stifling a moan. Motivated by adrenaline and a good dose of pain, I started it up right away and rolled out of the lot, heading for home.

I had a lot of thinking to do.

A Light in the Dark

I drove the long way home, making random turns here and there to throw off any tails I might have picked up. However paranoid that may sound, it's a habit, which has kept grief from my doorstep so many times in the past I've lost count. It was often enough to make the extra gas spent worth it. Once I felt comfortable, I aimed the car toward the east side of town, and home.

Stiff and sore from the long drive, my wounds screaming the entire way, I pulled onto my block at last. I hit the automatic garage door opener and pulled inside. Out of the car, I went to the inner door and felt the familiar tingle of the scanning mechanism as it washed over me. Identification complete, I stepped into my kitchen. Home sweet home.

My first stop was the fridge. I pulled it open and snatched a cold beer. I twisted off the top and took a deep swig as I went into the living room, moaning in satisfaction at the first swallow. I'd needed a drink.

"Rough day?"

I shrieked like a little girl when I heard the willowy soft voice, but if anyone asks, I'll lie about it. I fumbled my beer and it fell to the floor, splashing out onto the carpet like a foamy volcano. I ignored it as it certainly wasn't the first to end up there, and looked to see who'd spoken. Rachelle Knight sat on the couch.

"Jesus, woman! You *can* call, you know? What's the point of having telepaths if you're gonna pop in uninvited?"

"I wanted to speak to you in person," she replied. After a moment's hesitation, her wide hazel eyes appraising me, she commented, "You look horrible."

"Thanks. You too." That wasn't actually true. She looked pretty good even though I prefer women with a little more meat on their bones, not to mention a few decades younger. Though not my usual type, Rachelle carried all the grace of a super-model minus the revealing clothes, much to my regret. With no visible flesh of any perverse value to focus on, I dropped into my old recliner and stared at the spreading puddle on my carpet. This day just kept getting worse. Spilled beer and zero cleavage. Was there no mercy?

As always, Rachelle seemed a bit lost, vapid. I used to believe it was a side effect of her connection to the supernatural world. Recently, however, I'd come to believe she'd just been a little *too* experimental back in the sixties. I could picture her at Woodstock, flowers painted on her face, offering the goods up to Jimi Hendrix, looking for an experience.

I stopped my thought process there. There were just some things that didn't need to be imagined. I was treading dangerously close.

After a minute of awkward silence and her glancing about the room as I wandered about inside my head, she got down to business. "As you know, Abraham sent me to check the gates." She laid out a small map of the city on the coffee table.

I waited a few seconds after her voice trailed off, but it didn't seem like she intended to continue. "And?"

Her eyes focused. "The gates themselves are stable. I sense no abnormal fluctuation in them. It would appear nothing of any significance has passed between the dimensions recently." She tugged at the ends of her black hair for a bit before starting again, her other hand tapping at the map. "However, I have located three points off the grid where I believe the dimensional wall has been breached. I feel as though some great psychic trauma has been inflicted in these places, but I cannot be certain as to what caused it." Rachelle's face was lined with doubt, the creases deep.

"Why not?" I'd never seen her look so uncertain.

"Something interferes with my senses. I feel it pushing back against me, distorting my perception like nothing ever has before. One moment I can feel the Demonarch's presence seeping through, the next there's nothing; a void. This is not natural." She looked at the ceiling, her hand held up drawing invisible symbols in the air. "Though I cannot determine what lurks behind these abnormalities, I can be certain of one thing. There is much power to be found there;

a dark, malign power."

I sighed and leaned back in my chair. "Great."

She pointed again to the map, her finger lingering at each location in turn. "The occurrences happened in that order, each two days apart. The last occurred sometime today."

"So you're thinking they're connected and might happen again?"

Rachelle nodded as she rose to leave. I stood as well. She gestured to the table. "Seek out these breaches and find out what's behind them. I've informed Katon, so expect his assistance as soon as he is able." She turned away from me.

She waved her hand and I felt a sudden rush of magical energy coalesce inside the room. I took a step back as a tear began to open in the dimensional wall. Bright colors flooded out of the crack as it widened. Sparks of energy fluttered along the seams until the hole was large enough to accommodate Rachelle. I could see one of the DRAC offices through the shimmering veil of the tear.

"Be careful," she told me as she stepped into the portal. Once through, it closed as quickly as it had opened. A breath later, it was as if she'd never been there.

I rubbed my eyes to clear the spots that had sprung up from witnessing the dimensions merging. Once I could see clearly again, I looked to the map.

I growled when I realized where the markers were. Not surprisingly, all three locations were deep inside Old Town. If something bad was gonna happen, you could pretty much guarantee Old Town was where it'd go down.

Distraction over, I felt my injuries crying out for attention. I pulled my bloody and torn sweat jacket off with a grunt and dropped it on the floor beside the now empty beer bottle. My shirt followed. I examined my arm and hand, both cuts deep and festering. An unhealthy blackness bubbled in the wounds like heated tar. I went to the bathroom and looked at my back in the mirror. The cut, while long, wasn't very deep. I sighed, grateful for small favors.

I hated magically-forged weapons.

It's bad enough my ex-wife sent a bunch of goons after me, but to arm them with the tools to allow them to *actually* kill me, was going too far. Unfortunately, I didn't have time to hunt her down and wring her gorgeous succubus neck. I promised myself though, if I managed to avert Armageddon before it got too far along, I'd make the time.

Pushing away my petty, but oh so satisfying thoughts of revenge, I went to the bedroom. I walked to the back corner of the room and moved my nightstand to the side. Lifting the carpet below it, I rolled it back to reveal the tiled under-floor. I tapped on the corner of one of the innocuous tiles and it popped up, then I set it to the side. From the hole beneath it, I plucked out a small, felt Crown Royal bag. With my prize in hand, I went to the bed and sat down.

From the bag, I pulled out a handful of small, glass vials rubber-banded together. I slipped one loose and set the rest gently on the bed. I shook the tube and watched as the reddish-black liquid roiled inside, moving about within the vial like a lava lamp. Once it settled, I popped the rubber stopper off and took a sip.

In an instant, I felt a surge of energy as the blood—Lucifer's blood—ran down my throat. I replaced the rubber stopper as quickly as I could, my hands twitching like an epileptic's all the while. I set the vial down just as the shakes started to wrack my body. A moment later, it felt like my skin was on fire. Sharp, tingling spurs of agony danced across my body as the blood took hold. And as fast as they started, the pain and shakes ended. A warm tickle replaced the rest, its fingers fluttering soothingly over my flesh. Goose pimples broke out everywhere as the warmth settled into my crotch. I shuddered as I felt myself harden against my will. A moment later, the feeling drifted off into a vague numbness. I drew in a deep breath and let it out in a loud sigh of relief.I looked to my arm and watched as the wound churned, a healthy redness creeping in to evict the black. In the span of minutes, the sickly darkness had been cleansed away and the cut began to pull itself closed. I examined my palm and the same process had nearly finished there, only a pulsating red line remained. I stretched, testing my back, the shallower wound already healed. A moment later, the other two were closed as well, leaving behind no trace of injury. The pain passed as well. I gave silent thanks to my uncle, wherever he was.

The blood had been a gift from Lucifer given to me long ago when the roles of demons and angels had been more clearly defined.

"All things in their place," he would say.

I longed for those days. Life had been so much easier when I knew who my enemies were. These days it was everyone for themselves. Trust was a commodity traded on the open market, to be bought and sold on a whim. Ambition had become the new religion whose dogma had no place for compassion or mercy. No wonder God and Satan left.

My mood soured by the day's events, I decided work was the best distraction. I bundled up my uncle's gift, leaving the partially used vial out, and returned the rest to their hiding place. They had more uses than just healing and it was comforting to have one close at hand. I never knew what kind of trouble might pop up, so it was best to be prepared for anything.

I took a quick shower to wash away the blood and dressed for action. Black pants, black T-shirt, black boots. Beneath the shirt I wore a thin, small-ringed mail shirt, which a LARP (Live Action Role Playing) pal of mine weaved together. While far from the best protection in the modern age of guns, it would help ease my mind should I run into any more of my ex's cronies. Clothed, I checked to ensure my spare .45's were loaded, then slipped them into a double holster shoulder rig. I buckled an ammo belt on and covered it all up with a black jacket. I looked in the mirror and grinned, ready to rock. I threw the horns up and stuck my tongue out, head-banging.

Unable to think of an excuse to stay home any longer, I headed out. Since I couldn't tear open a dimensional portal, which would transport me in a blink of an eye like certain other people, I took the car. Blasting Cradle of Filth's, *Godspeed on the Devil's Thunder*, I rode out.

On the Trail

Just as the sun started to set, I pulled up outside the second location, a rundown warehouse deep in the south end of Old Town. The first, an abandoned strip mall, turned up nothing. It was obvious *someone* had been there recently, but the area had been swept clean. Too clean. I couldn't find a dust bunny if I farted in a corner.

Giving in once more to paranoia, spoiled bitch that she is, I parked the car a block over. I walked the long way around the block just to be sure. Back at the warehouse, I examined the chain link fence surrounding the property. Like most everything else in Old Town, there was nothing secure about the place. The fence had several sections where the links had been cut and peeled back, leaving room to slip through without much effort. I took that as an invite.

I went through the fence and glanced around the empty yard, looking to see if I could pick out any kind of security system that might have noticed my entry. Satisfied there wasn't any, I made my way toward the warehouse. I opened up my senses and reached out, sending invisible tendrils in search of the supernatural.

Like all demons and devils, I have the

innate ability to sense the psychic footprint left by a supernatural being's use of power. Because magic is not of the natural world and must be drawn from the caster's realm of influence, most often through the Demonarch, its use bruises the dimensional walls that separate the planes of existence. The more power drawn through the wall, the greater the damage left by its passage.

From the feel of it, this place had taken a serious beating.

I reined in my senses, pulled one of my guns free of its holster, and crept toward the warehouse. As I got closer, I noticed the big rolling door at the docks stood open. I pressed myself against the wall and worked my way toward the ramp, listening. Unable to hear anything that might indicate someone was inside, I ducked low and moved up the ramp as quietly as I could.

Though the sky darkened at my back, there was still sufficient light for me to see inside. Row upon row of empty metal shelves ran from floor to ceiling, their wares long gone. Past them, I could make out a small office. Still not hearing anything but the hurried rush of my nervous breath, I went inside. I walked along the line of closest shelves, making my way toward the office. I glanced all around, but nothing moved in the dusky gloom. Just like the first location, it was obvious someone of power had been here too, and not long ago.

Despite the mish-mash of graffiti—gang tags, Iron Maiden song lyrics, and an almost literate homage to my uncle—I saw none of the usual trappings that came along with an abandoned warehouse. No trash lying about; no empty quart bottles, used condoms, or discarded food wrappers. Nothing to show any of the usual vacated-warehouse residents had been here in years, despite the tags claiming it as so-and-so's turf and the complete lack of dust.

I closed in on the office situated in a clearing in the forest of shelves. Shards of shattered glass littered the floor, standing out bright in the dim light. I could feel the magical footprint lurking about the office without even trying. Something big happened here, just like Rachelle said. Hoping to figure out what, I pressed myself against the cubicle wall and peeked inside. While barren of furniture, the 10'x10' space was far from empty. A large star surrounded by a circle was painted in black on the floor. Scattered about inside the circle were a handful of half-melted candles. Large burn marks scorched the cement floor at four points of the pentagram. Unable to get a clear view, I went inside to have a closer look.

As I entered the office, I caught the subtle, tangy scent of burnt flesh. While it smelled enticing, like driving by a barbecue joint, it wasn't a good sign. I tightened my grip on my pistol and walked along the outside edge of the pentagram. At each of the scorch marks, there were small traces of what appeared to be melted candle wax. I knew better. This was the flesh I smelled.

My nervousness building, I kept looking to see what else I could find. In one of the corners were piled two sets of steel manacles. I picked a set up and examined them. On the cuffs, as well as spiraling down the length of chain, were etched silver, magical restraining symbols. I whistled. Runes like these were only used to bind the most powerful of supernatural beings. It took an impressive amount of magical energy to forge cuffs like these and even more so to ensure they worked on a reasonably powerful being. Whoever used them was the John Holmes of magic. They were packin'. That they left them behind was even more an indication of power. You just don't throw away things like these.

While hesitant to take them with me, worried their owner might change his mind and come looking, magical restraints like these were hard to come by. Besides, I'd be lying if I said an image of a naked Scarlett, chained to the wall of my bedroom with these babies didn't spring to mind. The stir in my pants made my choice that much easier. What can I say? I'm a dog. Woof.

As hard as it was, pun intended, I got back to business. I picked up the second pair and slung them over my shoulder. With nothing more to examine inside, I left the office. Outside, I glanced around the rest of warehouse, but couldn't see anything else that might be related to the breach. Believing I'd seen everything I was going to, I started for the exit.

I didn't get very far.

Just as I reached the end of the clearing, I heard voices coming from the docks. I clutched tight to the manacles to keep them quiet, and ducked around the back of the office. From there, I ran toward the shelves at the back of the warehouse, hoping the office walls would block my retreat. I got lucky. Sort of. I made it to the shelves, but without any merchandise, there was little to hide behind. I crept back into the shadows and dropped to the floor. Prone, I listened as the voices came closer. A moment later, the speakers popped into view.

Through the open front door, two men strolled into the warehouse. I didn't recognize them.

The taller of the two was dressed casually in loose-fitting jeans and a dark flannel shirt, a light jacket overtop. He was wiry thin except at his torso where he was abnormally thicker. He must have been wearing a vest.

The second, who couldn't have been any larger than five-six, was dressed a little more professionally. He wore a pair of black slacks and a white button-down shirt. He, too, wore a light jacket over his stocky frame. He probably had Kevlar underneath too, but it was hard to tell. Both were clean-shaven with short-cropped, military-style haircuts. Both were armed. While I couldn't see their guns, I could tell by the way they walked they were carrying. There's a certain swagger men affect when they've got the reassurance of a firearm and the will to put it to use. These guys had it in spades.

I held my breath as they walked toward the office and looked about, scanning the gloom. After a minute or so, the short one called to someone still outside where I couldn't see.

Seconds later, an older man entered the warehouse, his cowboy boots clicking as he walked. He had long, wild gray hair with a matching beard, which rested heavily on his chest. I couldn't help but picture Santa Claus. I caught myself looking for reindeer. He wore a loose-fitting earth-tone shirt and blue jeans that did little to hide his bulk. At about six feet, he easily weighed two hundred eighty pounds, but it was clear by how he moved it wasn't fat lurking beneath his country couture. He had that big, bad biker look to him. The kind of guy you just don't want to fuck with.

And there I was.

He walked casually up to the other two, his narrow eyes taking in the scene. He started to say something, then went silent. His eyes widened. Right then, I felt the almost imperceptible tingle of a magical scan.

He knew I was there.

Without hesitation, he pointed me out, shouting to his goons to get me. I felt so unloved. It took them but an instant to orient on me, each fanning out with his gun drawn.

Since there was no point waiting to get shot, I popped up, letting the manacles drop to the floor as I drew my own guns. I didn't wait for a clear shot, I simply started blasting. Stuck in the back end of a warehouse with no cover, I wanted them on the defensive. It worked. The little guy ducked behind the office without firing a shot. The wiry one snapped off a couple quickies as he scrambled to find shelter in the darkening warehouse. He wasn't even close to hitting me.

The wizard stood his ground and glared at me. He was a confident fellow; too confident for my liking.

I aimed at his chest and pulled the trigger. I saw a flash of sparks as the bullet struck an invisible barrier, deflecting away before it could hit the wizard. I sighed. No wonder he was so confident.

He walked forward with a smile, his hands held out as if to imply no threat. I knew better. The stocky goon ran over and positioned himself behind the wizard, taking advantage of the old man's shield. Pretty smart of him. Thinking it was time to get moving, I left the manacles where they lay—my inner perv screaming obscenities at me the whole time—and drifted off toward the darkness. The same direction the other goon had gone. I didn't get far before the lights came on.

The wizard had cast an illumination spell and the whole warehouse was suddenly bathed in a yellowish glow.

I ducked down to make myself a smaller target, the wiry goon only about fifty feet to my right. He leveled his gun when he saw me, but didn't shoot. I held both of mine out, one aimed at the goon, the other the wizard for all the good it'd do me.

"I don't know who you are, but you're not welcome here," the wizard said with a southern twang. He came off calm and calculating despite the drawl. He knew I was more than just some random trespasser. "You work for Baalth? I can sense his stench on you."

Damn he was good. "Hardly," I answered, kind of at a loss for words. Hard to believe, I know.

"If you don't work for Baalth, who do you work for?" He continued to edge forward, the goon behind him drifting along with him.

"I don't think that's any of your concern."

He shrugged. "Doesn't really matter none, I reckon. But you saw something you shouldn't have so that ties my hands. There's only one way to go from here."

"You know, I'm getting real sick of being threatened." That would be the third time today. I could feel my cheeks starting to burn. "How about you tell me who *you* are and why you're here since you're feeling so damn chatty." I get mouthy when I'm mad. It's one of my better character flaws.

I could see him mulling it over. "Why not? The name's Henry McConnell. That there is Mike." He pointed to the wiry goon nearest me, then gestured to the one behind him. "This here is Mario."

His name struck a chord. "Henry McConnell, The Gray?"

He broke into a smile. "I don't much go by that these days, but yeah, that'd be me."

Things just kept getting better and better. The Gray had been one of Abraham's earliest recruits. I'd never met him or even seen a picture, but I'd heard stories. None of them good. He was there when the pro-Armageddon forces went after DRAC the first time. From what I'd been told, he held his own. Pretty damn impressive, all things considered. Unfortunately, more so for me than him, he turned out to be an opportunist with little loyalty to anything but his own self-interest. When Abraham needed him the most, he hitched a ride out of town and disappeared. He'd picked an interesting time to reappear.

I kept my attitude in check, the best I could, while I weighed my options. Once again, I was way out of my league. That seemed to be an ongoing theme lately.

"Well, Henry, I'm not really looking for a fight, so if you don't mind, I'll be on my way." I took a slow step backward, angling to keep as much of the shelves in the way as I could.

"Not so fast." He matched my retreat with a step of his own. His staring, blue eyes seemed to look right through me. "Since you say you're not with Baalth, which I tend to believe, how'd you find this here place? You didn't just stumble onto it. You had to have been clued in somehow." His smile got wider. "There's not a whole lot of folk with power enough to spot the dampener wards I set up or who'd need to send a mutt to check it out. So, if Baalth didn't send ya, Abraham must have."

Powerful *and* smart. Shit. The look on my face must have given it away.

"Well, howdy. I'd heard rumors DRAC had reformed, but could never prove it one way or t'other. This'll make the boss's day."

He could only mean Asmoday. I was in it deep and sinking fast. "Glad I could help, but I gotta go."

Knowing I didn't stand a chance going head on with McConnell, I chose the lesser of two evils. I went after Mike. I dove forward firing. A professional, I hadn't surprised him. He dodged to the side and returned as good as he got. Almost. My first shot him dead center in the chest. I heard his breath billow out, but knew his vest would hold. My second, however, caught him in the neck. He gurgled and fell back, clutching his throat.

His first shot whistled past my ear. His second slammed into my shoulder just as I hit the end of my dive. Unfortunately, the chain shirt I was wearing was great against blades, but it didn't do much to stop a bullet. It ripped right through it. I let out a groan as I tumbled off balance and slid into the shelves, coming to stop with a crash. I jumped to my feet as soon as I stopped moving. Though the wound hurt like a good case of the clap, I'd had worse. Wounds that is, not venereal diseases.

Although...

Never mind.

A little disoriented by the fall, I looked for McConnell and company. I spotted them just in time to see Henry finish the final flourish of a spell. His hand flashed a brilliant gray and a split second later it hit. It hit hard too. Like a Mack truck without brakes hurtling down a San Francisco street, a wave of force smashed into me. I went blind from the pain, my thoughts scattered about my mind like so much detritus.

I flew backwards, crashing through the metal shelves. I felt the first couple as they snapped, banging against my head and shoulders, but the third, fourth, and fifth were just a vague blip on my pain radar. The sixth and seventh didn't even register. I also didn't notice when I'd hit the ground nearly forty yards from where I'd been struck. I did kinda feel the nearest shelves topple down on me, but just barely.

Good thing they weren't too heavy. I pushed them off and sat up, suddenly noticing the spreading stain of blood across my hips and crotch. My head clouded by the impact, I frantically checked for wounds. There were none. I checked again, feeling myself up as I wondered how I could be bleeding yet not injured. It took me a second, but the light came on, however dimly.

The vial. The fall had broken the tube of Lucifer's blood. Just great.

Now contaminated, the quickly drying blood was useless the minute it was free of the vial. My ace in the hole was nothing more than an embarrassing menstrual stain on the front of my pants. Knowing how little of the precious fluid I had left, I almost cried. The sound of a bullet bouncing off the shelf behind me caught me mid-sniff and reminded me I wasn't alone. I shook my head, trying to rid it of the cobwebs. They didn't seem all that interested in leaving, but I didn't have time to argue. I had to move.

I crawled to my feet, my bruised and battered body complaining the whole time, the nerves coming back to life. I saw Mario working his way toward me through the wreckage, McConnell at his back. The light in the room had faded, but I couldn't tell whether the illumination spell had ended or it was just my eyes. I figured I'd worry about that later. I raised my gun to take a shot and realized my hand was empty. Disoriented, I looked to the other hand. It too was missing its gun. Hell of a time to lose both weapons.

Without thinking, something I do so often it's frightening, I grabbed a chunk of twisted shelving and hurled it at my pursuers. While far from a perfect throw, it was close enough for government work. McConnell and Mario sidestepped the awkward projectile easily though. I just stared at them as Mario raised his gun. I found myself wishing I had one of those.

Fortunately, my instincts took over where my brain left off. I heard the crack of the pistol and saw the flash, but before my mind could figure out what all that meant, my body dove for cover. I barreled through the mass of broken shelves and tumbled out the other side as Mario's bullet pinged somewhere behind me. The sound clicked something on inside my head and the fog started to clear. Through it all, something felt weird about the whole situation. It felt surreal. Not right somehow.

I moved off further through the maze of shelves, deeper into the darkness, doing my best to circle toward the front entrance. Mario and McConnell cleared the debris and followed, veering off to keep me from reaching the exit. The goon popped a shot off here and there as they followed. They rang out through the gloom, ricocheting nearby.

Once the gears in my head found their rhythm

again, I felt sure the darkness was natural and not some reflection of my damaged skull. I presumed that's why Mario had such a hard time hitting me in the minimal cover of the warehouse. But again, something seemed off. His shots seemed hurried, desperate almost. As I thought that, he fired off a few more rounds in my general direction. It was like he hoped to get lucky. Not on the first date, buddy.

I worked my way around another shelf and nearly shit myself when I tripped over Mike's body. Focused on McConnell and Mario, I hadn't been paying attention to where I was. I stifled a nervous laugh and relieved Mike of his gun. He wouldn't need it anymore. It wasn't the supernatural slayer my piece was, but it'd do for now. I searched him for spare rounds and came up with a couple of cartridges, stuffing them in my pockets and scurrying off as I heard my pursuers closing in. A few more shots pinged nearby, drawn by my movement. I kept my head down and crept in the direction I remembered the door being. Through it all, I still had the sense of something wrong.

Right then, it hit me.

When McConnell arrived, it had been all confidence and overwhelming superiority. Now, I didn't get the same sense. Mario popped off shots almost at random, trying to hit me in the dark while McConnell hadn't done anything since he knocked me across the room. Don't get me wrong, it was a hell of a shot, but it was far from fight-ending. He'd even let the light spell drop, which was more a detriment to him than to me. Why would a wizard who once stood his own against a horde of raging demons and angels rely on gunmen to take me out?

He was holding back on purpose.

Or maybe he wasn't.

Indecision is a hobby of mine.

It was time to test a theory. I took off my shoes, set one aside and tossed the other in the general direction of the exit. It landed with a quiet thud, but it was enough. I heard a hiss from the darkness followed by the rapid crack of gunfire as three quick muzzle flashes split the dark, illuminating Mario's position. Gotcha. I took a moment to aim, then double-tapped the trigger.

Mario cried out as the first bullet struck him, presumably in the vest. His cry was cut short as my second hit with a wet thwack. There was a thump followed by the clack of his gun as they both dropped to the concrete floor. In the blackness next to him, I heard a gasp, then the slap of booted feet running. I oriented on the sound, realizing McConnell was running *away* from the exit, further into the warehouse. Thrown off by his choice of directions, I held my gun out in front of me and chased after him as fast as I could, dodging through the maze of shelves.

There was a loud boom as something struck the

corrugated metal roof of the warehouse. I stopped and looked up just as a huge section of the roof was peeled back as easily as a piece of aluminum foil. A brilliant light suddenly illuminated the warehouse, shining down through the hole. Blinded for only an instant, thanks to good genetics, I could make out a shape in the center of the glow.

And what a shape it was.

Scarlett floated toward the floor, her wings trailing behind her, more a manifestation of her power than a physical set. She looked every bit the avenging angel as she descended, Everto Trucido clutched in her hand. The only thing that could have made the moment more majestic was if she had been wearing a skirt.

Suddenly, I remembered what I was doing before my libido kicked into overdrive and looked again for McConnell. The room bright with angelic aura, I saw him just as he reached the warehouse office. He flung the door open and hurried inside.

With no idea why Scarlett was there, but grateful for her presence, I shouted for her to follow as I ran for the office. As I neared it, a green light exploded inside the tiny building, seeping out through the door and broken windows before it faded. Unsure of what happened, I held my gun out before me and whipped the door open.

The room was empty.

"Damn it!" I shouted as I ran around the back of

the office, looking to see if McConnell had slipped out that way. He hadn't.

"He's gone," Scarlett said, sheathing her sword.

I wondered if Captain Obvious needed her cape. "Where the hell did he go?"

Scarlett walked up behind me, glancing into the office. She shrugged. "He used the circle to transport himself away. He could be anywhere."

I growled, having not realized the ritual circle could be used as a makeshift gate. I thought McConnell was running low on energy, but his having to use the residual magic of the circle to escape meant he was on empty. I could have taken him out had I been faster. Damn. That would've earned me one hell of a pat on the back from Abraham. Now, a hole in my shoulder and a headache were all I had to show for it. Fortunately, all that would fade fast. The bullet was already being pushed to the surface as the wound healed beneath it.

Irritated, I turned to Scarlett. "What are you doing here?"

"I went by your house, but you weren't there. I saw the map and figured you'd be at one of the locations marked on it. It didn't take much to find you from there."

"So you just broke into my house? Does no one have any respect for privacy anymore?"

Scarlett smiled. "Given how I arrived to find you under attack by Asmoday's men, I'd think you'd be more grateful."

"I guess it's too late to add 'thou shalt not break and enter' to the list of commandments, huh?"

She just laughed, more at me than the joke.

I shook my head. "Anyway, since you're here, you can help me. Tell me what that circle was used for." I pointed to the office.

"Besides helping your bad guy get away?"

I took a deep breath and held off a second before I answered. "Yes, besides that."

With a look of feigned indifference on her face, Scarlett went inside the office. She no doubt wanted to know just as much as I did, maybe more. I could see it in her eyes. Pretending patience, I stayed at the doorway as she dropped to her knees in the circle, focusing. I watched as she rocked back and forth, reaching out. The wave of her senses washed over me like tendrils of her hair tickling my skin. I tried my hardest not to be aroused. It wasn't enough. What can I say? I'm easy.

Unlike my mystical sense, which has all the subtlety of a jackhammer on crack, Scarlett's could peel away the layers of supernatural occurrence like a fine-tuned MRI machine. She could easily pick out the faint traces left behind by wizards, which I would have missed, their footprints buried in the blurry mass of magical stimuli. Her sensitivity had a downside though. She felt everything so much deeper than I ever could.

I saw her green eyes go wide. Her hands flew up to

cover her mouth as her senses dropped. She collapsed. I raced to her side. Her breathing was labored and her whole body shook.

"You okay?"

She took a moment, slowing her breath, before she answered with a tentative nod.

"What did you see?" I asked, helping her to her feet.

She rubbed at her eyes as if to wipe the vision away. "There was an angel held here." Her shaking hand pointed at the circle.

I looked to the piles of melted flesh and a shiver ran down my spine. I felt cold. Numb. I knew the ritual had been elaborate, the manacles and dampeners a sure sign, but I would have never thought Asmoday capable of capturing an angel. It put things into perspective.

You see, while the old world demons like Asmoday were once angels, they lost a part of their power in the fall. It was the cost of their betrayal. That power was spread amongst the Angelic Choir, ensuring a measure of equilibrium against the Demonic Horde that bolstered its ranks with allies both supernatural and human. With Armageddon hanging over our heads, it was never good to see the balance shift toward the dark. At least now it made sense why McConnell was so short on magic. The capture and torture of an angel had to be exhausting, even with a demon doing most of the heavy lifting.

"Do you know who it was?"

Scarlett shook her head. "No, but I can feel his torment. His agony infests the very air. I can taste it with every breath." She looked like she was gonna be sick.

"What is there to gain from this?" It was too much of a coincidence for this not to be related to Asmoday's attempted coup against Baalth, but for the life of me, I couldn't see how the two were connected.

Neither could Scarlett. "I don't know." Her answer was little more than a whisper. Her eyes flitted about the room, taking everything in. "Whatever he intends, Armageddon is the final goal. He never forgave God for his fall." She said the last as if it explained everything. I guess to her it probably did.

She raised her hand, moving it through the air as if waving in slow motion. "The dimensional wall has been savaged here. It would take little more to collapse it completely."

Not entirely surprised, considering my reasons for being there, I extended my senses to better see the damage. "Jes—" I cut myself short knowing how sensitive Scarlett was about using the Lord's name in vain.

The invisible barrier separating the dimensions from one another had been badly battered. It felt like it had been mauled by a bear. A very, very, very pissed off bear on PCP. Deep psychic slashes had shredded its substance, leaving the core bare to the supernatural world. I could sense Hell seeping through from the other side. I'd never seen such carnage.

"We must stop Asmoday," she proclaimed, her eyes steely, staring off at nothing. I could feel her rage.

Seeing the opportunity to aim Scarlett, not as if she really needed the motivation, I took it. "Abraham thinks Asmoday intends to take out Baalth."

That got her attention.

"I think it's in everyone's best interest Asmoday be put down. Baalth can wait for another day."

Her eyes narrowed and locked on mine. "Do you do this for Abraham or for Baalth?" She could be quick sometimes.

I saw no point in lying. "A little of both, but I'm mostly doing it for myself." I shrugged as her face went slack, disappointed. "I know it's hard for you to see the gray between the black and white, but the truth is, Asmoday is the greater threat to the world. Baalth, for all his bluster, is in no hurry to bring about Armageddon. I don't put it past him to hold it in reserve as a sort of end game scenario, but he fancies himself the new Satan. He wants his own little Hell on Earth and he's not gonna bring about the end if it doesn't benefit him. Asmoday has no such qualms."

She sighed. Though she tried to keep her face neutral, she had to have known she was being manipulated, but she couldn't find a flaw in my logic.

"You win. I'll leave Baalth alone, for now." She raised her eyebrows to emphasize the *now*. "Do you have a plan to deal with Asmoday?"

I shook my head. "Not really, but I'm not known as the brains of the organization." I raised a finger to ward off the snarky reply I saw forming on her lips. "I'll hand over whatever I have to the Council and they'll decide the best way to go about handling him."

"Let us be on our way."

"Not so fast. I have one more location to check out. I'd hate to think I missed something we could use to put Asmoday away. Care to tag along?"

Impatient for revenge, but seeing my point, Scarlett nodded.

"Okay. Let me round up a few things, then we're on our way."

I worked my way back to where McConnell blasted me and retrieved my guns and shoe. I then went and found my other shoe and grabbed the manacles before returning to meet Scarlett at the door. She looked at the cuffs with one eyebrow raised.

"And just what do you plan to do with those?"

A million and one fantasies flashed through my head in the span of an instant. Every one of them had something to do with her naked and a metric shit-ton of Astroglide. I just smiled.

"Nothing."

Revelation

We drove to the third location in silence. Scarlett stared out the window, extending her senses as we neared the site. She turned a slight shade of green as we pulled up outside the abandoned church, which corresponded to the map. It wasn't a good color on her. It also didn't bode well for what we were going to find.

"A devil and an angel are sitting in a car..."

"Shut up." Her mood hadn't changed.

"Just trying to lighten things up a bit, sheesh."

She glowered at the rundown church, her fists clenched so tight her knuckles almost glowed. "They have defiled a house of God on top of all their sins."

I chuckled. "They're demons, it's what they do."

She snorted, ignoring my comment. "I sense no one inside."

I looked up at the building, admiring its architecture despite its battered appearance. I'd always liked the aesthetic appeal of churches; the sharp angles and Gothic spires, the intricate knot work shielding the stained glass windows. They always remind me of a horror flick. The good psychological ones, not the gore fests they try to pass off these days. This one was no different. I could feel the wrong committed here. My own senses were rattling off the chart. I tempered them to keep from being overwhelmed and wondered how Scarlett was doing with it all. The furious look on her face kept me from asking.

"But they've been here." I turned the car off and got out. I checked my guns and headed for the church, Scarlett at my heels.

Like the warehouse, the doors stood wide open, but I sure didn't feel welcome, not that I ever did at a house of God. It's not like He and I were enemies per se, despite my bloodline, but I could never be confused for one of the faithful. Stopping Armageddon was a personal, selfish kind of thing. I wasn't doing it to curry favor with the Almighty, wherever He might be.

"How about you go in first?"

Scarlett huffed and led the way. It wasn't that I was scared or anything, I just liked watching her walk. The church lights silhouetted her figure nicely.

Difficult as it was, I pulled my eyes from Scarlett's ass just as we hit the entrance. I saw her shiver, then felt a sudden chill myself as we passed through the door. She looked back at me and I could tell by the way her eyes narrowed, glistening like tiny daggers, she wasn't pleased. Without a word, she headed deeper into the church, slipping through a set of intricate double doors. I took a second to look around.

Like most every other church I'd been in, the entrance opened up into a small, pleasant foyer filled with comfortable sofas, small plants, and plenty of end tables covered in propaganda leaflets. Hallways extended to the left and right leading to the offices, classrooms, and kitchen. Like Scarlett, I knew there was no reason to search those rooms. If there were anything to be found, it'd be in the main cathedral. I followed her through the door. For once, my eyes were on the room rather than her.

An aisle of red carpeting ran down the center, splitting the room in half, wooden pews on each side. At its end sat a small stage with a podium at its center. A giant wooden statue of a crucified Christ loomed above it. Normally, I would go out of my way to avoid looking at it. I hated those things, the way their eyes seemed to follow me around. Today, however, I didn't have to worry. Its face had been mutilated by what looked like a hammer of some sort and splashed with thick, oozing blood. This particular statue wouldn't be doing much staring. It was a bitter kind of comfort.

In front of the stage lay another pentagram like at the warehouse. Scorch marks on the floor told a similar story. Edging closer to it, I could see the same tiny piles of burnt flesh. Whoever he was, our little captive angel was having a very rough few days, being dragged around town and tortured.

Scarlett stumbled and dropped onto a pew. I heard her sob, her sensitivity getting the best of her.

"You all right?"

She shook her head, her hands covering her face.

I could tell she was hurting. Even my own dull senses were stung with the residual magic released here. It was a lot like being covered head to toe in pissed off fire ants. I could only imagine how bad she felt. I moved behind her, placing a reassuring hand on her shoulder, hoping she could take some comfort from the touch. Though I tried my best not to look down her shirt, I apparently suck at being sympathetic.

"Same thing here?"

Scarlett drew in a few shuddering breaths and answered. "Worse."

I had a hard time believing that. "How so?"

"The dimensional wall is threadbare, even more so than at the warehouse." She glanced about. I knew her senses examined the wall, but I wasn't interested in following suit.

"There has been a power transfer here like I've never seen before. I know of no demon capable of such a feat." I felt her pulling her senses back, her eyes glazing over with despair.

I stepped away from her and paced the aisle, trying to motivate my brain. I knew Asmoday was powerful, and bolstered by McConnell, there was no doubt he could pull off some serious feats of magic, but nothing capable of crippling the dimensional wall. How had he done it?

I growled and stopped pacing, staring up at the blinded Christ. "Got any ideas, buddy?" He didn't answer. Foregoing any hope of divine intervention, the sense that God no longer prowled these halls, even in spirit, prevailing, my eyes roamed the church, taking in the somber mood.

The statuary lining the walls all stood with their eyes to the sky, their hands held out in welcome. Outside, I heard the rumbling of thunder and felt the faint tingle of electricity in the air. The hairs on the back on my neck stood on end as the reverberations faded away. There was a storm coming.

"Come on, Scarlett. Let's go. I can't think in here."

I went over and helped her to her feet. She was a wet rag, all but lifeless. It took a few minutes, but I finally got her up and moving on her own.

Thunder crackled again and the lights flickered as we headed for the exit. Scarlett seemed in a daze, walking numbly beside me. We stepped outside just as the first few drops of rain struck the ground. Not interested in getting soaked, I hurried her to the car and helped her inside. As I was shutting her door, I caught a glimpse of lightning as it forked across the heavens, striking something off in the distance. I smiled, the image reminding me of my childhood.

When I was young, my mother would tell me lightning was God's way of protecting humanity from the fallen ones. As demons were most likely to do their dirty work in the dark, especially in the midst of a storm, the angels would hurl lightning bolts down to illuminate the earth and expose the demons to the faithful. Raised human in the early years of my life, I didn't know any better than to believe her. While I learned differently later, I still remember the fear, which filled me every time a storm rolled in, of the black clouds swallowing the sky. I could picture demons lurking in every shadow, creeping up on me, my only salvation the kindness of lightning-hurling angels. I was so naïve back then, but so was most everyone else. People were simpler.

I chuckled aloud as I went around to my side of the car. The clouds had broken and the rain started to come down as I slid inside, shutting it out. That's when it hit me.

"Son of a bitch!"

Scarlett turned to me, her eyes wet and angry, clearly not interested in listening to me complain. "What?"

"I know what Asmoday is doing."

Her anger dissipated instantly, replaced by eager curiosity.

"He's using your angel as a lightning rod."

Scarlett looked at me like I was insane. She did that a lot, but this time she looked like she meant it. "What are you talking about?"

"Think about it. Asmoday doesn't have the raw power Baalth has. There's no way, even with his wizard's backup, he can compete with Baalth. So what can he do to sway the odds in his favor?"

"I don't know, which is why I asked you what you're prattling on about." Scarlett snarled. Patience was another trait she lacked. Good thing she was pretty.

I just laughed. "Look, I don't have any crayons to make this easier for you, so pay attention." She glowered at me like she wanted to rip my tongue out. I ignored the threat in her eyes. "Think about your nature, that of angels. God knew Lucifer's army would always outnumber his own, the lure of the dark and all that. So, to cope with the offset he granted you the ability to draw upon outside energy to improve your effectiveness against the Demonic Horde."

I could see comprehension beginning to dawn. It was a beautiful thing. I should have been a teacher. I'd have gotten all kinds of tail, but I digress. "So, unable to draw upon additional power on his own, Asmoday is using your angel to draw it for him."

Scarlett's cheeks flushed. "He's using him as a battery?"

"Looks that way."

"But how does he hope to use the energy? No true angel of the light, however badly tortured, would side with Asmoday. He's wasting his time."

I shook my head, marveling at her naiveté. "This isn't about your angel changing loyalties, Scarlett. It's about his life. All Asmoday has to do is kill him."

All the color drained from her face. "He...

he wouldn't dare." She clearly hadn't thought that possible. I knew better.

"I'm sure he would. And on his death, all of your angel's power would cede to Asmoday, giving him the easy edge over Baalth."

Scarlett sunk into the seat. "But we'd feel his death, me and the other angels. We'd know where he died."

"That's probably one of the reasons he's still alive. That and Asmoday's greed. He'll do his damndest to get the most power he can before he tips his hand." I felt the cold chill of an ugly realization. "If he succeeds, our little angel won't be the only one to suffer such indignity. There'll be more."

I saw Scarlett's eyes go wide.

"If he's able to capture and contain one of the Powers, what's to stop him from doing it again when he's twice as strong? Nothing." I answered my own question. "He'll feed off them until he's unstoppable."

Scarlett shivered, her arms wrapped across her ample chest. I shivered a little too, though I'm not sure if it was because of Asmoday's plot or from seeing her boobs nearly spill out of her shirt. I'm gonna go with a little of both.

"We can't let that happen," she whispered.

I nodded, my thoughts too scrambled to form words.

"I can't just sit here." Scarlett opened the door,

the scent of rain filling the car. "I need to find him before it's too late." There was determination in her sad eyes.

I nodded again. "I'll do what I can from my end. Keep in touch."

She shut the door without another word and burst into the sky, leaving behind a trail of shimmering light. She was gone in an instant.

Alone and feeling a bit vulnerable, I started the car and took off like a bat out of Hell. With a pretty good idea as to what Asmoday had up his sleeve, it was time to call in the cavalry. I headed for DRAC.

A Plot to Murder the World

After finding the closest teleporter, their location changed daily for security purposes, I arrived at DRAC headquarters. As usual, I stared up at the thirty tons of doom hanging over my head until my escort arrived. I was somewhat relieved to see some random member of security appear, rather than Katon.

I was led to Abraham's office in silence. I opened the door and was assailed by the delightful smell of Abraham's book collection. I glanced up to see the serious faces that lurked past the cluttered desk. Rather than indulge in the scent, I took my cue from their mood and closed the door and went inside, Abraham waving me to a seat. Rahim stood behind him, his dark eyes taking everything in. I nodded to the wizard, who replied in kind.

Unlike Abraham who came off as grandfatherly, or Rachelle who'd always seemed too flighty to be termed impressive, Rahim exuded power. Dressed in a dark business suit only a few shades lighter than his skin, he always reminded me of Darth Vader. Easily six-foot-eight, a good five inches taller than me, Rahim towered over everyone. His bald head gleamed in the light and his deep, Barry White voice carried an authority that spoke of confidence. He was not someone to be trifled with and knew it. So did most everyone else with any semblance of sense in their head.

"What did you find, Frank?" Abraham asked.

I shook my head. "You're not going to like it."

"Do I ever?"

He had a point. I shrugged at Rahim. "Looks like Asmoday captured an angel and is using him to draw power through the Demonarch. I think he's going to use it to challenge Baalth. At least that's where he'll start."

Rahim's brown eyes narrowed. Abraham's widened, his glasses reflecting his surprise.

"I found signs of rituals at two of the locations Rachelle pointed out. There was also substantial damage to the dimensional wall in both of those places. Scarlett believes it won't take much more to shatter it." I kept the part about finding the manacles to myself. No need to tell them everything. A boy's gotta have his secrets.

Abraham sunk down and stared at me, speechless.

Rahim had no such hesitance, taking what I told him in stride. "So, your cousin was with you? Did you send her after Asmoday?"

I wanted to burst out singing, *Let's Get It On*, but I controlled myself. "She showed up later, but yeah, I did. It didn't take much to get her worked up." An impure thought crept to mind, but I stayed on track. "I also ran into an old friend of yours." I gestured to both Rahim and Abraham. "The Gray."

Rahim cussed in a language I didn't understand and Abraham sunk even lower in his chair, running his hands through his gray hair.

"McConnell is involved?"

I nodded at Abraham. "He's definitely involved. The bastard and a couple of his goons tried to whack me."

They both looked at me like I was full of it.

"Seriously. If he hadn't blown his wad doing grunt work for that bastard Asmoday, I wouldn't be alive right now."

Abraham looked back at Rahim. "If McConnell is involved, we've inherited a whole new set of problems. Big ones."

Sheepishly, I interrupted. "Yeah, I think we have. He figured out DRAC is still functioning. I'm sure Asmoday knows by now, as well."

Rahim growled like a feral pit bull.

I raised my hands. "It's not my fault. For a cowboy, he's pretty damn quick-witted."

Abraham sighed. "You're correct, he is very intelligent. He also knows many of our current operatives. While his technical information is somewhat dated, it's enough to put our people at risk."

Rahim set his hand on Abraham's shoulder. It

was surprisingly gentle. "I'll check into it and see what I can do, Abe."

Abraham patted his hand in thanks. Just then, the door to the office swung open and Katon walked in.

"I know what Asmoday is up to." His face was smug, confident.

I chuckled and reclined in my seat. It felt good to one-up their prized assassin, not that I'm petty or anything.

"As do we," Rahim responded without emotion, motioning for Katon to sit. "Frank figured it out from evidence he gathered."

Katon strolled over and dropped into the chair beside me, giving me an approving nod. I felt giddy inside, such high praise.

"All right, tell me what you've got. I'll let you know what I found."

Humble as always, I deferred to Abraham. Katon remained quiet, only nodding here and there until he'd been told everything I had already passed onto the Council.

Up to date, he added what he knew. "Trigg is correct, Asmoday has captured an angel. His name is Glorius, one of the Powers."

"I still don't understand how that's possible." Abraham wrung his hands together.

Katon shrugged, as uncertain as the rest of us. "Despite The Gray's assistance, Asmoday shouldn't have the ability to contain Glorius normally, let alone after he powered him up further. There's something else at work here, but I have no idea what it could be."

"We need to find out before Asmoday tears a hole in the dimensional wall and we're overrun with Dread Fiends," Rahim said.

"Not to mention what will happen if Asmoday absorbs Glorius's soul. Either situation would be a nightmare. I shudder to think of the horror that would befall the world if either came to pass." Abraham took off his glasses and rubbed at his temples. He looked worn out today.

Rahim turned to the assassin. "Katon, find Glorius before Asmoday can steal his soul. Kill the angel if you have to, but do not let that demon get his hands on Glorius's power." He waved De Peña off. Katon left without a word. Rahim turned to me. "Set up another meet with Baalth. Tell him what we know and do everything in your power to convince him he needs to become more active in his own defense. The stakes have been raised."

"I'm not sure he'll care much. I had to trade a favor just to get him to cooperate the first time. Only the missing God knows what it'll cost me this time."

Rahim turned cold. "You'll pay it, whatever it takes." I gazed into his eyes, but I couldn't see anything resembling compassion. "A united DRAC *might* have been able to fight Asmoday to something resembling a standstill before, but with the factors in place now, we stand no chance. We need Baalth if we are to have any hope of staving off Armageddon."

My ass hole puckered. It knew what was coming, pun intended. Even guys in prison didn't get screwed this often.

"After considering what you've told us and adding Rachelle's theories to the mix, we have less than two days before Asmoday makes another power grab. We need to hurry."

I sighed and nodded. What the hell? If I was gonna die, why not go out with a bang? I stood and said my goodbyes and headed off to set up a meeting with Baalth.

Again.

The Continuing Downward Spiral

Less than pleased by the arrangements of our last meeting, I held out for something less confined, more neutral; Memorial Park. Set near the center of our lovely desert town, El Paseo, a short but comfortable distance from Old Town, the park was a sprawling oasis in a sea of blowing dirt and tumbleweeds. With rolling hills and wide open tracts of green grass and trees, the park was the perfect place to have our little sit down. It was quiet and out of the way.

I chose a spot on the highest hill that gave me an unobstructed view in each direction. From there, I could see all three of the intersecting roads, the railway line that passed along the edge of the park, and all the high-dollar surrounding houses. I was feeling pretty confident I'd made the right choice.

I should have known better.

Almost imperceptibly, there was a rustle behind me. I spun about just as a figure burst from a nearby trash can and hurtled toward me. Before I could even draw my guns, the figure crashed into my chest, driving the breath from my lungs. I caught a glimpse of silver arcing through the air as I tumbled to the ground. It didn't take a genius to realize it was a weapon.

And I was no genius.

I hit the ground rolling, kicking my feet out at the apex to make space. It was just enough. I struck my attacker as he tried to drop down on top of me, catching him in the arm. Off balance, he stumbled forward and I saw the blade of his knife sink into the ground. He growled as I hopped to my feet, his eyes meeting mine. I got a good look at him while he pulled his knife free.

Dressed in all black, from head to toe, there wasn't a lot to go off of. There was enough though. The cold gray eyes that peered at me through the opening of the ski mask, shined with feral determination. Lean muscle rippled beneath the skin tight clothing, and though he couldn't have been much more than five-six, he packed a lot of meat on his solid frame. He held the knife with confidence, waving it before him as he approached. It clearly wasn't the first time he'd put a blade to use. I was hoping to make it his last.

He must not have ever heard the saying: *Never bring a knife to a gun fight*. I went for my .45's. His blades out, he got off first. He closed the distance in a single leap, the blade flashing in a wide X before me. I felt a slight tug at my chest as I jumped back to avoid being cut open. Still reaching for my pistols, my hands came up empty. At the same time, I felt something slide down the back of my legs and land with a soft thump on the ground. Unable to slow my momentum, I tripped over the gun belt whose straps had been severed, and tumbled backward. I caught my balance after stumbling about five feet. Like a bad joke, my guns sat on the ground, splitting the distance between us. I could see the faint outline of a smile beneath his mask.

"You have got to be fucking kidding me." I was getting real tired of being the catcher.

The assassin, on the other hand, was clearly still in the mood to pitch. He dove forward, whipping his blade toward me. I caught his wrist and answered with a quick, inside uppercut. He tucked his chin and took the shot without flinching.

Just my luck, the guy knew how to fight.

A straight kick reinforced that fact. His foot caught me in the solar plexus and sent me head-over-heels down the hill. Before I could adjust and turn my body into the roll, my head smacked the ground, all my weight behind it. Spots flashed before my eyes and the next thing I knew, I was laying face down on the cold, cement sidewalk.

I rolled over and hopped to a squat just in time to catch a boot to my jaw. Something phlegmy and wet spewed from my mouth as my head snapped to the side. The searing white light of pain blinded me as I spun about to land hard on my back. Dazed, I was beginning to think I wasn't winning the fight.

I opened my eyes as the assassin came to stand over me. My blurry gaze met his. I could feel the savage coldness in his eyes. He intended to finish the job.

"Who?" I asked, hoping for a second to catch my breath.

He waggled a finger at me and wrapped his hand around my throat, holding me in place. He lowered the knife toward me slowly, making sure I knew it was coming. That's when I got a good look at it. It was a long boot knife and down its length was carved a series of magical runes. I recognized it instantly. It was the same one Eenie had used on me earlier.

"Veronica," I muttered, his hand doing more to hold me down than choke me. Her name dripped off my tongue like bile. The assassin just nodded and tapped the tip of my nose with the blade. Bingo.

Anger rose up in me like a volcano, blasting away the cobwebs in its fiery wake. I held it in check until the assassin's blade neared my eye, then I exploded. Both hands wrapped around his knife wrist and I bucked my hips like he was the best lay I'd ever had. With every ounce of strength I could muster, I wrenched his arm to the side and swept him. He slammed onto his back and I mounted him, sitting on his chest and locking my legs together underneath to keep him there. I twisted his wrist even further, leveraging my weight behind it. The knife slipped free of his hand and bounced off down the sidewalk as I bent his arm backward. I heard a muffled snap as I dislocated his shoulder. He was a tough son of a bitch because he didn't even cry out, but I could see the pain in his eyes. I knew I had him.

I didn't wait for him to recover. Like Chuck Liddell on a tear, I started teeing off, raining down punches in bunches. He took the first two well enough, thrashing to get out from under me, but my third shot shattered his nose. He let out a moist grunt as blood squirted up from beneath the mask and blinded one of his eyes. I didn't let up. I kept banging away, my fists smashing into his face like sledgehammers, until I felt his resistance cease. I hit him a few more times after that just to be sure, his consciousness having faded about twenty seconds earlier.

Not content to simply avoid being assassinated, and feeling mighty vindictive, I got up off the guy and went to retrieve the knife.

"Try to kill me, will ya?"

I walked back over and slammed the blade into his chest without hesitation, piercing his heart. His eyes popped open and he stared up at me, his throat rattling, trying to voice his surprise. Nothing came out. I could hear the sizzle of his blood and see it bubbling black where the blade entered. I snarled and pulled the hood from his head. While I didn't recognize the guy, it was more than clear he was a demon, a minor one, but a demon nonetheless.

"See you in Hell." I laughed, amending my statement. "Oh yeah, no I won't. You won't be going back. You're dead forever." I leaned in closer, pressing my mouth to his ear. "Hope that bitch was worth it."

I stood up and spit on him as he twitched his last. I saw his chest heave once and settle, his final breath expended. Less than a second later, I felt my skin tingle while the hairs on the back of my neck stood at attention. A sudden warm flush ran the length of my body. I moaned as the feeling, way too pleasurable given the circumstances, set in. Thinking I'd been poisoned or something, my whirling mind raced along with my pulse. My crotch throbbed and felt like it was gonna explode. That's when I realized what was happening. I was experiencing a soul transfer.

I stood still for a minute, letting the transfer run its course. I could feel it burning through my veins, passing on the assassin's strength and vitality, his very essence. My pains were pushed into the background, only to disappear a moment later. When it was all said and done, I felt better than I ever had before.

No wonder demons got off on killing one another. It was like taking a handful of Viagra and getting a sloppy hand job from Jessica Alba. I wanted more.

Before I could get too carried away with my analogies, a black Cadillac Escalade with tinted windows rolled up and stopped a short distance from me. I grumbled to myself and took a deep calming breath as I waited to see what was next. A second later, I had my answer. The doors swung open and Baalth and Marcus stepped from the vehicle. Marcus, of course, had his gun out, pointed in my general direction.

Baalth clapped. "Well done." He gestured to the body on the sidewalk. "You're no longer a virgin. You've popped your soul transfer cherry."

"While you sat there and watched. How naughty of you." I was starting to think Baalth had a hand in the attempts on my life. While the assassins, both the longhairs and the demon fellow, had confirmed it was Veronica, I imagined she wasn't doing it alone. There was too much going on around Baalth for it all to be coincidence. I'm no firm believer in serendipity.

He shrugged. "If you can't handle a lowly demon by yourself, you're not worth saving."

I ignored him and snatched the blade, wiping the blood off on the corpse's shirt. I slipped it into my waistband, making a show of it. I glared at Marcus, testing his resolve. He stared back without flinching.

"Relax, Frank. You called me, remember? I'm not here to fight." He waved Marcus off, sending him back to the SUV. As his goon returned to the vehicle, he gestured for me to walk with him. "There, now tell me why we're here."

I sighed, putting my suspicion away for the moment. It wouldn't make things easier. "Asmoday has captured an angel and has been using him to draw power from the Demonarch."

A quiet hiss, and almost silent drawing of breath, was his only reaction. That was the only time

I'd ever seen Baalth appear even remotely concerned. It lasted only a quarter second before he regained his composure. In that instant, I learned an awful lot about what we were facing.

"Continue."

I did. "As I'm sure you've figured out, he's going to use that power to come after you."

"So, what do you want from me? I've already engaged Asmoday. As we speak, my men are seeking out his and wreaking as much havoc as we can without drawing human law enforcement attention."

That was demon-speak, which meant he was doing only just enough to fulfill his contract to me, and not a pubic hair more.

Even knowing what Asmoday intended, and its consequences for him personally, Baalth still played the role of uninvolved. Gotta hand it to him, he was one smooth operator. Even on his death bed, he'd be wracking up favors. I turned to face him so he could see how angry I was.

"You're playing a dangerous game, Baalth. This isn't some petty coup attempt you can put down with guns and goons. Asmoday has drawn so much power from the Demonarch the dimensional walls are crumbling in its wake." I saw his eyes narrow. It was clear he hadn't noticed, or hadn't realized the extent of the damage. "The fact he hasn't already butchered the angel and stolen his soul to come after you tells me he intends to draw even more. It's likely his next attempt will shatter the wall and free the dimensions to merge. What then?"

He didn't answer.

"Fine, I'll tell you what." I poked my finger into his chest. He took it well. I didn't lose it. "Heaven and Hell will flood into Earth and all of creation will explode with war. Everything you've worked for since Lucifer disappeared will be washed away. If you survive, big *if*, you'll be beholden to Asmoday as he'll have the biggest dick in this pissing contest of yours. How do you think he's gonna treat you after all you've done to thwart him? Let me tell you how. You're gonna be his bitch. I hope you like taking it up the ass, buddy, because that's how it's gonna be from here on out."You finished?" Baalth put his hands on his hips and raised his eyebrows. His eyes glowered at me. I could feel emanations of power wafting off him as his anger simmered inside.

I thought about continuing for a second, but I figured I'd pushed my luck far enough. "Yeah, I'm done."

"Good." He remained calm, much to my surprise. "I don't know what your organization has planned, but I'm sure it hinges on my hitting Asmoday before he strikes at me." He paused to gauge my response. I imagine my face told him everything he needed to know because he continued. "I will do as you ask, but be warned, given the circumstances, I cannot commit the entirety of my resources to this. I must hold them in reserve to defend myself should you fail."

I groaned quietly, knowing that was the best I was gonna get. At least I didn't have to trade another favor to get it. "Fine, but you've got to do it soon and it's gotta pack a punch. We've only got about a day and a half before Asmoday kicks down our house of cards."

Baalth nodded and waved to his men. The Escalade pulled up alongside us and the back door swung open. I saw Poe peering out at me with cold eyes. Marcus glared at me from beyond the mentalist, his gun visible in his lap.

"I'll do what I can, but after that, you're on your own." Baalth climbed into the SUV. "Make it count." He closed the door and the Escalade sped off. I watched until its taillights disappeared before I relaxed.

"I guess it's just you and me now." I turned to the assassin's body. It wasn't there. "Or not." In its place was a pile of clothes soaked in a thick black goo, which resembled tar. Albeit nasty, it sure saved on my having to dispose of a body. My buddies at the local cemetery would appreciate the break, I'm sure. They were good guys. They let me dig a lot of holes.

Presuming the assassin was smart enough to not carry any clues as to the whereabouts of Veronica, I left his mushy remains behind and went up the hill. Fortunately, my guns were still there. I could just picture some homeless guy stumbling onto them and going on a rampage at a liquor store. That would just make Abraham so happy.

Bum crisis avoided, I scooped them up and headed for the car, kicking over every trash can I came across. I didn't have the time to deal with my succubus ex-wife, but I reiterated my earlier promise to myself. The first spare moment I got, she was going down.

And I didn't mean in a good way.

Behold the Light

I had just started the car when I heard a whispered voice. I jumped at the sound and spun around, searching the vehicle. There was no one there. Then I heard it again, this time more clearly inside my head. I laughed when I realized what it was.

Rather than use unreliable cell phones or two-way radios whose signals could be interrupted or intercepted, DRAC uses telepaths to contact their members. They have several on staff, their abilities varying from a range of a few miles all the way up to global and dimensional communication. As such, DRAC could call any of their people without the fear of eavesdropping. The only real drawback of the system was it only worked one direction. I couldn't contact them through the link. That and it was rather disturbing hearing someone else inhabiting the same space as my mind. I always felt dirty afterward. More so than usual, that is.

I answered aloud. I never quite got the hang of thinking an answer. It always got muddled up with whatever other thoughts were rutting about in there. Let me tell ya, the last time I tried, the telepath got way more information than she ever wanted to know.

Trust me. It was real bad timing on her part. I heard she turned a beautiful shade of magenta and went rushing off to the bathroom. She doesn't handle my calls anymore.

It's too bad, she had a sexy voice.

Abraham's not so sexy voice echoed inside my brain, interrupting my reverie. "Frank?"

"I'm here."

"Rachelle has picked up a massive spike in magical activity near where the other three incidents occurred." A map image appeared in my head, showing me the location. It wasn't too far from where I was. And of course, it was in Old Town. I was getting real sick of that place. One day there'd be a barrel of gasoline and a match with Old Town's name on it.

"It's a little soon, isn't it?"

"Magic isn't an exact science, Frank. You know there's no way to be sure. Just head over there and see what's happening. If Asmoday is drawing more power, we need to stop him. Katon and Rahim have been informed and will be there shortly."

"All right, I'm on my way." The Lone Ranger to the rescue. I couldn't get the image of being scalped out of my head as the telepath broke the connection.

I hit the gas and headed out. Less than five minutes later, I rolled up near the address. As usual, I parked a block or so away and walked over. No point in advertising I was there. The site turned out to be another abandoned warehouse. I sighed when I saw it. Things hadn't worked out so well at the last one so I didn't expect it to be much better this time around. I debated on waiting for Rahim and Katon, but I didn't know what kind of time schedule I was working with. So, rather than risk being too late I decided to go it alone. Besides, if I died in the line of duty they'd call me a hero. I'd get a better epitaph, at least.

You gotta have priorities.

I extended my senses and let the psychic feelers wander out. I could tell there had been some sort of magical outburst here, but the footprint didn't feel the same as it had at the other locations. That could only mean one of two things. One, this was a trap. No big surprise there. Or two, this incident was unrelated to our Asmoday problem and I was walking in on something I didn't want to deal with at this point. Neither was appealing. I guessed the only way to find out was to go inside.

I drew one of my guns from my waistband, bitching to myself about not having a holster anymore, and went in through the open gate. The yard was windblown, with debris scattered along the base of the wire fence. Despite the fact the scene felt and looked different than the other locations, I couldn't let my guard down. I ran to the docks and crept up the ramp slowly. At the top, the rolling door stood open. I had this strange sense of déjà vu hit me, broken only by the fact that the lights were on inside the building and there weren't any of the long lines of shelves like the last place had. Too late to worry about it, I took a deep breath to calm my nerves and went inside.

Less than fifty yards into the barren warehouse, a man stood staring at me as I approached. I recognized him immediately. It was Asmoday. My first guess this was a trap was right. Chalk one up for me.

Tall and lanky, Asmoday was dressed in an expensive, black business suit, cut to his thin figure. He wore an understated black and red tie, which hung from his narrow neck, a gold upside down cross pinned in the center of it. Light-complected, his full beard and short hair were jet black, so much so shimmers of blue appeared in them when he shifted under the lights. His lean face looked chiseled in wood, cut with sharp lines and delicate angles. His brown eyes, so dark as to appear black, settled on me. I could feel the weight of their stare. If ever a man truly fit the description of sinister, Asmoday was it.

"Come in Triggaltheron, I was hoping it was you who would arrive first. I wanted to speak with you." He waved me forward.

Damn demons and their penchant for given names. Some people say true names give the wielder power over the named. That's superstitious crap at its finest, but it definitely makes a guy uncomfortable when someone knows you well enough to name you fully. It sets a defensive tone to the whole encounter.

I walked up to him, shaking my head. "Said the spider to the fly."

"Come now, do you truly think so little of me?" He feigned hurt.

"I gotta say I'm not exactly a fan of anyone who lists wiping out existence as their top priority."

"But it's in our nature. Are we not what God has made us to be?"

He had a point. Damn demons. I hated these philosophical arguments. I always lost.

"What do you want, Asmoday?"

He didn't hesitate to answer. "To know why you've turned away from your uncle's path. He had such high hopes for you."

I tried my best to keep my expression neutral. I doubt I succeeded. My acting skills made Keanu Reeves look expressive.

Years ago, when Lucifer came to me and told me my true nature, he threw my world into chaos. Raised by my mother until I was fifteen, I had no clue I was part devil. I had known I was different, but not even in my worst nightmares could I have imagined what I really was or what plans had been made for me.

You see, while I was eventually able to accept my lineage, that wasn't the worst of it. After decades of acclimating to Hell and learning about the abilities my heritage would one day grant me, I was told of my destiny. I was to be the next Anti-Christ. Talk about a head trip.

"Lucifer's path was never mine."

Asmoday shook his head. "You turned your back on your uncle, snubbing his inheritance. You passed on the greatest gift of power since God willed Lucifer into existence and for what? So you could pretend to be human?" He laughed, his voice melodic yet arctic cold. "There is no room for you amongst humanity. They would just as soon cast you to the pyre like the witches of old before they would ever accept you. You are pariah."

"Thanks for talking me up. I feel much better now." The truth hurts sometimes.

A semblance of warmth softened his features. "While your opportunity to take up the mantle of the Anti-Christ has passed, there are other offers to consider." His eyes locked onto mine. "Embrace your true self. Join me and let us bring about the final days together, as your uncle decreed. Make him proud."

I'd always wondered what I'd given up, and for what. Life hadn't exactly been all blowjobs and free porn since I'd returned to Earth. It had been rough. For as long as I could remember, I'd had to fight for every scrap that crossed my plate, for every penny that kept me off the streets. I'd passed up the chance at power unimagined, the means to make all my sordid dreams come true.

"Accept my offer and I will grant your friends at DRAC clemency. I will spare their lives and give them a place of honor in the new order. I will even spare your angelic cousin, if that is what you desire."

I couldn't help but think about it. I could save my friends and family and make something of myself. It appealed to me, I can't lie. The part of me related to Lucifer called for me to say yes, but all I could see was my mother's face.

I shook my head. "I can't." I'd always been too human.

He sighed, his shoulders sagging, and reached out to me. "I will not extend my hand again, Triggaltheron. Take it now or be swept away by the tides of Armageddon."

"I guess I better get my surfboard out of hock."

He pulled his hand back, clenching it into a tight fist. "You will regret this."

"It's kinda hard to regret something when I'm dead." A shiver ran down my spine as I spoke. Being a realist can be a serious downer sometimes.

Asmoday took a step back. "Then our business is concluded." He met my eyes again. I could see disappointment in his. There was a terrible certainty as well. "Farewell, Triggaltheron. We will not meet again."

Ah crap. I wasn't so dense I didn't recognize a threat when I heard one.

Asmoday's form wavered and turned indistinct,

swallowed by a swelling mist of blackness. In a great plume of whirling obsidian, he drifted up and through the roof of the warehouse leaving behind an inky black cloud. At the same time Asmoday rose up, four shafts of brilliant white light descended. I squinted and put my hand up to shade my eyes as the shafts coalesced and took form. When the light faded, four angels stood before me. None of them looked thrilled to see me.

Dressed in flowing white robes and barehanded, the angels began to fan out and circle around me. I could tell by the look in their gold eyes, they weren't here to convert me. They were planning to go Old Testament on my ass.

A lot like demons, angels trended toward simplicity in violence. They didn't rely on a bunch of modern weaponry, in fact, they rarely used anything more than a sword, preferring to crush their opponents with their bare hands. They restricted their magic use to augmenting their strikes or to deflect blows, and occasionally they might toss out an energy blast if it seemed reasonable, but they liked their combat up close and personal.

The opposite of humans, who'd refined hand-to-hand down to an art, supernatural fighters were all about sheer, unbridled brutality. They loved to brawl. Ugly, cold, and efficient, there was no science to it. By the look in the eyes of these guys, they fit nicely into the stereotype.

Though I had a damn good idea how this was gonna go down, I didn't wait around to see it played out. I started strafing. Sweeping to the left to avoid them getting behind me, I started firing, drawing my second pistol as I moved. I guessed they didn't know what kind of ammo I was packing because they charged recklessly forward into the hail of gunfire. Didn't take but an instant for them to realize that was a mistake.

The closest angel, who stepped to the front of the line, took three in the chest at close range. Each bullet hit with a solid, bone-shattering thud. He stopped in his tracks, his eyes wide as spurts of shimmering yellow-gold blood sprung from the wounds.

I held my fire, waiting to see what effect my guns had before I committed any more bullets. Never having the opportunity to shoot an angel before, I wanted some assurance it'd be effective before I blew my wad. As such, I didn't leave my fate in the hands of DRAC's demon-forged bullets. I kept backing toward the exit, but I couldn't tear my eyes from the scene unfolding before me.

The wounded angel put his hands to his chest and looked down, muttering something incoherent. He collapsed an instant later. The other three went to his aid, covering him in comforting hands. It wouldn't be enough. One second they were fluttering above him whispering words of encouragement, the next they froze, their faces going slack. Each raised his tear-stained face to Heaven and let loose a wailing dirge that rattled the dust from the rafters. That was my cue to get the hell out of Dodge.

I popped off a few more shots as they lowered their faces to glare at me, murder in their eyes. While I did, a ripple of energy tickled across my skin. As I'd just recently experienced it, I recognized the feeling instantly. It was the soul transfer. I'd forgotten it worked with angels as well.

"Damn it," I complained just as the flush of orgasmic energy rippled through me, halting my retreat. My eyes fluttered closed.

An instant later, in the throes of what amounted to the equal of the best sex I'd ever had, one of the angels slammed into me. I almost didn't feel it. I did feel the wall though, as we smashed through it. Surprisingly, it didn't really hurt much.

Carried by the tackling angel's momentum, we flew about a hundred feet out across the parking lot. We came down hard, the angel maneuvering me through my daze to take the brunt of the landing. We hit the asphalt with a fleshy slap, tumbling into a roll. After about fifteen feet and a serious case of road rash, we came to a stop. Turned out, I ended up on top. Even better, thanks to the ongoing transfer, my wounds had barely opened before they were stitching themselves shut. Man, I loved this stuff. I decided to go for seconds.

With a smile so wide it hurt my jaw, I put my

gun to the forehead of the angel beneath me.

"Repeat after me. If I should die before I wake, I pray for Trigg my soul to take."

You'd think I'd have learned from all the movie villains who get beat while monologuing. Guess not. Before I could pull the trigger, I caught a kick to the face. Apparently the transfer had run its course because I felt every bit of that one.

I heard my nose snap and felt a warm gush explode from it. Lightning bolts of pain shot through my eyes and I flew backwards and landed in a heap. My head felt like used Jell-o.

You figure it out.

I knew I couldn't just sit there so I jumped to my feet, raised my guns and started blasting away at random, spinning in a tight circle. My eyes were so blurry everything was a wet blob so I aimed and shot at the darker blotches as I got to my feet. Meanwhile, I blinked hard and shook my head, hoping to clear my eyes without having to pull one of my guns from service. I managed to sluice a bit of the moisture away just as a shadow engulfed me. I growled at my stupidity.

I had forgotten angels could fly.

I never had a chance. From above me there was a rush of wind just as two vice-like hands seized my shoulders. I felt myself spun about and pressed face first to the ground, a steely weight pinning me down. I was about to start bucking when I realized the maneuver hadn't been aggressive. On top of that, I felt a woman's boobs pressed into my back.

At least I hoped they were a woman's. It could have been a really fat guy, but I preferred not to think of that possibility.

Right then, I felt the air pressure change. My lungs burned as the breath was ripped from them. My gasp was drowned out by the sonic boom that ripped open the sky as if a thousand thunder storms had been unleashed at once. I heard the sound of wrenching steel buried beneath the cacophony of destruction and smelled the tangy scent of burning wood and metal on the heated air. A heartbeat later, I felt the temperature drop about thirty degrees and the ground danced beneath me. I held on for dear life. Through it all, the boobs were an ever present comfort.

It ended a moment later. Everything had gone quiet. It was as if the world had been put on mute. I felt the restraining grip relax as my captor rolled off me. I opened my eyes and turned to see who'd held me. I met Scarlett's green eyes. Her face was pensive and she seemed none too pleased.

"Was it good for you?" I asked.

She shoved me away and stood up, making an ugly face. The moment ruined, I sat up and looked to the warehouse.

It was gone.

All that was left was smoldering ruin. Like a

miniature Nagasaki, the place had been nuked into non-existence. Twisted metal and pieces of smoking concrete lay scattered about the perimeter. The asphalt surrounding the warehouse was slagged into a black soup that glistened with tiny sputtering firelights. The destruction was impressive. I glanced behind me to see who'd pulled the trigger.

Rahim Alakha stood rigid with his hands extended toward the warehouse, wisps of white smoke emanating from his dark fingers. The whirling glow of his eyes faded as I watched, then disappeared. He drew in a deep breath and relaxed, his arms dropping to his side. He walked over to us, shaking his arms out as I climbed to my feet and stood beside Scarlett. Katon joined us a moment later as I put my guns away.

"Way to go, Oppenheimer." My voice sounded wet and thick, thanks to the blood draining down my throat. "So much for low profile."

Rahim shook his head. "I think the appropriate response would be to say thanks."

"I was doing all right."

He looked at my face and smirked. "I can tell."

Scarlett drew my attention. Her eyes were wet. "An angel died here. What happened?"

"You saw them when you got here." I tried to look sympathetic, but I'm sure you can figure out how well that worked. "I showed up and Asmoday was waiting with a sales pitch. I told him to take a hike and the next thing I know four of your brothers pop in and start coming after me. I did what I had to." The death had hit her hard, but she didn't say anything about it. I think she was starting to understand it was a sign of things to come in our new age. It didn't help to dwell on it.

Katon went to examine the wreckage as Rahim turned to me. "Asmoday has angelic assistance." It was more of a statement than a question. I think he was disappointed more than surprised. "It looks that way. It's too much of a coincidence for it to be otherwise. He threatened me and bailed just as the winged goon squad arrived."

Katon shouted from the remains of the warehouse. "There's a body."

"Only one?" I asked back. I'd figured the other three fled when Rahim blasted the warehouse based off of Scarlett's comments, but it didn't hurt to be sure. I was hoping Rahim had gotten the rest. I didn't want to run into them again.

Katon nodded as Scarlett raced to the downed angel's side. Rahim went after her. I took a deep breath and followed behind. As we reached the dead angel, Katon turned to me.

"Three in the chest." He nodded in silent approval. "Guess our forgers need a pay raise too."

Scarlett growled at him and knelt down beside the body. She cradled the fallen angel's head in her lap, her tears flowing freely. Katon took a step back to give her room, realizing he'd upset her. After a moment, she looked up at me, anger flashing in her eyes.

"This is Israfil." As if telling me who he was changed anything.

I recognized the name, though. He was the angel destined to sound the horn that ushered in Armageddon.

"That blows." I couldn't help myself.

Furious, she bared her teeth, the green of her eyes whirling.

I raised my hands to ward her off. "They came after me, Scarlett. It's not like I wanted this." The lie tasted bitter. Yeah, I admit I lost a little control after the first soul transfer, but it wasn't like I sought them out to kill them. They attacked *me*. "Besides, they're working for Asmoday. I'm sorry if I hurt someone you know, but if he's pro-Armageddon, he's an enemy, plain and simple. That applies to all of them. That's just the way it is." I tried my best to look apologetic. I never realized how hard it could be.

She sighed deeply, her expression softening as she put it all into perspective. Her anger at the angel's death made way for sadness. She gave a shallow nod.

Rahim, who'd stayed out of our philosophical debate, stood surveying the scene when he suddenly went rigid. He looked up with seeking eyes. Scarlett turned to the sky as well, her face slack with surprise.

"Move away from the body," Rahim shouted, his voice filled with reedy tension.

I was gone in a flash. Anything that could spook Rahim was something I didn't want to play with. Even Scarlett abandoned Israfil's body and retreated with us. I watched the dark sky to see if I could determine what was coming our way. I didn't have long to wait.

Brilliant sparkles of light illuminated the night, washing the stars away. I shielded my eyes from the brunt of the glare and kept watching as thousands of glowing beams struck the ground at once, then dissipated. A nebulous cloud of swirling energy floated toward us, the air crackling. A chill settled around us as I heard what sounded like singing. It was amorphous, yet beautiful. I realized who it was.

Gabriel.

He appeared in all his glory as I thought his name. The cloud reached the ground and broke apart, drifting away to reveal the archangel. Like the stories of old, he looked every bit the archetypical angel; flowing long hair, bronzed skin, and perfect chiseled features. Dressed in an ivory white breastplate emblazoned with a gold cross, a bejeweled sword at his side, he smiled at us. It was the smile of a predator. I saw no hint of God's mercy in it.

His majestic wings, made of shimmering golden light, folded behind his back and faded away as he knelt beside the downed angel, his face going blank. He set his hand upon Israfil's chest and bowed his head, muttering a quiet prayer. To whom, I had no idea. It wasn't as if God was listening. A moment later, he stood and returned his attention to us. There was no longer even the pretense of kindness, the smile gone from his face.

"You have struck down one of the Lord's faithful." His eyes settled on me.

Not willing to be bullied, I stood my ground. "I can't imagine God would be real happy to know your angel was cavorting with demons."

Gabriel didn't look surprised. "God is forgiving. And in these difficult times, I have no doubt He would reward those who serve His desires so fervently, be they angel, man, or demon."

"The end justifies the means, huh?" I could feel my anger getting the better of me.

Scarlett stepped in. "We know not God's will, Gabriel." That had to hurt for her to admit.

The archangel laughed. "No, *you* do not know His will. *You* whose bloodline is tainted by the Devil's seed could never understand His holy plan." He sneered at her. "Do not speak to me, for your very voice curdles the blood in my veins. You are a demon in all but name."

That wounded Scarlett deeper than any blade ever could. In one sentence, Gabriel had taken her pride from her, wounded her to her very core. Despite how much of a pain in the ass Scarlett could be, Gabriel had no right to speak to her like that.

It made me angry.

"Your God is gone, His relevance with Him." I stepped toward Gabriel. "His plans and desires don't mean shit anymore. Had He cared, He would have told us what He wanted instead of leaving us to figure it out. So don't go being all self-righteous like you have a clue, some secret insight into what God wants. We all know damn well know you don't. You're as much in the dark as everyone else."

Gabriel matched my forward step with one of his own. His hand settled on the pommel of his sword. "Spawn of Lucifer. Do not presume to speak of that which you cannot understand. God shall be a part of the faithful forever. It will be in His name I carve the tongue from your blasphemous mouth."

Rahim stepped between us. I could tell that was the last place he wanted to be. I had to give the guy credit for stepping up though. "Had you intended to strike us down, it would have already been so." He gestured to Katon, who grabbed my shoulder and pulled me back. I didn't resist much. "So saying, why have you come?"

"You are wise, wizard." Gabriel's hand slid away from his sword. The smile crept back to his lips. "Armageddon is a foregone conclusion. God has seen fit to bring it about and so it shall be. After which, there is to be a new Genesis, a rebirth of all which is good, righteous, and pious. I would rather not be forced to destroy the misguided among you because of a misunderstanding. You and your people, with but a few exceptions—" He turned and looked at me. "—are good people. You do what you believe to be right, but unintentionally, you work against God. I am but His servant, yet I know His will as if it were my own. He would be merciful to you, and as He would be, so will I."

"And God desires the end of world?"

"It has long since become obsolete. The humans wage war under the guise of false gods, false beliefs. They pervert His holy texts with their petty schemes and defile the planet as well as each other. They commit atrocities in the name of God, which cannot be forgiven. They ravage the land, murder the children, and rape the tenets of His holy faith. Could He desire anything less?" He paused a moment, waiting for an answer. None came. "The time has come for a reckoning."

Rahim drew in a deep breath and let it out in a whistling sigh. "What would you have us do?"

"Stand aside. Let the demons bring about their own end and allow Armageddon to move forward. This age is past. What stands before us is the true glory that God has promised. We will bask in the light of our Lord as Adam once did, knowing no evil, shame, or desire. At the end of our existence is yet another, more befitting our status as servants of the Lord."

Son of a bitch! It was right then I realized how Asmoday had been able to capture an angel for his little science project.

Gabriel had done it for him.

"You speak of treason yet you hand over one of your own to Asmoday in order to further your cause."

Rahim and Scarlett hissed in unison as what I'd said sunk in. It made perfect sense. I'm sure we were all surprised I was the one to figure it out.

Gabriel's eyes narrowed. "Glorius serves willingly. He understands his sacrifice will be the catalyst that brings about Armageddon. He was honored to give up his life so God's will could be realized."

"You sent Glorius to Asmoday?" Scarlett screamed at him. "He's being tortured!"

"Glorius serves God. His pain is nothing compared to that of the world. It will soon end, ushering in a new age unburdened by sin. He will be revered, as was Christ. He accepts this. He would have it no other way."

Scarlett just stared, unable to speak. I could, but for once, I decided not to. I didn't have anything good to say.

Rahim took the opportunity to step in. I could see by stiffness in his shoulders, the slight hunch in his stance, he was getting ready to fight. While I had always respected the man, his willingness to stand up to Gabriel earned him the 'Biggest Balls of All Time' award.

"With all due respect, I cannot deny my heart, nor can I ask it of those who stand by my side." He bowed, but his eyes never left Gabriel's. "With God gone, I cannot in good faith follow the word of any who claim to speak for Him. It is to His word alone I must cling to and I have not yet heard His call for the end. I'm sorry, but I must stand against you."

"So be it, wizard. I know you to be a man of faith, but you have been led astray. I will look for you at the end of days where you will be given one final chance to stand up for your convictions, however errant they may be." He nodded to Rahim. "It will be an honor to face you on the field of battle."

In silence, Gabriel lifted the body of his angelic companion and cradled him in his arms. Despite all our bluster, no one moved to stop him. He looked to us and I could see the disappointment in his eyes. He bowed his head and his mystical wings spread from his back. With one powerful flap, he sprung into the air, a cool breeze whipping about us in his wake. In a blink of an eye, he was out of sight, obscured by the dark night. I could hear the collective sighs of those around me.

"We're fucked." I said it, but I knew everyone around me was thinking the same thing, albeit probably less crudely.

Scarlett waved her hands about like she was having a seizure, clearly having a hard time coping with all we'd learned. She turned away and I thought I heard a sob. I didn't have time to check on her before she too leaped into the air and flew away. Once she was gone, I turned back to Rahim and Katon.

"So, is my assessment correct?"

Rahim didn't respond, but Katon laughed. It was one of those laughs you usually associate with people who have lost their minds. I think Rahim was kinda surprised it didn't come from me.

"Gabriel's involvement with Asmoday definitely ups the stakes," Katon answered after he'd gotten his chuckles under control. "Even if we had Baalth's full cooperation, we'd still be underpowered. I've yet to find where they're keeping Glorius, so they've still got a card in play. For that matter, I'm not even sure taking him out would make a difference now. If what Gabriel said is true, he could just as easily find another angel to sacrifice himself."

Rahim interrupted. "Keep looking for Glorius. While I don't know about what, I got the sense Gabriel wasn't being entirely truthful. There's some other piece to the puzzle we aren't seeing."

"Angels lie?" I scoffed.

Rahim ignored me. "Katon, return to the hunt. If we can at least delay their plans, it will give us the opportunity to seek out a more permanent solution."

The vampire nodded.

Rahim summoned his energies, sending Katon

away in an explosion of glistening energy. Rahim turned back to me. "While I've no specific directions to help guide you, keep mucking about and see what you can find."

"Mucking about? Is that the official term for what I do?" I gave him a dirty look. "Frank Trigg, professional mucker. He's one bad mucker-trucker."

Rahim shook his head, a sly smile on his lips. "You are good at what you do, Frank. And what you do best is stumble upon trouble. I'd hardly call that a skill."

"Yeah, well...your grandfather was a goat herder. What would you know?"

He laughed, his eyes sparkling. "At this point, I seem to know very little. That is why you are so very important. Amongst the ignorant, you are king." He mimed setting a crown upon my head. "Find us something, Frank. We're desperate," he told me, his tone turning serious.

"If only you were a woman, that kind of talk would really get me worked up." I rolled my eyes, pushing aside the image of Rahim as a woman. I shuddered.

He patted me on the shoulder, a genuine smile gracing his lips. "Be safe. Let me know what you find." With that, he teleported away, leaving me behind with the wreckage and one hell of a case of the heebie-jeebies.

Alone, I took a moment to think, difficult as that was sometimes. I was used to being behind the eight ball. My entire devilish life had been built around the premise of getting screwed and not in a fun, porn star way. It was most often in the prison kind of way, getting sucker punched and waking up with a sore ass with some big guy named Bubba sitting on the bunk smoking a cigarette and heating up a branding iron.

Mostly human, I had always been the underdog when it came to dealing with the demons and devils of Hell, but this was different. Caught up in a war where the combatants were an archangel and two of Lucifer's top lieutenants, I felt like France. All I wanted to do was raise my arms and shout, "I surrender." I was feeling way outclassed, but I had an idea.

It wasn't just a few of us who would suffer if Armageddon came to pass. It would be everyone, human, angel, and demon alike. So thinking, it was time to call up some reinforcements.

Welcome to Hell

Back at home, I stumbled inside, manacles in hand. Certain they'd come in handy at some point, I stashed them where they would be the most useful; the bedroom. I placed them in a box beneath the bed for safekeeping and quick access, right beside the jumbo tube o' lube and my inflatable Jenna Jameson doll. One could never tell when the need to restrain a supernatural being might arise. I'd rather be safe than sorry.

Just thinking about how I'd use them got my blood flowing. Unfortunately, it wasn't just my crotch that was throbbing. My nose was killing me. So to fix that, I dug out a vial and took a sip of Lucifer's blood. Within moments, I was healed and much happier for it. I wrapped the vial in a washcloth, to help protect it, and stuffed it in my pocket. I hoped it'd fair better than the last one. I couldn't afford to keep losing the things.

Finished with my healing, I peeled off my bloody shirt and examined the chain mail underneath. Between the hole blown in the shoulder and all the damage it'd taken when I was tossed through the walls, the chain shirt was barely hanging together. The links had begun to unravel. I pulled it off, realizing it wouldn't do me much good in the shape it was in. And since I didn't have time to meet up with my Medieval Renaissance pal to get it repaired anytime soon, I tossed it to the side. Regrettably, it was the only one I had. I slipped on a shirt and hoped I wouldn't need the chainmail. My cynicism laughed at me.

Cleaned up and as ready as I was gonna be, it was time to go.

I went to the spare bedroom of my house and opened the door. Long ago, I had converted the room to accommodate something other than visiting relatives, something far more useful. I didn't feel bad about it as the only family I had was Scarlett and it's not like she would be popping in to stay over. Not willingly, at least.

Painted all black, the room seemed to swallow what little light the bulb in the hallway gave off. On the floor was an engraved silver circle, surrounded by electric lights in the shape of candles.

What I lacked in magical power, I made up for in ingenuity.

Actually, it had been Lucifer's idea. He had always been the brains of the operation.

Anyway, I flipped the switch on the wall and the candles flickered to life. I shut the door, waited a moment for my eyes to adjust to the dimness, then went and sat in the middle of the circle. I picked up the small knife, which lay on the floor, and took a deep breath as I glanced around the room, feeling a bit apprehensive. I felt weird. It had been quite a while since I'd been in here last. A fine layer of gray dust covered everything. I wondered if it would still work with Lucifer gone. I figured, what the hell? I didn't really have anything to lose. It would work or it wouldn't.

I used the knife and poked a finger. After tossing the blade to the side, I reached down and squeezed a drop of my blood onto the circle, willing it to life. I immediately felt a surge of magical energy and saw the edges of the circle shimmer. I smiled as the gate came online, silently thanking my uncle for not taking all of his power with him.

I closed my eyes and thought hard about my destination. Once I had it fully envisioned, I willed myself through the gate. In an explosion of energy and willowy blackness, I arrived a moment later.

I was in Hell.

The smell of burnt flesh and brimstone stung my nose as I drew in my first breath, grinning all the while. For all its notoriety, it felt good to be home. I glanced around the monstrous cavern halls to gain my bearing and smiled when I realized I'd appeared exactly where I intended to, the Sixth Plane. The circle had worked perfectly despite the trauma inflicted upon the dimensional walls. I wasn't sure it would, but I was sure glad it had. Pessimism ran deep in me.

I looked off in the distance and saw where I needed to be. Carved in black stone, and decorated in the gleaming white skulls of the enemies of its master, the castle cast an imposing shadow in the reddish-yellow light. While glad to be back, I knew I didn't have time to waste reminiscing, so I headed off. It only took me a few minutes to reach the castle, the roads and fields empty.

That was a little disconcerting.

It had been over fifty years since I'd been in Hell last, but I hadn't imagined it would have changed so drastically in such a relatively short time. Normally, the Sixth Plane would be bustling with activity. As one of the more lenient Circles, the Sixth attracted the most adventurous of Hell's denizens, which lent it an energy that couldn't be found anywhere else. Culturally devoid and entirely lacking in morality, the carnival atmosphere prevailed. If there was something taboo you wanted to see, touch, taste, or fuck, the Sixth was where you went. There was very little that couldn't be experienced there.

I know most people would picture the entirety of Hell as being such a place, but that's not true. In general, it's an ordered society with a civilized, albeit somewhat tormented, populace. It's not the rampant serpent's nest of evil it's made out to be. That's all a story made up by the Church to keep the believers in line.

There are, of course, those parts best left alone if you value your life and sanity. Places even the denizens of Hell would rather not think about, but as a whole,

Hell is little different than Earth. It's drier, hotter, and entirely subterranean, but otherwise pretty similar. It is, after all, populated by the same people.

To see the Sixth so devoid of life was disturbing. I'd spent many raucous nights here sowing all manner of seeds. Today, it felt like I was visiting a grave. Lucifer's departure had taken away more than just Hell's leader. It had taken its spirit as well. I shuddered and returned my focus to the castle. I didn't like the feelings that were being dredged up.

Once at the castle's gate, I called out. I stood there for several minutes twiddling my thumbs, but there was no reply. Worried the war had taken its toll on the seat of power of the Sixth, I called out louder. Once more, there was no response.

Discouraged, I turned away from the gate and glanced out across the sputtering lava fields. They churned and bubbled in slow motion, the thick scent of sulfur from their gurgling exhalations tickled the back of my throat. I looked to the coal caves where those souls still serving penance would toil beneath the biting whip of the field masters. They too were empty, devoid of life. Even the sky seemed lifeless. The black clouds hung immobile, thick and threatening. It was as if Hell were holding its breath. Saddened, I looked once more to the gate. A pair of glowing red eyes stared back at me.

"What is your business?" the wrinkled face that

peered down at me from the top of the wall asked.

Startled, it took me a second to answer. "I've come to see the duke." The door guy must have been new. He didn't seem to recognize me. Admittedly, it had been a while since I'd stopped by. I guess I couldn't hold it against him.

"He's not to be disturbed."

"I need to speak to him. It's of grave importance."

The servant seemed unmoved by my grandeur. "Nothing is of importance if the master does not declare it so. Go away." He stepped away from the wall, out of sight.

"I am Triggaltheron, nephew of Lucifer." Though I hated dropping my uncle's name like that, I needed inside. "I must speak with the duke." I tried my best to sound important.

I guess he wasn't impressed, as he didn't return. Fifty years ago, I'd have been let in so fast I'd have incurred whiplash. Today, my name and heritage didn't carry enough wind to raise an ass hair. How quickly the past is forgotten.

I sat there for a minute longer until I decided I wasn't gonna be let in. I'd have to make other plans. Just as I turned to leave, I heard a loud clack and the gate began to slowly rise. I looked back to see the great double doors behind the gate pulling open. Once both had cleared the way, I saw the servant waving to me from inside. I hurried through before he could change his shriveled mind.

Short, hunchbacked, and looking far too old and feeble to be of much use, the servant gestured for me to follow him. His sharp nose and disfigured arms made him look like an under cooked chicken. I doubted even Colonel Sanders would find him attractive. He hobbled along toward the main keep as I caught up.

"So, you're the fool who refused Satan's offer to be the Anti-Christ?"

That's just what I needed, the help questioning my life choices. "Yeah well, the hours sucked and there weren't any health benefits. What can I say? I could do better."

He looked at me like I'd just praised the Pope. "You utter such blasphemy." A smile crept to his twisted, cracked lips. "It would explain why Lucifer held you in such high regard."

I think I blushed.

We traveled the rest of the way in silence. At a pair of ornate double doors made of bone, we came to a stop. The servant tapped on the door and a basso welcome roared out. The doors swung open and I was ushered in.

The room beyond looked suspiciously like a church. A great red carpet led down the center of the room, rows of red velvet chairs lined either side. At the far end was a raised dais, a monstrous throne on top. The subtle scent of singed meat hung in the air, wafting up from the fleshy candles, which circled the room. My stomach rumbled.

Seated upon the throne was an old friend of my uncle, one of my mentors in the days when I lived in Hell. Duke Forcalor. He lifted his chin a bit and narrowed his eyes as I approached. He looked as regal as I'd remembered.

Clothed in the finest silks, he seemed the paragon of comfort. His long white hair was tied back tight, lending him a youthful appearance. His clean-shaven, unlined face added to the illusion. He waved me forward, his eyes sparkling. He seemed glad to see me.

"Come in, come in, young Trigg." He remembered how much I hated my full name. It warmed my heart. "It's been ages since I've seen you. How are you?" He gestured to a nearby chair.

I gave a quick bow of respect, then dropped into the seat. "As well as I can be." I tried not to sound too pessimistic. "How are you, my friend?"

"I'm wonderful, just wonderful." He looked me over, an eyebrow creeping up. "I sense a burgeoning strength within you." He paused a second, examining me further. A bright smile lighted across his face. "You've blooded your hands."

Though I knew it was a compliment, I felt a hint of shame well up. "I hadn't really intended to. This war..." I left my sentence hanging.

He nodded. "It comes to us all, in its own time. Do not regret what you cannot control. Our existence is a violent one. We can do little about that. Relish what time you have and do not let your enemies dictate your emotions."

Forcalor had always been a soldier, but he longed for peace. He had acknowledged his role in life, though he would never accept it. Unlike the majority of demons, the duke took no pleasure in death, or in destruction. He held no animosity for the angels still on high. In fact, he envied them. He did only what he had to do to survive, nothing more. 'Live and let live, lest the wolves come knocking at your door,' he'd always said. And he'd meant it. That made my mission even harder.

"I'm sorry to be so direct, but I need your help."

He leaned back in his throne. It was clear by the look on his face he'd already known that. Why else would I come to Hell now that my uncle was gone? He gestured for me to go on.

"Asmoday has enlisted the help of Gabriel in his efforts to bring about Armageddon."

Forcalor squinted. He hadn't known *that*, or at least he put on a good act. Like with most demons, it was hard to tell the difference between their lies and the truth.

"Between them, they're drawing power from the Demonarch, using an angel to store it until Asmoday can claim it as his own. He intends to kill Baalth." I paused to let him take everything in.

"With Baalth's power alone, Asmoday would be a formidable opponent. Add in what they've stolen from the Demonarch and he would be nigh unstoppable." The duke rubbed his hands together. I could tell he was thinking about the possible consequences of such a brazen move. "It makes no sense Gabriel would allow Asmoday to claim such power. It does nothing to benefit him, quite the opposite, in fact."

I didn't understand it either. "They've also badly weakened the dimensional wall through their rituals. It may soon break open, but I'm sure you've noticed."

"I'd sensed the damage, though its cause was a mystery to me." He shrugged. "However, I trust in the wall to hold. It is far more resilient than most think. They'll have to do much more to it before they run the risk of its collapse."

That, at least, was a dab of good news floating in a sea of shit. "Even so, Asmoday is on the short track to bringing about Armageddon, wall or no wall. We're hanging on the edge here."

The duke leaned forward and met my eyes. His mischievous smile sparkled. "Aren't we always? What is it you're asking of me?"

Here came the hard part. "I know you'd rather remain uninvolved, as has been your wont since Lucifer vanished, but the time for neutrality has passed.

Asmoday is on the cusp of ending the world and those of us who know, don't have the means to stop him. We're all looking at being dead or enslaved, and that includes you."

Forcalor sat back, but said nothing. I couldn't read his expression. It was frustrating.

I continued. "I know this is a lot to drop in your lap, but I've nowhere else to turn. You're the only person I know who has the power to challenge Gabriel, giving us a shot at taking Asmoday down."

"I have much to lose in a confrontation of that magnitude."

"You have much more to lose if you do nothing." I couldn't tell if I was getting anywhere. It was like trying to talk a woman into giving it up. The answer was always no until you weighted the offer sufficiently. "Defeat Gabriel and there's a chance you can return to Heaven." The bait had been cast. I was looking to reel in a whopper.

The duke's eyes glimmered. "How so?"

I felt a nibble. "Without God around, Gabriel is the final word in Heaven. Show the Angelic Choir his true intentions and take him out before he can drag them down, and you'll be hailed as a hero. You'd be welcomed back in a heartbeat." I stopped talking. I didn't want to overplay my hand.

Forcalor grinned wide and clapped his hands. "You've learned well."

"I had an excellent teacher." I lathered it on thick.

The duke laughed at me. "Had your teacher been so good, he would have taught you when to stop."

I shrugged apologetically. We both knew I was a 'C' student at best.

"I will assist you, but as always there is a price to pay for my help."

Oh great, here we go again. I knew I didn't look excited at the prospect of selling another piece of my ass. "Of course there is. Put it on my tab."

He called his servant to him. Old and chatty arrived with contract in hand. The little guy handed it to me and I took it without too much complaint.

I looked it over real quick. It didn't matter how close Forcalor and I were, you never, *never*, signed a contract with a demon without reading the fine print. I ran down the line; favor to be repaid later; first born son; blah, blah, blah; standard. I bit my hand and made my mark. It's a good thing self-inflicted wounds healed quickly, otherwise I'd have some seriously mangled hands with all the wheeling and dealing I'd been forced to do lately.

My ass in yet another sling, I handed the contract to the duke.

He looked it over and smiled. "We have a deal." The servant handed him a small, black box. From within it he pulled a round gemstone, glistening blue in the dim light. He passed it over to me. "Understand first I can only aid you once, so choose your moment wisely."

Hey, look at that, a catch.

He saw my disappointment. "Like any good teacher, we cannot help but continue the lesson."

"With all the hot teachers banging their kids these days, why'd I have to get stuck with you?"

"Consider yourself lucky. Were your teachers these women you so profess your lust for, you would most certainly be fucked. Given the current circumstances, what could they do for you?"

I gave him the golf clap. "Good one." Snappy comebacks were not the duke's strong suit.

He chuckled before continuing. "I cannot simply confront Gabriel without provocation. I must be drawn into the fray. More importantly, I must be drawn in by him."

I groaned as I thought about the logistics. "It's not like he's gonna rush down here and pick a fight. By the time he does return to Hell, the damage will have been done."

"It's really not complicated, Trigg. My favor is that you serve under me until this conflict is resolved."

I didn't quite get it. I'd failed my Infernal Politics class. "Not sure I see what you're getting at."

"As my servant, an attack upon you by Gabriel is an attack on me."

"Uh, so I've got to get him to come after me?" That wasn't exactly what I'd planned when I thought this whole scheme up. I was looking for a way to avoid having to mix it up with Gabriel. Now, I was gift-wrapping my ass for him. My simple plan was becoming way too complicated.

"In essence, yes, but you must not initiate the confrontation. I cannot defend you if he is in the right in your conflict. You must find a way to provoke him without appearing to do so."

"Excellent." For a guy who rarely gets laid, I sure did get screwed a lot. I was beginning to regret having come here.

"Speak my name once the conditions of our agreement are met and I will come to your aid. Keep the gem close, for it is the portal through which I will arrive."

Strapped for time and having gotten all I was gonna in the way of help, I stood. "Thank you. For everything." I bowed to Forcalor, trying my best to hide my disappointment. I really was grateful, I had just come there hoping for more direct help, fool that I am.

Duke Forcalor stood and extended his hand. I took it. "Should our fates align, we will see each other soon. If not, it was an absolute pleasure to have known the only man to have ever refused the office of Anti-Christ." He smiled wide. Devils loved rebellion, just as long as it's not them you're rebelling against.

I took my leave and left the castle, Forcalor's servant showing me out. In a daze, I went back to the arrival point to trigger my departure. On the walk there I wondered if, what with all the holes I'd been digging myself into lately, I needed a longer shovel.

Confession

B ack on Earth, I didn't have a whole lot of faith in what I'd done. While the duke would honor his word and come to my aid, the conditions he set were going to seriously limit my options in ways I hadn't planned for. I'd hoped to pull a fast one, using our relationship to get a freebie, but I should have known better. Forcalor didn't get to be the Demon Trainer because of politics. He got it because he was a good demon. In the end, he'd proven once again why he was the teacher and I was still the student. He'd been given the opportunity to return to Heaven while I got shipped back to the front lines and offered yet another chance at coming home in a body bag.

Life was so unfair.

My brain in a haze, I left the house and stopped off for a cup of coffee. I needed a fix.

I hustled down to the Coffee Hut and ordered up a grande latte. After mortgaging my house to pay for it, I dropped down onto a way too colorful couch whose design challenged my manhood, to enjoy it. Just as I took my first sip, I felt a booming presence in my head.

"Where the hell are you?"

It was Abraham and he sounded pissed, the telepath projecting his emotions through the link. "I'm at the Coffee Hut. What's up?"

"Stay there, I'm on my way. We need to talk."

I felt the connection sever. A chill ran down my spine when it did. It'd been a long time since I'd heard Abraham angry. It didn't bode well for me. I took another sip and saw him outside the store windows, coming inside. He wasn't wasting any time. The lines in his face were etched in stone, his eyes narrow and dark behind his glasses. I could see the pulse at his temple dancing like a two dollar stripper. His upper lip curled when he saw me, waving for me to come outside. The door hadn't even closed when he stomped back through it, the bells jingling wildly.

I set my cup on the table and followed him out, feeling like a kid who had just been called to the principal's office. Abraham went around the corner into a narrow alley without looking back. Reluctant, I went after him. Halfway down it, he stopped and turned to face me as I caught up.

"What were you thinking?" His voice trembled. His glasses were misty. I almost expected steam to come out his ears.

Considering all the things I'd done that would warrant that question, I wasn't going to walk into an admission of guilt until I knew what he was referring to. "What do you mean?" I'm all about not incriminating myself. I had the right to play dumb, and by Starbucks, I was gonna exercise it.

He shook his head. "Forcalor."

"Oh, *that*." Rachelle must have been watching the gates still for him to know about my trip so soon afterward.

"Yes, *that*," he growled. I thought his head was going to explode. His cheeks were a deep shade of red. "Why on earth would you drag another demon into this confrontation? Do we not have enough problems with the ones already here?" I started to answer, but he waggled a finger to cut me off. "I swear, Frank, I sometimes wonder just how dedicated you are to avoiding Armageddon."

That stung. "Hey! Don't go there. I've gotten my ass kicked for the cause more often than I can count." Insert 'how high I can count' jokes here. "I've spent the last thirty years putting my head in the cross hairs, shedding blood for you guys. I've even killed for you, so don't you dare question my dedication."

Abraham stared granite-faced at me for a moment, then sighed. The tension in his expression eased a little. "You're right. I'm sorry." He put his hand on my shoulder. I felt it shaking. "I just don't understand what you're doing. Forcalor has no loyalty to us. By involving him, you've opened the door to God only knows what."

"That's just it, Abe. He's the wild card we need. Asmoday won't be expecting us to go to Hell for help and we need someone who can take on Gabriel.

The duke is our guy."

It was clear he wasn't convinced. "Can we trust him?"

I laughed. "As much as we can any other demon. For that matter, as much as we can Baalth." I hated throwing that in his face, but I wasn't gonna take shit for something he'd set the precedent on. "At least Forcalor and I have a contract, so he'll live up to his end of our deal. After that, things are up in the air, but that's not any different from how things are now." I shrugged. "Besides, isn't my connection to Hell one of the reasons you brought me into DRAC in the first place?" I figured I'd try some of stuff they call reason. I heard it works sometimes.

"Yes, that is true." He did his best Spock impersonation. "However, some advanced warning would have been nice. We might have found another way to go about dealing with Gabriel without engaging another of the old guard demons."

"Maybe, but you and I both know we probably wouldn't have before it was too late. For all DRAC's talents, Gabriel is beyond us. That's a fact." I met Abraham's steely gaze. He knew I was right. "Forcalor is our best bet at neutralizing Gabriel while minimizing the cost to us, after the fact. Like it or not, we're out of our depth here. We need the duke."

Abraham shuffled in place. I could tell he was thinking about what few options were left to us.

He didn't look happy with any of them. "We will play the cards we have been dealt." He gently pushed me forward. Abe was a man who knew how to bow out gracefully. "Since I interrupted yours, let me buy you another cup of coffee. I could use a bit of the mud myself. It's likely to be a long day."

He was still mad at me, but I could tell he at least understood why I did what I did. Abraham was a good man, but he felt things too deeply, took things too personally. He carried the weight of the world on his aching back and every day it wore him down further. He'd envisioned the end of the world and no matter how hard he tried, he couldn't see the way to save it. It had to drive him crazy. Every time he closed his eyes he saw existence crumble, like a sand castle being swept away by the rising tide. But Abraham was a warrior. He would stand his ground until his vision either showed him the way to salvation or his heart stilled within his chest. Sadly, I believed it would be the latter that came to pass first. I hoped he'd find his peace before that day came.

"Sure." I strode a short step behind him as we headed out of the alley. I could see how tired he was.

When we reached the street, I heard a screech of tires as a black van shuddered to a stop in front of us. I went to pull Abraham out of the way as the side door slid open and we were staring down the barrel of several guns.

One of them just happened to be mine.

"Get inside, gentlemen," Marcus told me through a toothy grin. "The boss wants to see you."

Ambushed

Crouched on the floor of the van, I stared up at D'anatello wishing upon him the worst plagues and venereal diseases known to demon-kind. Abraham sat beside me, staring off into space. Though as brave as anyone I'd ever known, he didn't look up to being kidnapped. I couldn't blame him.

"Let Abraham go. He's got nothing to do with our arrangement." I spoke to Poe, bypassing the hulking moron who pointed my stolen gun at my head.

Poe shook his head, his face a mask of cultured neutrality. "I'm sorry, Mr. Trigg, we cannot do that. Baalth has requested we bring both of you to him. That is what I must do."

Stripped of my guns yet again, I thumped the back of my head against the van wall in frustration. I wasn't willing to risk Abraham's well-being just to buck Baalth, so I stayed put and tried not to let my emotions get the best of me. We rode the rest of the way in silence.

A short time later, the van came to a stop and we were herded out. I stepped outside, staying close to Abraham and looked about. Rows upon rows of marble headstones spread out before my eyes, poking up out of the verdant green field that stretched out for acres. A large mausoleum painted in delicate shades of pink and gold stood in the center, casting its shadow over us. The bastards had brought us to Restland Cemetery. I knew the place well as it was where my buddies worked and I had been here more times than I should admit. After hours though, there was no one here to see us, working or otherwise. To the left of us were two freshly dug holes. Baalth stood beside them like a preacher offering up Last Rites. He waved us over. I could tell by the way his eyebrows met in the middle he was angry. I can't say I cared all that much.

"What the hell is your problem, Baalth? We were in the middle of saving your ass, but I guess that doesn't mean anything to you. I don't appreciate you dragging us out here."

"And I don't appreciate you involving Forcalor in our business." He postured up and stepped into my face. "What possible reason could you have for bringing *him* into it?"

It seemed like everyone was on the ball today *but* me. "How'd you find out about that?"

"Let's just say a little bird told me. Now answer my question."

What's the world coming to when you can't even trust the ugly servants to be loyal? Tired of being on the receiving end, I dug my heels in. "Fine, I'll tell you why. Your best buddy Asmoday has gone on and found himself a new friend, one with wings, a great big halo, and one hell of an inferiority complex." The confused look on Baalth's face was very satisfying. "I'm talking about Gabriel. The two of them are working together to put their collective boots in your ass. You might want to start making room."

Baalth looked to Abraham. "Is this true?"

Abraham nodded. I snapped my fingers in Baalth's face. "Over here, big fella. You haven't earned the right to speak to him."

Baalth growled low in his throat. "Be careful, Triggaltheron."

"Or what? You'll kill me? Oh wait, Asmoday is already working on that and he's bringing his holy enforcer to preside over the funeral. I do feel better though, knowing I'm not gonna be the only guy getting stuffed into the ground. Maybe we can be roomies." I gestured to the open graves. "That's the reason I made a deal with the duke. We need an equalizer."

Baalth paced, his fists clenched tight. "What's his angle?"

I laughed. "Don't worry, big guy, he doesn't want a piece of your not-so-humble little pie. His mission is to take on Gabriel, leaving the rest up to us. And by us, I mean DRAC, since you're too busy running to contribute to your own deliverance."

"On the backs of slaves, kingdoms are made." A smug smile graced his lips as he stopped his pacing. "Don't worry, mutt. I'll do my fair share when the time is right."

A chill ran down my spine. I didn't like the way that sounded. "What's that supposed to mean? What do you have up your sleeve?"

He shook his head. "You just live up to your part of the deal, and I'll worry about my end."

I let it go, knowing I wasn't gonna get anywhere. Baalth was nothing, if not stubborn. My pushing him would only cause me further grief. "Now that we're finished with the pissing contest, I need addresses for some of Asmoday's real estate. A few of the juicier ones would be best."

Baalth raised an eyebrow.

"Relax. I'm not looking to move in. I'm just looking to put a little pressure on the bastard."

He nodded and waved Marcus and Poe over. He turned and whispered something to the mentalist as Marcus glared at me. Poe scribbled some locations down on the back of a business card and passed it to me. I pocketed it without looking.

"Anything else?" Baalth asked.

"Yeah, how about you have Tweedle-Dumb and Tweedle-Poe give us a ride into town so we can get back to work."

"I think we can manage that." He turned to D'anatello. "Return Frank to wherever you found him." He added, "In one piece, as much as it pains me to say."

Marcus snorted, before gesturing to the van. Abraham started to head that way when Poe reached out and laid a restraining hand on his shoulder.

"You'll be staying here, Mr. Solano."

"No he won't." I growled, going back to retrieve him.

Marcus stuck the gun in my face. I stared into the black barrel, my anger building. One of these days...

"Abraham will remain with us, for a while," Baalth told me with a crooked smile. "He and I have a lot to discuss while you're off saving the world."

I took another step forward and felt the cold steel of the barrel bite in as Marcus pressed it against my forehead. I was willing to risk being shot if by doing so I could rescue Abraham and I think Poe realized that. He pulled another of my confiscated guns out from beneath his jacket and pressed it into Abraham's side.

"I have nothing but respect for Mr. Solano, but I will not hesitate to end his life should you continue being uncooperative, Mr. Trigg."

I'd never seen Poe with a weapon before, but I knew he meant every word he said. He had always been a cold fish. Even worse, he was a mind-reading cold fish. I hated the thought of leaving Abraham behind. It's not that I was afraid of what they *might* do to him. I was afraid of what I *knew* they were gonna do.

Abe waved me off. "I'll be fine, Frank. Have Rahim mobilize DRAC as necessary and do what needs to be done to end Asmoday's threat. You have more important things to worry about than me."

"I'm not leaving you here, with *him*." I pointed to Baalth.

"I won't hurt him, Triggaltheron. I have more respect for him than that." He gave a nod to Abraham, then looked back to me. "Go and find the angel before Asmoday makes a meal of him." He shooed me away. "I've prepared a surprise for our demon friend that should meet your needs sufficiently. I'll contact you with the specifics when the time is right."

I felt torn, but if I didn't focus on the job at hand, it wouldn't matter where Abraham was. We'd all be dead. "Make it fast, Baalth. We're up against the clock here."

"I understand our time restraints fully." He smiled wide. "Now handle your business, Frank."

Marcus pushed me toward the van. I went grudgingly, looking back at Abraham, fighting the urge to go back for him. I could tell he didn't like the situation anymore than I did, but he was a trooper. He'd do whatever it took to save the world, even if it cost him his life. I just didn't want to see it come down to that.

"If you harm him, Baalth, Asmoday will be the least of your worries," I shouted as I was pushed into the back of the van.

Marcus closed the door behind me, making the smart choice of remaining outside. I wasn't sure I'd have been able to restrain myself had he climbed inside with me. That would have made things messy. As it was, I'd let Abraham fall into the hands of the enemy and it didn't get much worse than that. No, scratch that. It was gonna get worse. Even if we managed to save the world, Rahim was gonna kill me.

I rested my head on my knees as the van pulled away. I felt like shit leaving Abraham behind, but he was right. I had a job to do. The fate of the world rested on my shoulders.

Now would be a good time for a miracle.

Boiling Point

The van dropped me off at the alley where Baalth's men had abducted us. At that point, I wasn't so much mad as I was worried. I couldn't get Abraham out of my head. I slammed the door to the van shut and started to storm away when the driver called out. I spun around, waiting to see what last minute BS Baalth had set into motion. My cynicism didn't play out this time. In the driver's hand was one of my pistols.

"Baalth thought you might need this." He tossed it out the window to me.

I caught it and sighed, looking it over. At least they didn't steal them both. I thanked the guy as he drove off, stuffing the gun into my waistband and pulling my shirt over it. It wouldn't help to be seen waving a gun downtown. I didn't need any more problems. I had far more than enough on my plate already.

Feeling out of touch, and not a little bit adrift, I decided contacting DRAC would be my best bet. I went to a nearby phone booth and dug some change out of my pocket. I deposited fifty cents and called one of the dummy corporation numbers that would put me in touch with DRAC. I gave them the call signs, before hanging up. A few seconds later, I felt my head tingle, Rachelle's wispy voice reverberating inside my head.

"What can I do for you, Frank?"

I paused for a second, not sure how to tell her what happened. I edged toward the alley and turned to face the wall. It wouldn't do to have people think I was some lunatic carrying on a conversation with himself. "I've some bad news. Baalth has kidnapped Abraham."

I felt her concern through the connection. "Is he well?"

I tried my best to sound sincere. "I don't think they'll hurt him, but I'm not sure he's okay, exactly."

"I'll alert Rahim and Katon. They can help retrieve him."

"I don't think that's such a good idea. Abe thinks we need to stay focused on the task at hand. If we veer off to rescue him, we put the world in danger. He doesn't want that on his conscience. Sadly, I agree." I hated saying that, no matter how true it might be. "Baalth said he intends to stick to his word and go after Asmoday. He'll pass on the specifics of what he intends before it goes down. I'll forward them on to you as soon as I know."

I could hear the hesitation in her voice. She understood the situation, even if she didn't like it. "Then we will stick to the plan." I knew leaving Abraham in Baalth's clutches was tearing her up as much as it was me, maybe even more so. I'd always imagined the two had a thing for each other. The pain in her voice all but confirmed it. I felt like a schmuck.

I changed the subject to avoid rubbing salt in the wound. "Have there been any more magical hot spots popping up, recently?"

"The last one to occur was Asmoday's trap."

"What about the gates? Any traffic through them?"

"The usual travelers, but no one out of the ordinary. I've been keeping a close watch hoping we'll stumble across something, but so far there's been nothing."

I shook my head, trying to think of a way to track Asmoday down before it was too late. A thought popped into my head, hard as that may be to believe. "What about any dead zones? You were telling me Asmoday was using some sort of magical dampener to mask the magic he was calling up. He'd have to activate them before he actually performed anything, so that'd give us a small window of detection. Have you noticed any areas where your senses drop off, maybe?"

She took a second to think about it. "I hadn't noticed any, but I hadn't been looking. I'll start another scan and see what I can find. Is there anything else?"

"Yeah. Can you please send a message to Scarlett and ask her to meet me here? I know you're not supposed to do stuff like that, but I don't have time to try and track her down. I need her help with this."

Fortunately, Rachelle wasn't a stickler for the rules when it helped the cause. "Of course." She paused.

I figured she was just off in her own world, so I waited patiently. A few seconds later, she continued. "Be careful, but do what you must. I'm sure Abraham will be fine." She cut the contact before I could respond. I thought I heard a quiet sob right before the connection was severed. That only made me feel worse about Abraham's kidnapping, it being my fault and all. I am a horrible friend.

Sick to my stomach, and no longer in the mood for coffee, I figured it best to get off the street while I waited for Scarlett. I wandered around the corner and back into the alley where Abraham and I had been ambushed. I paced back and forth for a while, replaying the scene where I'd left Abraham behind. My conscience gnawed at me as I thought about the things I could have done to avoid it. Caught up in my head, I barely heard the quiet squeak of brakes at the opposite end of the alley. I looked up to see a gray van parked there, the side door sliding open. I watched in disbelief as the Black Metal trio hopped out and started toward me.

"Not again," I muttered to myself. You gotta hand it to them. They were nothing if not persistent. Not in the mood, I snarled. They were pissing me off.

I looked the motley crew over as they stalked forward. Meinie had recovered from his injuries, no doubt thanks to Veronica and her gifts. He'd paid for that help though. His face was unhealthy thin, almost skeleton-ish. His clothes hung loosely from his narrow frame. He'd probably lost twenty pounds since I'd last seen him, pinned between the van and dumpster. The other two looked a little better, but not much. My ex-wife had left her mark on all of them. They looked used up, desiccated. Though in their case, looks were deceiving. As long as Veronica had her psychic hooks in, they were a threat. Stronger, faster, and armed with magical weapons, they could take me out, given the chance.

As they spread out across the alley, I noticed Eenie had replaced the knife I'd confiscated from the demon assassin with a samurai sword of some sort. I imagined it was wrought by the same supernatural hands that had created the weapons the other two wielded. I wasn't interested in finding out.

Unlike the last time, when they'd caught me unarmed, I was prepared to fight. As they got a little closer, I whipped my gun out and went to work. I pumped three rounds into Meenie. The first two slammed into his chest, the third crashed into his nose. He didn't even have time to scream as the back of his head exploded in a spray of crimson tendrils and gray chunks. Before his body hit the ground, I was firing at Eenie. He caught two to the face. In a flash, his head was like a melted candle, streams of ruby pouring down his neck.

As his friends crumpled around him, their

weapons clattering to the ground, Meinie closed on me. His eyes were like two pieces of coal, simmering with rage. He was looking for vengeance, but I was ready. He swung his short sword in a wide, downward arc, which I easily sidestepped. The blade bit into the cement, throwing up sparks as I moved behind him. Before he could spin about, I shot him in the back of the knee. He screamed like a banshee as his leg buckled and he fell, face first. I was on him like white on rice. My next shot was to his wrist, the bones shattering on impact. His sword bounced from his hand and skittered across the ground to land a few feet away.

I added insult to injury. I stepped on his broken wrist and pressed the barrel of my .45 hard against the base of his skull.

"E Nomine Satanas, motherfucker." I pressed harder, his face grinding against the rough pavement. His grunted moans made me happy. "I know my ex is a hot little number, but trust me, nothing she's got is worth dying for."

He muttered something incoherent and bucked against me. Despite his wounds, he was still pretty strong, Veronica's magic coursing through his veins. I increased the pressure on his wrist and leaned my weight into my gun. After an initial groan, he went quiet. He was smarter than he looked.

"I'm trying to give you an out. Don't give me any more of a reason to kill you than I already have.

Do you understand?"

I could feel his resistance crumbling as he thought about his options. He grunted affirmative.

"Good. Now play nice and I won't have to blow your balls off, you hear?"

He gave the thumbs up gesture with his good hand and I took a step back, kicking his sword further away as I did. Moaning, he pulled himself into a seated position, his back against the wall. He looked up at me, his eyes awash with fear, his body too dehydrated to form tears. But for all his bravado, he hadn't signed up to die.

"How'd you find me?"

"Veronica told us where you'd be."

"How did she know? Is she working with Baalth?"

He shrugged. "No idea about Baalth. All I know is she said she could track you. That she knew where you'd be. I don't know how she does it."

I thought I did. As a succubus, Veronica was drawn to the essence of life. She fed on it, devoured it, leaving behind an empty husk. I don't mean just our marriage either. She'd always been able to seek out the most potent of humans to feed on, but it had been more of an instinctual thing. It happened without her conscious control. At least it had. We'd been separated for the last twenty years. A lot could change in that time. The possibilities were intriguing.

"It's too scrawny. You'll have to throw it back," a voice from behind me said, interrupting my thoughts with a start.

I turned to see Scarlett strolling up to me.

"We're gonna have to stop meeting like this." I gestured to the alley. "People are starting to talk."

As usual, she just laughed at me. It made me feel like the loser at the bar who'd be stopping off at the all-hours quickie mart for magazines and hand lotion on his way home.

"Don't tell me you needed my help with this?" She pointed to Meinie.

"No, I think I've got this one handled. I actually needed you to help fry a bigger fish." Keeping an eye on Veronica's wannabe assassin, I pulled the business card out that Poe had given me and handed it to her.

She looked it over. "What are the addresses for?"

"Those are a few of Asmoday's local interests. I'm hoping you'll look after them. I'd hate to see anything happen. You know, like a raging inferno or an accidental carpet-bombing."

"You think he's at one of them?" She couldn't help but smile at the thought of raining down her righteousness on Asmoday.

"I doubt it, but if you make a big enough mess, he might pay a visit."

"Ah, you're looking to draw him out."

I nodded. "Either him or one of his cohorts,

preferably one from on high. If they're busy protecting his interests, they aren't off destroying the world."

"That's a simplistic presumption."

"Simple is what I do best. Besides, I'm not choking all my chickens in one basket."

Scarlett looked at me like she didn't know whether to laugh or be offended. I could tell she was leaning toward the latter.

"Just pay a visit to those addresses and let me know what happens. I'll handle the rest. Oh, and do me another favor."

She raised her eyebrow.

"Can you take those things with you?" I pointed to the collection of weapons scattered amongst the bodies. "I don't have time to stash them somewhere safe."

She nodded and scooped them up in a hurry. Not one to resist the opportunity to blow something up, Scarlett waved and shot up out of the alley, leaving me alone with Meinie.

He sat there with wide eyes as he watched the golden trail of her passage fade away.

"Come on. We've got places to go and succubi to see."

He shook his head, sweat pasting his greasy hair to his face. "I can't do that. She'll kill me, man."

"You ever see the movie *Deliverance*?" His eyes grew wide. Apparently he had. "If you don't get up and move your ass little piggy, I'm gonna whip out my banjo and make you squeal, you feel me?"

He raised his hands in surrender. "I'll take you, man. I'll take you."

"Good choice."

I grabbed his healthy arm and hauled him to his feet. Twisting it behind his back, I dragged him to the van and shoved him inside. I hopped in the back and closed the door, settling in. To be sure I had his cooperation I jammed my gun against the driver's seat hard enough so he could feel it through the padding.

"Drive."

With a resigned sigh, he started the van and drove off. Good thing for him it was an automatic.

I leaned back in my seat and stared out the window. It had been a long time since I'd seen Veronica and it was obvious she wasn't taking the divorce well. I wasn't looking forward to the reunion, but if she could do what I thought she could, it would be worth the trip.

Besides, I might even get laid.

'Till Death Do Us Part

"This is as far as I go, man," Meinie told me as he brought the van to a stop near a seedy strip of No-Tell Motels at the south end of Old Town. "She's in room 112, bottom floor near the ice machine."

"You'd better not be lying to me."

"I'm not, I promise. I'm done with it, dude."

That wasn't possible, but I didn't bother to tell him that. Once a succubus got her claws in a guy, he was as good as dead. What she had to offer was more addictive than any drug imaginable. I don't care how good a woman was in bed, the things Veronica could do would put the best lay to shame. The feelings she evoked with just a whisper could curl your toes and make your ears wiggle. She could make a heterosexual man listen to Clay Aiken and like it.

I was starting to get aroused just thinking about it; Veronica, not Clay, just so we're clear"Fine, but I swear if I ever see you again, you'll spend your last few moments singing soprano. You get me?"

He nodded enthusiastically.

I ground my gun into the back of his seat once more out of spite and slid the door open. I hopped out and looked toward the hotel. I felt my chest grow tight as I thought about seeing Veronica again. There was a lot of water that had passed under that bridge and most of it smelled like raw sewage. I wasn't sure I was up to jumping back into it, however temporary the swim was.

Meinie, not waiting to see how things turned out, gunned the van and took off, squealing the wheels as he took the corner way too fast. He was gone in a flash. He was the smart one, apparently.

No longer concerned with him, I headed off toward the hotel. I figured Meinie might give Veronica a heads up I was coming, but I didn't care at that point. If she still wanted me dead, she'd have to do it herself.

I slipped around the side of the building and approached her room. Not giving myself time to get nervous, I knocked on the door. I did it lightly to avoid it sounding like a cop knock. It must have worked. The door swung open and Veronica stared out at me, her eyes wide with surprise. She looked even better than I remembered.

She had on a pair of black biker boots that ran to the calves of her painted-on blue jeans, which hugged her in all the right spots. She also wore a tight, wife-beater T-shirt, which barely contained her bra-less chest. The sight of which got my blood to flowin'. My eyes roamed up her body, taking it all in, much to my libido's delight.

Her taught arms rippled with lean muscle beneath the colored lines of extensive tattooing that covered their entirety. The brilliant colors and

Asian-themed artwork ended at her collarbones where her long neck led up to her shocked face. Her big blue eyes stared at me from above her scrunched button nose, her head framed in a halo of short, wild black hair. The look of surprise quickly vanished to be replaced by the hard lines of her fury.

"Frank. You son of a bitch," she growled.

Before I could open my mouth to defend my mother, she clocked me. Throwing a sneaky uppercut, she caught me flush on the chin. I heard my teeth clack together as my head whipped back, knocking me off balance. I tumbled into the parking lot, fireworks exploding in front of my eyes. Face to the asphalt, I mumbled an incoherent complaint as a thin stream of my blood trickled from my mouth and pooled beneath me. I'd forgotten how hard she could hit.

I rolled over to talk just as her boot crashed into my ribs. I felt my breath whoosh from my lungs as I slid back across the lot a few feet, scraping away layers of skin. I instinctively curled up to protect myself from further injury, but kept my eyes on her. I wanted to see the next shot coming.

"I'll kill you!" she shouted. I'm not sure whether it was a good thing no one was around to witness her kicking my ass. Not that it would matter much. In Old Town, people tended to ignore everything that didn't involve them, or they couldn't profit from. I wasn't gonna get any help from the locals.

A few giggles maybe, but no assistance.

Furious, she kicked me again, her boot slamming into my arms. While it stung, it didn't do much damage. I caught my breath as she kicked again. This time, I grabbed her leg and twisted. She went down, rolling away from me as I jumped to my feet.

"Come on now, can't we discuss this like adults?" She growled low in her throat and flung herself at me again. "I guess not."

She came at me like she intended to tackle me. I let her close, then just as her shoulder connected with my stomach, I wrapped my arms around her waist and lifted. I spun sideways and let her go, using her momentum to throw her into the ice machine. She let out a grunt as she slammed into it, the sound drowned out by the crash of falling ice, knocked free inside. She righted herself and glared at me, her eyes sparkling with rage.

"Look, I don't want to fight."

She ignored me and stalked forward, her hands raised like a boxer. I sighed, shifting my own stance, resigned to the fact we weren't gonna work our differences out peacefully. I really didn't want to fight her. It's not like I was all that concerned about hitting a woman, I am part devil after all, but I always had a hard time hurting those I cared for. For all our problems, I couldn't help but think of the good times we'd shared. Admittedly, most of them involved her face shoved into a pillow, but that's beside the point. They were good times, for me at least.

She clearly didn't feel the same way. She closed and threw a left. I moved my right to defend against it and caught a kick to the liver instead. I stumbled back with a hiss, angry at myself for falling for her feint. She'd gotten better. That didn't bode well. She'd always been a scrapper, but she'd been sloppy, undisciplined. It wasn't something she really needed to learn considering her feminine charms ensured she had an army of men to do her dirty work for her. The fact she had taken the time to learn how to fight properly meant my task here was going to be harder than I thought. What a surprise. Nothing was ever easy for me. Why should it start being so now?

She didn't give me any time to recover before she pressed her attack. She came in fast, throwing a nice combination of punches. I blocked the first two, but the third slipped past, catching me in the temple. Once again I saw stars, my legs doing the chicken dance beneath me. She laughed and took advantage. She drove a straight right into my nose. I felt the crack as once again the cartilage in my nose shattered. Ice pick-sharp pains shot through my eyes as they welled up with tears.

"Bitch." I growled as I stumbled back, getting angry, but she wasn't finished with me. She charged forward, throwing a flurry of punches and kicks.

I managed to defend against a few, but most of them connected with solid thuds. She drove me back toward the hotel, her fists a blur of violent motion that rocked my head back and forth, blurring my vision even further. My skull rang like a bell.

I felt my back slam into the wall. With nowhere to retreat to, my face a train wreck of swelling contusions and bleeding cuts, I needed to do something to turn the tide. As Veronica closed on me, I dropped down and slipped a punch, causing her fist to crash into the cinder block wall behind me. I heard her grunt, but didn't wait to see if it slowed her any. I popped back up and head-butted her. My forehead collided with her nose and I heard a loud snap. She shrieked and stumbled back, clutching her face as blood seeped from between her fingers.

Not interested in giving her time to recover, I leaped forward and grabbed her by the arm. With every ounce of strength I had, I spun her about and flung her through the window of her room. The glass shattered, exploding into a million shards of glittering razors that slashed at her as she flew through, landing in a heap on the hotel bed. I waited a second for the shards to clear, then dove in after her, landing on top of her, my weight pressing down.

I knew there was no reasoning with her, especially now that things had gone so far, so I did what I had to get through to her. Crouched on top, I slugged her in the face. I followed that up with another, then another, pinning her beneath me. She squirmed and cursed me as I rained down blows, her hands tearing at me to get me off her. One after another, I punched her until her face looked like a slab of tenderized meat. By about the twentieth shot, her struggling resistance at last gave way to whimpering compliance and I stopped.

She looked up at me, her blue eyes filled with pools of crimson, interspersed with tears. Her clawing hands, giving up their useless defense, now gripped me like steel vises. I stared down at her, meeting her sad, beaten gaze with my own. She moaned, part pain part something else, and pulled my head down. With a passion I'd not experienced since our wedding night, she kissed me.

Though I knew her as well as anyone, I had to admit, I hadn't thought my plan would work considering our history. You see, succubi are not like most women— or more correctly, they aren't like what any woman would ever admit to being—in that they are drawn not only to power, but to the display of said power. The bigger the display, the better. Able to control men with but the merest sliver of their sensual capabilities, they find themselves bored easily so they seek out those who offer them the most challenge. The harder the pursuit, the more they invest themselves in the chase. Due to the nature of succubi, the man who can conquer one physically also conquers the succubus's heart. Though that didn't make things perfect, our failed marriage a good example of that, it certainly made things easier in the wooing process.

I reveled in the kiss, letting her tongue run amok inside my mouth. Through the heat, I could taste the intermingled blood of our wounds and as disturbing as it might sound, I found it arousing. I pressed down onto her, leaning hard into the kiss. It'd been a long time since I'd been with a woman. At least, it'd been a long time where the encounter didn't end with me pulling out my wallet, so I did my best to savor every second.

I felt her grinding her hips into me, setting off rampant sparks in my crotch. I shuddered in pleasure and ground back, working myself into a frenzy. I could feel the warmth, radiating outward from our conjoined crotches, tingling up through my limbs. I tore my mouth from hers and pushed her head to the side, diving into the crook of her neck, kissing and biting.

She hissed in pain and pulled away, shattering the moment. I sat up in a rush, taking my weight off her. I looked down at her beautiful face, although it was really hard to call her that at the moment considering the amount of swelling and bruising present. I felt a little bad, I had to admit.

"Uh...hi." Her voice was raspy and wet sounding, but nothing could hide its sexiness.

"Hi yourself," I replied, a little at a loss for words,

all the blood somewhere besides my brain.

"No hard feelings?"

"For what? Sending assassins after me three times? Trying to kill me?" My mouth went on autopilot. I have foot-in-mouth disease.

"You sent me back to Hell, how'd you think I was going to react?" Her look turned hard as she pushed me away.

I rolled off her and sat on the edge of the bed. I raised my hands in surrender. "You're right, I probably had it coming, but what did you expect? I came home to find you in bed with the cable guy. You didn't even have the decency to get us free HBO."

"Hello. I'm a succubus, that's what I do. You knew that when you married me." She sat up, glaring.

"Knowing you use sex to retain your strength is one thing. My walking into the bedroom to see some strange guy's hairy ass bouncing up and down as he pile-drives my wife is another thing entirely."

She shook her head. "You always were too damn sensitive, not to mention insecure. That's one of the reasons I left you, not counting the unexpected, forced visit to Hell. And just so you know, it took me fifteen years to hitch a ride back to Earth thanks to your uncle shutting most of the damn gates down." She put her hands on her hips and glared at me. "I was with you because I loved you, not because you satisfied my needs as a succubus."

Ouch. I felt my hard on retreat. "That's just cruel."

Veronica laughed. "Get over it. You know damn well I can't feed off you because of your genetics. Don't get all butt hurt over it. It just wasn't going to work. I needed more than you could provide."

Bah. Women. Can't live with them, can't bury them deep enough to avoid prosecution. I tried to act like I was cool with her logic. I wasn't, but I didn't want her to know that. I went on auto-redirect. "Anyway, I didn't come here to stir up old memories."

"Then why did you come?" She ran her hand over her battered face and winced.

"Meinie told me you tracked me, knew where I was all the time."

She looked at me with quizzical eyes.

I sighed and explained. "You know, one of the longhairs you were sleeping with to get him to kill me?"

"Ah, okay. What about it?"

"I remember your life-sensing abilities were pretty limited, so how'd you do it?"

She snarled. "A lot has changed in the last twenty years, Frank. I've gotten better at everything I do." She licked her swollen lips.

Like an idiot, my thoughts started to wander. I reined them in as flashes of past perversions burned their sinful images into the screen of my mind. "How good is your tracking these days?"

"Quite good. I tracked you easily enough, didn't I?" She looked me over like a piece of meat. "Although I have to say, it helped you've gone and upped your power a few notches since we last crossed paths." I thought I heard her purr.

"I've seen a bit of action, lately." Of course, it wasn't the kind of action I wanted to see. "So, if I were to ask you to track someone for me, could you do it?"

"Depends." Her eyes grew wary. "Who's the mark?"

"An angel. He's no one you know, but I really need to find him." I didn't want to tell her too much, but I tried my best to convey the importance of what I was asking of her. She picked up on it pretty fast.

"What's in it for me?"

I couldn't help but laugh. Like every other supernatural being in my life, they all wanted their cut. Shit, for that matter, so did all the humans. Veronica was no different. "What do you want?"

She smiled, knowing I'd given in too easily. She'd figured out I needed this favor badly so she was gonna make it worth her while, regardless how it turned out for me. Satisfied she had me by the short and curlies, she decided to drag it out. "I'll think about it for a bit. Right now, I'd like to get cleaned up and find a way to heal."

I heard the less-than-subtle hint in her words. She knew about the vials Lucifer had given me and was maneuvering to get one. I kept the fact I had one on me to myself. "I think we can work something out." I didn't mind giving her a bit of my uncle's blood, but I sure wasn't gonna do it before I got something in return.

"I'm feeling a bit exposed out here in Old Town. Why don't we go back to my house and finish our discussion there?"

A hint of a smile graced her lips. "Of course. Let me get my things." She dropped off the bed and started stuffing her belongings into a couple of small suitcases. She was traveling light. I guessed she'd thought her assassins would finish the job quickly. She should have known better. I'd always been pretty good at disappointing people. You'd think she'd remember that, being married to me and all.

I'd called a cab while I watched her pack, my car still at Coffee Hut. I didn't imagine Meinie would swing back by to give us a ride. Too bad, he seemed like a nice enough fellow. He had good taste in music, at least.

Once Veronica was finished, I grabbed her bags and headed outside with her. Much to my surprise, it was only a few minutes until the cab pulled up at the curb. The cabbie must have been desperate for a fare to have arrived so soon. The look on his wrinkled face when he saw us told me he thought he'd made a mistake. I didn't give him the chance to change his mind. I gave him directions and a healthy cash incentive to get us there fast. Money talks and people listen. He heard me loud and clear. We were on the road in a flash.

I glanced at Veronica and despite the bruises and bloodstains marring her face it was still very apparent why I'd been so attracted to her in the first place. Her sharp features lent her a classic beauty that even all the damage couldn't completely hide. It didn't hurt I could see down her shirt. She turned and smiled at me, sliding down in the seat to snuggle beside me. I put my arm around her and sighed. It felt like old times.

No matter how everything else turned out, no matter how bad things got, no one could take away the happiness I felt. With her boobs pressed into my side and her hand on my lap, the end of the world was a distant memory.

Retribution

For the first time in days I felt relaxed. I held Veronica's lithe body tight against me, feeling the warmth of her presence. Even though she'd tried to kill me three times, there was a sense of comfort that seemed to override all of that, a feeling of righteousness born of past intimacy. At that moment, it didn't matter what either of us had done, it was as if we'd never parted. All that mattered was we were together. Or maybe it was that her hand, resting on my crotch, kept twitching. Regardless, I was feeling pretty good.

That, of course, meant something had to ruin it.

Without warning, Rachelle's voice exploded inside my head. "Frank!"

I winced, jumping in my seat. Veronica sat up and looked at me like I'd let one rip. I could see the cabbie staring at me from the mirror, his eyes nervous. I tried my best to grin like nothing happened and turned into the seat so my voice would be somewhat muffled. I still didn't trust trying to think my response, especially not with Veronica there stirring up my libido.

"I'm here." Veronica raised her eyebrows, her eyes going wide. The cabbie just shook his head, no doubt regretting picking us up. I couldn't say I blamed him.

"We've been attacked." I could hear Rachelle's thoughts trembling. "Squads of Dread Fiends have struck at DRAC installations all across the city. Even worse, they've gone after our members at their homes."

I hissed. "Is everyone okay?" I knew when I asked it was a foolish question.

Dread Fiends were the shock troops of the Demonarch. What they lacked in brains, they more than made up for in ferocity. More beast than anything, they were bred to fight, born to kill. They did both quite well.

I could hear the hesitation in her voice. "We've yet to assess the damage, but I fear for the worst. There are many of our brethren still out of contact. The fiends attacked in waves, picking targets spread too far apart to allow for quick or organized responses." She paused, then continued as if having just been given new information. "Rahim has formed a search and repel party, but he is not optimistic he will be in time."

I turned to look at Veronica. By her reaction, it was clear my face reflected my concern. "What do you need me to do, Rachelle? Should I join up with Rahim?" Veronica must have realized what I was doing because her eyes narrowed and she sat back, listening and waiting for me to finish. She'd seen me do it before. The cabbie just drove faster. He knew crazy when he saw it and he wanted us out of his cab as fast as possible.

"There is little you can do, Frank. DRAC's

headquarters are secure once more, and Rahim will do what he can for our people. Just be on the—"

I didn't hear the rest because the cabbie stomped on the brakes. In unison, Veronica and I slammed into the divider between the seats. I felt a solid thud as the side of my head smacked into the plastic, pinning my face against it. My thoughts scrambled, the connection with Rachelle was lost.

We bounced back as suddenly as we hit, the car coming to a screeching halt. The two of us ended up in a tangled heap of limbs on the seat. It was like the game Twister, only minus the awkward sexual connotations.

"What the fuck are those things?" the cabbie shrieked, pointing at something in the street I couldn't see, terror in his quaking voice.

I didn't even need to look to know what he was asking about. With my luck, it could only be the Dread Fiends Rachelle was talking about. I whipped the door open and dove out, screaming at Veronica to do the same. She didn't hesitate. On my heels, she hit the asphalt right after I did. Moving forward, I slapped the hood of the car and gestured for the cabbie to retreat. He wasted no time, grinding the gears into reverse, cursing the entire time. Spanish truly is an expressive language. With a choking cloud of burnt rubber swirling about us, I turned to face the fiends as the cab hurtled to safety.Clearly not human, four Dread Fiends stood in front of us as multiple rows of sharpened, rotten black teeth grinned in their cadaverous mouths. Their leathery skin glistened with moist putrescence as a bubbling, yellowish-green fluid oozed from their pores. I wrinkled my nose as the bitter scent of rancid flesh wafted over us. I tried not to gag as it settled thickly in the back of my throat.

Though I'd seen many of the fiends before, it'd always been off in the distance. Their place was the far reaches of Hell, the soul pits, the torment fields. They didn't mingle with infernal citizens, they were kept apart. I'd never had the odious pleasure of being so close to one of them. It wasn't on my to-do list, that's for sure.

Their elongated faces were chiseled in hard bone beneath shaggy mops of knotted, coal-black hair. Sharp yellow growths burst from beneath their waxy skin in bunches, making their faces look like the bastard sons of skeletal porcupines. Their oval eyes shone with an unnatural orange glimmer, focused to a murderous fine point on us. Thick muscles rippled across their wide torsos as they crouched and crept toward us, the sharpened talons on their hands twitching in eager anticipation of the blood to be spilled. Our blood.

Less than thrilled about the prospect, I backed away slowly, pushing Veronica behind me as I angled toward the cover of a nearby abandoned tenement. They had no intention of letting us go. With ravenous snarls, which sent dancing shivers rattling down the length of my spine, they charged.

I shoved Veronica toward the boarded-up building and yanked my .45 out of my waistband. In fluid motion, I swung the pistol up and squeezed the trigger as I went, foregoing accuracy for speed. Turned out, it really didn't matter how fast I was. I was rewarded with a hollow click of an empty chamber.

The gun had run dry.

I fumbled for another cartridge just as the first of the fiends reached me. I had barely ejected the empty clip, the fresh one nowhere near inserted, when the beast slammed into me. I likened the impact to being tackled by a Bullet Train; a stinky, greasy, hairy Bullet Train with claws. I felt my chest cave in as my legs, arms, and head were snapped forward only to whiplash back when we hit the wall behind us. Shards of brick exploded on impact, the wall cracking and giving way, tumbling down on top of us. A gray cloud of mortar dust choked the air as it billowed up around us.

I felt the pressure on my chest give way some as the fiend, which lay on top of me, shrugged off the wreckage and stood up. Without mercy, it reared back, its claws shimmering in the hazy light, and slashed at me. I closed my eyes and tried my hardest to sink into the ground.

Fortunately, I didn't have to rely on that highly overrated defensive maneuver. I heard a guttural gasp above me and felt the fiend pulled off, sliding past my feet, and then it was gone. I opened my eyes in time to see Veronica Judo-tossing the stinky critter back toward his companions. It was a beautiful sight to behold.

"Get up!" she screeched.

Not waiting to see if I listened, she disappeared, the remnants of the wall blocking her from my sight. The fiends dodged their hurled buddy, which rolled past them to land in the street, and shot off after her en masse. They must have thought I was done. I muttered a curse and crawled to my feet. My head pounded out a tribal rhythm as my eyes swirled inside their sockets as I stood. I pushed down the nausea that bubbled in my gut and stumbled out of the hole. Despite it all, I knew what I had to do. I had to help Veronica.

Outside, amidst the wreckage of the wall, I found my pistol. Without bothering to search for the loose clip, I pulled another from my belt and slipped it into the gun. I was priming the chamber just as the tossed fiend came lunging toward me to finish the job it started, its gnashing mouth spewing out graveled-throated growls. I showed it all the mercy it had shown me.

As quick as I could, I emptied the gun into the fiend. While my hands were shaking like a crack whore who needed a fix, my aim was true. One after another, each of the seven bullets ripped into the beast. The first struck it in the center of his face, which exploded in a spray of vile rot. Its head whipped back as the second bullet caught it in the neck, silencing its growled complaints. The rest struck in rapid succession, each a little lower than the last as the force of the one before redirected the momentum of its upper body. The last bullet hit it in the abdomen with a gurgling thump. Wide eyed, the fiend slid to stop in front of me, its ruined head at my feet. I heard the click of the empty chamber, my hand still squeezing away, as I stared down at the fallen fiend. It wouldn't be getting up.

Still shaking, I was reloading the gun when I heard Veronica scream, her voice harsh, panicked. Without hesitation, I bolted off after her. At least I tried to. More injured than I thought, I stumbled, finding it difficult to put one foot in front of the other. My legs felt like Jell-o, my whole body wracked with pain.

Unfortunately, Dread Fiends weren't like the rest of demon-kind. Their souls, their power, didn't transfer over on their deaths. I didn't get a healing boost from the ugly bastard I'd just killed and that was gonna make things hard, considering there were three of them left. Between the beating Veronica had given me and the fiend, I was already half-done. That was when I heard Veronica cry out again and I realized my weakness would mean both of our deaths. I couldn't let that happen. I resorted to something drastic.

As I ran, I dug in my pocket and pulled out the wrapped vial of Lucifer's blood. I gave silent thanks to my uncle when I found it intact. Frenzied, I tore the washcloth off and popped the stopper. In one big gulp, I swallowed the contents, tossing the vial aside. It shattered against the wall as I raced around the corner to where I'd heard Veronica's screams. What I saw turned my stomach.

In a whirling pile of demonic limbs, the fiends tore at Veronica like a pack of rabid hyenas on a fallen antelope. In the midst of it all, I could see her lashing out, fighting back against them. That gave me hope, albeit only a little. I sure wouldn't be betting the house on her survival.

"Take your hands off—" my shout went unfinished as the full fury of Lucifer's blood hit me, screaming through my veins.

My vision blurred and I felt my legs go out from underneath me. I hit the ground, my gun bouncing away across the asphalt. Numb and weak, I stared up at the out-of-focus fiends as they stopped their assault on Veronica and turned to glower at me. I got to my knees as the three barked amongst themselves, presumably about what to do. It didn't take them but a second to decide. They did what they always do.

They attacked.

One of the fiends grabbed Veronica and held her tight while the other two stalked toward me. I tried to stand to meet their approach, but felt my legs wobble hard. Once more, I collapsed. I started to worry. I'd never taken so much of my uncle's blood before. Though I knew what it would do in theory, I'd never had the courage to test it. Seemed I picked the wrong time for field trials.

Unlike when I had just sipped the blood, what I felt now was far from orgasmic. My veins burned as if molten lava rumbled through them. My skin felt two sizes too tight as my muscles throbbed beneath it, threatening to rip free. I could barely see through the haze that clouded my vision, my brain rattling about inside my head. I tried to stand again, but my body conspired against me. I felt heavy, as though someone had weighted me down with pocketfuls of lead. Unable to stand, I looked up at the fiends who smiled sharply back, realizing I was easy prey. I heard their teeth chatter and saw them pounce. I vaguely heard Veronica scream, her voice off in the distance, before the fiends were on me. I went down in a heap, incapable of holding them off.

I could see their claws tearing into me, but couldn't feel them. Spurts of blood shot from the wounds, splattering us all in a scarlet rain. It pooled beneath us. I saw hunks of meat torn from my legs and torso, flung about like so much refuse. I watched in horror as one of the fiends went for the soft bits, its claws sinking into the flesh on the inside of my thighs, its snapping mouth closing in. My nerves came alive like a roadside flare.

A screech like a million banshees filled the air, shattering nearby windows. Much to my surprise, it had come from me. The fiends paused, hovering above me, staring down in uncertainty as shards of glass tinkled down around them. I felt the pain of my wounds wash over me, but there was something else buried within it, something dark and ominous.

Something majestic.

As soon as the agony reared its head, it vanished, replaced by a soothing coldness that chilled me to the marrow. My mind and vision cleared a heartbeat later, my weakness vanished right after. Even more abruptly, I felt a power in me like I'd never felt before. It roared inside, straining against my rippling flesh to be free. I decided to oblige it.

I rolled away from the fiends, taking advantage of their confusion, and hopped to my feet. I laughed maniacally as I realized my wounds were healed. The missing chunks of flesh were regenerated in their entirety, leaving behind no trace save for the blood that still stained everything in dark shades of red and black. I clenched my fists, the cracking of my knuckles echoing loudly as I stared at the fiends. They simply stood there, uncertainty etched across their slack faces. I didn't wait for them to pull it together, I went on the attack.

I leaped forward and drove my foot into the ribs of the fiend on the left. I heard a muffled snap as the beast clutched its midsection and stumbled backward, bellowing a baleful howl. I didn't wait to see where it ended up. I threw a right cross that caught the other fiend in the temple, before it could react. The blow knocked it sideways ten feet, where it crashed into the wall. It crumpled, eyes wide and unseeing. I glanced over at the one that held Veronica and it stared back with wide eyes. It stood there motionless, doing nothing to threaten me or Veronica. The fiend with the wounded rib didn't have any such compunction.

It launched itself at me, its claws extended forward. As surreal as it was, and as clichéd, it seemed as though it was moving in slow motion. I grinned as I took my time to set my footing, preparing for its arrival. Once it closed, I stepped out of its path and cinched my hands onto its wrists, redirecting its momentum into the ground. The fiend smashed into the asphalt, its face leading the way. Shards of teeth and bone spikes sprayed in all directions at the impact, blood and bitter-smelling pus flowed right after. I heard a moist gurgle rumble from its throat as it thrashed about in agony.

Feeling less than merciful, I stomped down between its shoulder blades, my hands still wrapped around its wrist. I leaned my weight into it and rent its arm toward his back. I heard a pop and something that sounded like tearing paper as its shoulder came out of its socket, the tendons ripping free. It screamed and I shouted back, pulling even harder. I leaned further to the side, twisting its wrist again and its pained scream turned into an eardrum-shattering screech. I didn't let up as I felt the resistance grow tighter, then give way with a sudden snap. I stumbled off the fiend, regaining my balance a second later. I held a grisly trophy in my hands; the fiend's arm.

In shock from the grievous wound, the creature shook violently, but stayed where it lay. Thick black blood spewed from its ravaged shoulder and ran down the street like a gory river. Satisfied it was out of the fight, I turned my attention to the fiend I'd stunned earlier. It had just begun to gather it senses and pull itself to its feet. That was unacceptable.

I ran over to it, swinging the severed arm over my head. The fiend looked up just in time to see my weapon of choice. It cringed as the arm crashed into its skull. With a meaty thud, they collided, driving the fiend back to the ground. I discarded the arm, a surprisingly less effective weapon than one would think, and decided to go about this the old-fashioned way; pure and brutal ground and pound.

Not giving the fiend the chance to defend itself, I pressed down on the back of its head and drove my knee into its face. The impact smashed its jaw, teeth exploding from its mouth. I felt it go limp, but I didn't stop. Over and over again, I rammed my knee upward until the fiend's face was nothing more than a seeping puddle that dribbled down its chest in shades of reeking red and black.

Splattered in blood, my own and my enemies', I spun about to face the last of the attacking fiends. I was surprised to find only Veronica there, staring at me through a mask of cuts and bruises. She wobbled on her feet.

"Where is it?" I shouted, spinning around in a circle to find the missing creature. Veronica said nothing. She looked ready to pass out.

Unable to find it, I turned back to her, my rage subsiding. Fueled by the blood of Lucifer, my senses heightened, I saw her shiver despite my being thirty feet away. She didn't look too good. Her stomach and thighs had been raked apart, leaving behind bubbling wounds from which flaps of flesh and clothing hung in strands. One of her arms lay limp at her side, trails of crimson running down its length, dripping from her fingers. Her face had been brutalized, even beyond what I'd done to her earlier, making it almost unrecognizable. My heart sank as she limped forward. I knew she didn't have much time, her breath heavy in her lungs.

I snatched up my gun and raced to her side, scooping her up into my arms as gently as I could. I whispered sugared apologies to her as I took off full out down the street, trying my hardest not to jounce her about too much. After only a few blocks, her whimpered cries piercing my heart at every painful jolt, I came across what I needed.

At a stop light sat a beat up Chevy Impala, its muffler spewing black smoke, its sub-woofers rattling the trunk. I saw the driver slouched in his seat, bouncing his head in rhythm to the music, his arm hanging out the open window, oblivious to the world around him.

I ran up alongside the Chevy, shifted Veronica so I had a free arm, and reached into it, putting the car into park. The banger inside stared at me with wide eyes, at least as wide as the bandanna on his forehead allowed, while I yanked the door open.

"This is what you get for not locking your door," I told him as I snatched him out and shoved him down onto the street, away from the car. He tumbled back, uncertain of how to react. I'd caught him off guard. "And wear your seat belt next time." I wasn't in the mood to be witty.

I eased Veronica inside, from the driver's side, and slid in after her. I slammed the door shut just as the owner found his courage. He stepped up to the window shouting obscenities in Spanish, calling me out as he reached for the handle. Not interested in playing, I pointed my .45 at him. He took a quick step back, his arms raised in surrender. Like most wannabes, his courage fled once faced with the barrel of a gun. With no time to waste, I gunned the Impala and shot off down the road, leaving the *vato* in the dust. I saw him in the rearview mirror, jumping up and down, shouting. He'd found his eggs again.

Unconcerned with his antics, I was in a race for Veronica's life. I had to save her, especially if there was to be any chance of my having sex before Asmoday brought about the end of the world.

I didn't want to die horny.

The Precipice

B ack at my house, I screeched to a stop in the driveway. I hopped out of the appropriated Impala and raced to the passenger side to collect Veronica. Even in the short drive, she had paled a good deal. She was slumped down in the seat, lethargic. The blood loss had taken its toll, the seat beneath soaked in dark fluid. I pulled her out of the car and rushed to the front door. I fumbled in my pocket for my keys and after a heart-pounding moment where I'd believed them lost, I fished them out. I got the door open, calling out the password that would shut down the defensive wards in an emergency, and ran inside toward the bedroom.

Unceremoniously, I dropped her on the bed and tore into the hidden stash of Lucifer's blood. I yanked a vial free of the pack, and popped it open, leaving the rest on the floor. I knelt beside Veronica and fed her a couple drops of the blood, urging her to swallow. When she did, albeit weekly, I leaned back against the headboard loosing a sigh, having done all I could. From then on, it was all in the hands of my uncle. Well, it was all up to his blood, at least.

As I watched over Veronica, her eyes fluttering behind their closed lids, I tried to catch my breath. The rush I'd felt earlier was wearing off fast, exhaustion welling up to take its place. Like a thick, gray cloud of smog, I felt it coming on, choking my senses. I sealed the vial and stuffed it out of sight between the pillow and mattress as I fought to keep my eyes open. The frantic voice ringing about inside my head helped.

"Are you there, Frank?"

Good old Rachelle. "I'm here." I kept my voice low.

"What happened? Were you attacked?"

I nodded, then remembered she couldn't see me. "Yeah, we were. It seems Asmoday got the bulk rate on those Dread Fiends of his. We had four of them pop up. I managed to take out three, but one got away." I glanced over at Veronica. She twitched gently, squirming on the bed with her eyes closed, her face flush with color. I could see her wounds knitting themselves together, the skin bubbling and inching closed. I felt the weight of my conscience lifting itself from my shoulders. I really didn't want to be responsible for her death, my earlier testosterone-fueled anger a distant memory. I still cared too damn much.

"I'm glad you're all right, but I'm afraid there's more."

Not surprised, I shook my head. "What now?"

"The Dread Fiends were nothing more than a distraction."

"From what?" My heart started to pound. If the fiends weren't the worst of it, I was hesitant to know what was.

"While we were busy with Asmoday's pets, he was performing yet another ritual to draw power from the Demonarch."

I thought about that for a second, the words chilling, but yet they felt empty. There was something missing in the equation. "Well, we're all still here. The world isn't a flaming ball of smoking ash, so what happened?"

"I'm not exactly sure. With my focus drawn to the fiends, I failed to notice the dead zone that cropped up until the ritual was already complete." Her voice drifted off, coming back strong. "There was something different about it this time though, Frank. The footprint seems much smaller than it did at the last two locations, the scarring less drastic. I don't sense the same kind of damage to the dimensional wall, although there is some. It just doesn't seem like the same level of event."

"Another trap?"

"No. Katon has already surveyed the area. He found discarded ritual trappings there, yet nothing else."

"Maybe this has something to do with *when* the ritual was performed." I took a second to get my thoughts in order. My head was still pretty scrambled. "We'd estimated Asmoday had been tapping the Demonarch's energy every two days and it's only been about one since the last time. Could that have anything to do with it?"

There was silence on the connection as Rachelle contemplated the possibility. They really needed to pipe in some music during the pauses.

She chimed back up, sounding almost hopeful. "That may well be it. The previous power outputs had been on such a grand scale that it's possible Asmoday has been burning himself out each time he performs the ritual. It is quite tasking. That could explain the apparent reduction of this attempt.""It would also explain why Asmoday needs Gabriel's help, though it does nothing to explain why Gabriel needs his." I felt the bed shift as Veronica sat up, her blue eyes staring at me from above a wide, grateful smile. I grinned back, waggling a finger to request patience. She gave me a pouty-faced look, but nodded. I continued, lowering my voice again and stepping away from the bed. "If he's blowing all his power, we need to find him soon so we can take advantage of it. His greed is the only thing that's keeping us in the game."

"I agree. I'll convey what we've deduced to Rahim. Once we've figured out the course to take, I'll contact you."

"I've my own lead to follow up on, so I'll let you know if it pans out. Talk to you soon."

Rachelle said her farewells, breaking the connection. Once more, it was just me and the multitude of my own questionably sane inner voices bouncing around inside my head. Trust me. They're more than enough to keep me busy.

"Anything exciting?" Veronica asked, her voice still a little raspy.

Once again, I didn't really want to give much away. Our history aside, you just can't trust a succubus. "Just work stuff, that's all." I looked her over, her shredded clothing leaving little to the imagination. "Besides, the only exciting thing in my life these days is you."

She laughed, rolling her eyes. "Sure, buddy, whatever you say." She got up from the bed and sauntered over to me. "I do want to thank you for saving my life though. Those fiends had me. Another minute and I'd have been dead." She shivered, no doubt remembering them hovering over her, their claws tearing into her flesh.

I wrapped my arms around her arched back and pulled her close. "If you hadn't dragged them away, neither of us would be here. You're the hero on this one. I was just following your lead."

She drew in closer, pressing her body against mine in a ferocious hug. "Sounds like we both deserve a reward." She looked up at me and winked, her face all kinds of sultry.

I felt the seam of my torn jeans go tight as my mind ran amok with all the possibilities her statement conjured. She purred, rubbing against me, her hips gently swaying from side to side. I shuddered and pressed back against her, hard. She moaned low in her throat as she slid her warm hands beneath my shirt, her fingertips sliding under my waistband. Pulling me along, she backed up toward the bed unbuckling my belt as we went. At the bed, she yanked my belt from the loops and tossed it to the side, dropping down onto the mattress. In a feat of manual dexterity unheard of this side of Hell, she popped the button to my jeans and slid the zipper down in a fluid motion with one hand while she pulled me on top of her. I felt my gun slip from my waistband and heard it hit the floor. It didn't matter. I had a backup weapon, which was ready to go off.

Frenetic, she buried her mouth in my neck, snarling as she nipped and kissed her way across my throat, leaving behind a moist trail that pricked at my skin. I couldn't help but groan as her warm hand slid deeper into my pants, latching onto me, her grip tight and accommodating. I could feel the beat of my heart against her palm. Taking charge, she used her free hand to slide my pants down to my thighs before rolling me over onto my back. After giving me a grin, which would make a Cheshire cat jealous, she worked her way downward, strafing my chest and stomach with fluttering kisses. Her knees dropped to the floor as her hand continued its dastardly deed. I heard the clink of the vials as she bumped them, tugging my pants to my ankles with her free hand. I lifted my head to watch her ministrations, voyeur that I am. She had small hands. I was feeling pretty good about myself.

Though I knew I should be doing something more productive like finding Glorius and saving the world, I couldn't help myself. I was under her spell like I'd been so many times before. Unable, and more to the point, unwilling, to rein my libido in, I gave in to the yearning that made granite of my groin. I pushed all thoughts of Armageddon aside and let the pleasure wash over me.

My hands entangled themselves in Veronica's silky hair, wordlessly cheering her on. I arched into her, testing her willingness. Finding no boundary, I was consumed by the storm of our passion.

Through the haze of it all, my only coherent thought was, for a woman trained in the arts of Hell, she sure knew an awful lot about Heaven.

Coitus Interruptus

I lay back as Veronica went about pleasuring me, plying her trade. She was a pro. I'd forgotten how satisfying her touch could be. I hadn't realized how much I missed her affection, if what she was doing could be given such a sentimental term. She put all the other women I'd slept with to shame.

Not interested in opening old wounds, I told the voices in my head to shut the hell up about my feelings and encouraged Veronica to continue, my words coming out in grunts and groans. She obliged me by taking me to new heights, drawing me close, then pulling back, holding me on the edge. The bed shook beneath us as I clutched the sheets tight in my sweaty hands. I opened my eyes as her tongue flitted across sensitive areas and watched as the light fixture on the ceiling swung back and forth. Damn she was good.

I felt the rumble of thunder rattle the house as I neared the apex. It was then Veronica pulled away, sitting up on the bed, her eyes narrow.

"Did you feel that?"

I growled as I grabbed her arm, tugging her back down toward my crotch. She resisted. "Of course I felt it, now don't stop. I was almost there." Thinking she needed a bit of romance to regain her motivation, I added, "You're pretty."

She pushed my frantic, clutching hands away. "Not that, idiot. The house is shaking."

Frustrated, I only half heard what she said. "What are you talking about?" She didn't need to answer.

I felt the pressure in the room drop suddenly as a sound like a 747 firing its engines roared up right outside my window, vibrating the entire house. My lungs tightened in my chest as I felt a surge of supernatural energy coalesce somewhere nearby. There was a hell of a lot of it. Pants around my ankles, I dove for the floor dragging Veronica with me.

With an explosion of sound, the roof of my house was blown away, frenzied winds whipping above us. Shards of wood and tile flew past, caught up in the fury of the blast. The front walls followed a second later, furniture and household goods were swept along like an Alabama trailer park during twister season. I felt a wave of energy prickle my skin and pulled Veronica tighter against me in anticipation. We were going for a ride.

A gust of wind blew through the house, aimed lower this time, catching up everything in its wake. The bed tumbled over and the mattress landed over top of us with a thump as the magical tornado whirled through the room. Slid across the floor, we were slammed hard into the bedroom wall. The plasterboard shattered and gave way as we struck. The support studs creaked and cracked against my back, but they held. I cried out in pain as I was wedged against the boards, but nothing could be heard above the wail of the winds.

I felt a series of heavy impacts against the mattress that lay over us as more of the house rained down. I was suddenly glad of the extra money I'd spent on the quality bed as its padded bulk shielded us from further harm. With it blocking the majority of the wind's force, and the detritus that came with it, I rolled over and placed Veronica behind me. Her eyes were wide, frantic, looking for a way out. I couldn't blame her. I wasn't exactly feeling all that brave myself, but I knew this wasn't some natural disaster. Someone was trying to kill us. Worse yet, they'd interrupted us during sex. I felt my face heat up as I thought about how close I had been to getting off. I ground my teeth together as I looked down at my limp dick, the moment ruined. Someone was gonna die for this.

I pulled my pants up as the wind calmed outside our makeshift fort, the ear-splitting whistle dropping to a quiet whine, then to nothing. With the storm settling, I knew it was only a matter of moments until whoever blew the roof off would come looking to finish the job. Not wasting anymore time, I leaned past Veronica and kicked the remaining plasterboard away, opening a hole big enough for her to crawl through. The bathroom beyond was still mostly intact.

I whispered to her, "Go through there and stay low." I pointed to the hole. "I'm gonna draw our attacker away. Once I do, you get up and run in the opposite direction. Get down the street where it's safe and I'll find you when it's over. Got it?"

Veronica nodded. Her face was a knot of sharp lines and I could tell by the way she was shaking, she was scared. That sure didn't make me feel any better. Veronica was a tough woman and it took an awful lot to rattle her cage. The fact that she was afraid caused my own fear to well up and worm its way through my confidence. The voices gibbered inside my head, pleading for me to follow Veronica, to hide. I shouted them down as best I could. I didn't have time to be scared.

She leaned in and kissed me. "Be safe." With a last apologetic look, she squirmed through the hole and crawled out of sight.

I didn't waste any time. I slipped from behind the mattress, working my way over to my stash. I was gonna need a pick-me-up. My heart skipped a beat when I saw what was left of it. There, amidst the wreckage of my deflated Jenna doll was a dark, drying puddle. The wind had pushed everything against the back wall, the vials of Lucifer's blood along with it. Made of glass, the heavy furniture and debris had shattered the tubes, freeing the blood to become inert. I nearly cried.

Frantic, I dug through the mess, but there were no survivors. All of the vials my uncle had given me were destroyed, splattered across the floor and quickly turning to dust. The last trace of Lucifer's existence had been wiped away. I felt my face burning as I thought about what that meant. There would be no more quick heals for me, no magical advantage. Worse, I had lost my only connection to my heritage, all long dead or gone. Now, Lucifer truly was nothing more than a memory.

Furious, I pulled myself together and stormed out of the ruin of my house. I wanted to know who'd taken my uncle from me. I wanted revenge. Once past the rubble, I came face to face with the destroyer of my house and irreplaceable inheritance.

It was Henry McConnell.

My confidence took a dump.

"Howdy." He waved at me. "Seems you've ticked the boss off something fierce." A cloud of billowing smoke surrounded the area around my house and the street, cutting the view off from the other side.

"Well, ain't that an unfortunate pile of steaming bull puckey, cowboy." The rebel in me kicked into high gear, my anxiety spurring it on. "You can tell your boss he just interrupted the best blow job I've ever had and I'm not in the mood to give a damn about his feelings." I kept my head enough to start circling away from the house. I turned him so the wreckage was out of his field of vision to give Veronica a chance to escape unnoticed. He kept pace with me, but he stayed about ten feet away. His eyes remained locked on mine.

McConnell chuckled. Even his laugh had an accent. "Sorry to have bothered you, but you know how it is. When the boss man says jump, I ask how high. When he says kill the devil mutt, I ask how dead."

"Maybe I'm remembering it all wrong, but didn't we just do this not too long ago? If I recall correctly, it ended with you running off with your tail between your legs. What makes you think it'll end any differently this time?" Apparently my mouth felt the need to write a check it couldn't afford to cash. I'm not even sure Donald Trump could afford the bill I was racking up.

He shook his head, an amused smile on his lips. "The last time, I wasn't expecting you to show up. I was just there to pick up the chains the boys left behind. And besides, I was burnt out from helping the boss light up that angel he's got all trussed up. This time, I've got all my horses saddled up and raring to go." A tiny spout of fire sprung up from his palm and danced across his fingers as nimbly as a ballerina. He winked at me, the firelight glistening in his blue eyes.

I'd realized during our first run-in McConnell wasn't operating on a full tank, but I'd noticed too late to take advantage of it. I was regretting that failure now. If what he said was true, and he was fully charged, I didn't stand a chance.

"We can't discuss this?" I changed gears.

"Tain't nothin' to discuss. I got a job to do and I figure I better get on with it. It was nice meeting you, hear?"

I didn't waste a second. If that cowpoke wanted to put me down, he was gonna have to work for it. I dove forward, closing the distance between us, lashing out with a right. My heart jumped as I felt the satisfying thud of my fist collide with his mouth. He grunted and rolled away, redirecting most of the impact and stumbling back to give himself room. He wasn't getting off that easy. I stayed on him. I threw a low kick, which nearly buckled his leg, and followed it with a left hook. It caught him alongside the head, just above the ear, and I saw his eyes flutter. His legs gave way a second later and he dropped onto his butt. Thinking I had him and feeling rather optimistic, I moved to put a knee in his face.

His magic struck first.

With but a flick of his hand, he sent out a wave of concussive force. It slammed into me like a wrecking ball. I flew back before I'd even realized what'd happened. The pain hit me while I was still in the air. It felt like I'd been raped by a jackhammer, all romance aside.

Instinctively, I curled up just before I struck the ground, but it didn't help much. I crashed hard and rolled, more accurately defined as flopping, and bounced along the asphalt. I was in a white haze of agony when I finally came to a stop. My eyes wouldn't focus, my lungs burned with each shallow breath, and my body ached like it had been run through a hydraulic press. I lifted my head, fighting down nausea as I looked for McConnell. He was strolling forward, his eyes burning holes in me. My optimism crawled away to hide someplace I'd rather not talk about. I seriously thought about following it.

"I was gonna make it easy for you, boy, and kill you quickly." He closed, cracking the knuckles of his fingers as his hands clenched into fists. "Not anymore. You want to slug it out? I'm more than willing to oblige you." He gestured for me to get up.

I debated staying where I was. Without my guns, or my uncle's blood, I wasn't anywhere close to winning this confrontation. This was David versus Goliath, but only if David were a blind quadriplegic with asthma. I didn't even think I had that much of a chance. Despite all that though, it just wasn't in me to quit. I pulled myself to my feet with a groan, and met McConnell's eyes.

His face softened a bit, the hint of a smile creeping onto his bloody lips. "Glad to see you've got a pair on you." He settled into a defensive posture. It appeared he knew a thing or two about boxing. Just my luck, the old boy could fight.

"All balls, no brains, or so they tell me."

He chuckled, apparently having realized that already, and moved forward.

The talking over, we began to circle one another. Not expecting him to fight fair, I thought it best to get off first to see what I could make happen. I darted in with a jab and a quick, straight right. The jab clipped him and he adjusted, sweeping my right to the side. He countered easily, his hand speed much faster than I would have believed him capable of, and punched me in the liver. A flash of gray sparked off when he hit and my side exploded with pain, tendrils of it snaking down my leg and across my crotch.

I stumbled, barely getting my arms up in time to block the follow up. His fist crashed into my forearms, once more throwing up a flash of gray light. It was like he'd hit me with a sledgehammer. The bones in my arm throbbed, my shoulders stiffening up as I backed away.

He grinned, stalking me down. My prediction as to the fairness of the fight played out and I knew I wasn't gonna be walking away in one piece. I cast a quick glance toward the house and hoped Veronica had run like I'd told her. It would tear me up to think what might happen to her once McConnell was finished with me. I shook my head to clear away the images that popped up. I didn't want to picture the possibilities.

Driven to a rage by my way too active imagination, I lashed out. I threw a feint with my left, following it up with a kick to his ribs. My shin struck home with a thump, knocking the wind from McConnell. He gasped hard, doubling over, but he managed to catch my leg. With it leveraged against his side, he twisted hard and I heard a snap, his magically-enhanced strength making it easy. I screeched as stabbing pains shot through my calf, the bones of my lower leg broken.

McConnell lifted it up over his shoulder and dumped me on my back. I hit the asphalt with a thud, reaching down to cradle my right leg as he hovered over me.

"Any last words," he huffed, his breath still a little short.

I moaned against the hard surface of the street, rolling my head to look up at him. "Yeah." I did my best to smile through the pain. "You might want to watch your back."

He burst out laughing. "You think I'm gonna fall for tha—" A flash of red behind him cut him off.

He spun around, but was too late. Rahim let loose a burst of searing energy that smashed into him, blowing him a hundred feet into the air. I heard him land a few seconds later, crashing down through the roof of an aluminum storage shed in the yard next door.

"Are you all right?" Rahim asked with surprising gentleness in his voice. His upper lip peeled back into a disgusted sneer when he saw my leg, the bones protruding from the skin. He looked a little pale.

I shook my head. There wasn't time to do

anything else.

There was a squeal of aluminum being torn apart, then a flash of gray blasted through the neighbor's rock wall and streaked over my head, tearing into Rahim. He cried out as the force of the blow drove him back. Knocked off his feet, he slid along the asphalt, shredding flesh in crimson layers as he went. He tumbled to a halt and got to his feet, wobbling as McConnell stepped over the wreckage of the wall and stormed toward him. Rahim seemed dazed.

I shouted a warning as The Gray walked past me, unable to do anything to stop him. Rahim looked up just as McConnell let fly another burst of energy. The old wizard threw up a shield and reflected the blast, grimacing as he did. I could see his arms shaking from where I lay. No doubt McConnell could as well. He pressed forward.

Tenacious, he fired blast after magical blast, alternating hands and angles in an attempt to take Rahim out. Rahim was just as intent upon not being struck. He conjured shield upon shield, turning away each of The Gray's attacks, many at the very last second. Though he held his ground, I could see he was tiring. Sweat trickled down his face and he was breathing in deep, sucking gasps. It wouldn't be long until he missed a block. Things would be over for us both when that happened.

With no magic of my own to aid in the fight,

I thought about what I could do to help. Injured as I was, it wasn't much. I glanced back at the remains of my house and had an idea. Tearing the sleeve from my shirt, I wrapped it tight around my broken leg. I clenched my teeth to hold back my screams, doing what I could to work through the pain. The wound, like any caused by a supernatural being, wouldn't heal on its own so I couldn't expect it to get better. The best I could hope for was it didn't get worse. I tightened the tourniquet to keep the bones from shifting too much, rolling over onto my stomach.

As the battle raged behind me, I dragged myself toward the house. Each agonizing inch was like dousing my leg in gasoline and setting a match to it. The punctures, where the bone had torn through the skin, burned with searing intensity as it scraped across the unforgiving asphalt. Dirt and grease were being ground in, guaranteeing infection, if I lived long enough to worry about it. The bones twisted and turned inside the leg, grinding against one another with every shift of position. Tears streamed from my eyes and I bit down on my bottom lip to keep from calling attention to myself. An agonizing eternity later, the sounds of the magical duel muffled by the wreckage, I crawled into the house. Fortunately, given my current condition, the majority of the front rooms no longer existed. There was nothing but smooth tiled floors and open space. Compared to the street and the sandpaper surface of the sidewalk I'd had to cross to get here, this was like Heaven. Too bad I'd have to crawl out once I found what I was looking for. I stowed the negativity and continued on, hauling myself to the bedroom. Once inside, I headed for the back wall. Thanks to the wind assault of McConnell's, if I was going to find anything, it'd be there. Halfway across the room, where the debris began, I found it harder to navigate. Wooden splinters dug into my legs, their sharpened points piercing through my jeans and finding a home in the soft flesh. Glass shards snapped and cut deep as I crawled over them to reach the back of the room. Though there'd been a decent amount of blood oozing out of me when I'd arrived in the bedroom, there was now a lake pooling beneath me, a tributary running behind. I was beginning to feel the effect of the blood loss. My vision had begun to tunnel, the edges hazy and indistinct. My thoughts had become sluggish, chaotic; more so than usual.

Realizing how little time I had before I succumbed to my wounds, I dug through the debris with abandon. I ran my hands recklessly through the pieces of broken furniture and the shredded pieces of my house, searching for my gun. I was coming up empty.

I heard Rahim cry out from the street and redoubled my effort, only slightly reassured by the continued sounds of magical warfare. There wasn't much time left for either of us. I crept closer to the discarded mattress, digging through the wreckage. I had just about given up all hope, my thoughts wavering in my head, when my hand lighted on something cold and metallic. I sighed as I ran my numb hand over its surface, identifying it. I groaned. What little energy I had spiraled to nothing.

It wasn't my pistol.

I collapsed in defeat, the vestiges of my resistance crumbling beneath the weight of my despair. My vision narrowed further as unconsciousness came to call, whispering soothing lullabies. My eyelids, far too heavy to resist the pull of gravity, drifted closed. I felt the darkness rising up to meet me.

The end had come.

A whoosh of air startled me back to consciousness. I lifted my weary head and forced my heavy eyes open. There in front of me, laying flat upon the mattress was Rahim. He didn't look so good. The places where his clothes had been burnt away by The Gray's magical blasts, scorched and bubbled skin shone through. Patches of deep red and even blacker burns stood out against his natural dark hue. He lifted his head and met my gaze. I saw something in his eyes I'd never thought I'd see there.

Fear.

There was also disappointment in equal amount. I think he cared more about being beaten by McConnell than he did about dying.

Before I could say anything, I felt a gust of wind whip by as a pair of snakeskin cowboy boots dropped to the ground a few feet in front of me. McConnell turned and grinned as I peered up at him through fluttering eyes. Though his face looked a little worse for wear, puffy eyes, bruised, swollen cheeks, he didn't look anywhere near as bad as Rahim did. That was a sobering realization.

"There you are. I'd wondered where you'd gotten off to. Figured you crawled off to die. Glad to see I was wrong," he told me. "Give me a second to take care of your buddy here, then you and I can get back to business." He chuckled and stepped to Rahim, energy building at his hands. Gray sparks fluttered to life. "Don't worry, old boy, I'm not going to kill you. Not yet at least. The master could use a strong conduit like you. It'd sure save me a hell of a lot of grief."

Though I knew there was nothing I could do, I couldn't just lay there without trying. I moved to get up, sliding my elbows underneath me for support. That's when I felt the cold steel of something clutched in the death grip of my left hand. I wracked my brain to figure out what it was while I quietly tugged it toward me through the debris. The increasing hum of McConnell's magic covered the sound. He was charging up the batteries to be sure he could put Rahim out. I could feel the power washing over me. He was loaded for bear. Time was running out.

Unable to think clearly, I pulled the thing from beneath the wreckage and stared hard at the interlocking links. A second passed, and another, as I implored my brain to engage. Just as The Gray raised his hands to smite Rahim, it suddenly did. I held a pair of the magical manacles in my hand; the same chains that Asmoday had used to bind an angel.

With nothing to lose, Rahim and I already dead in my mind, I mustered up the final remnants of my strength and pulled myself into a crouch. I hissed as I drew my broken leg up underneath me, but it held, barely. McConnell heard me and glanced over his shoulder. His eyes sprung wide as he saw what I held. He whirled around extending his arm toward me at the same time I leapt forward. The timing was perfect.

The cuff hit his wrist and clacked shut as I tumbled to the ground clutching the other end. The dancing gray flames, which swirled at his palm, blinked twice, then died, dispersing without so much fanfare as a fart in an empty room. McConnell screamed, his voice shrill and crackling, as his free hand clawed at the manacle, trying to remove it. With the opportunity presenting itself, I sat up and snapped the remaining cuff over his free wrist. It clicked closed with a solemn snap.

The look on his bearded face, the quivering lower lip, his twitching eyelid, was priceless. He looked like I'd just sexed up his horse. That alone was worth the beating he'd given me. When I look back on my life, the twisted, agitated look on his face was an image I'd always remember. I might even masturbate to it on occasion considering the amount of pleasure it brought me at that moment. It was that good.

"That's gotta suck."

I fell back with a smile, too exhausted to hold myself up any longer. His eyes swiveled to me. They were like two simmering coals, flickering red. I didn't know what to expect when I'd slapped the cuffs on him, but I had thought it might physically restrain him as well as neutralize his magic.

Seems I was wrong.

He growled low in his throat and drove the point of his boot hard into my stomach. I gasped as the blow knocked me back into the wall, my lungs aching. With no mercy, he pulled his leg back and soccer kicked me in the face. My head snapped back, spider-webbing the plaster of the wall behind me as my mouth filled with the tangy taste of blood. My skull rang like an old brass bell and my jaw throbbed, but I noticed something as it did. Earlier when he'd been beating me, each blow was crippling, bone-jarring. It was like being hit by a speeding truck, but now, his blows seemed like love taps in comparison.

I smiled big and wide, no doubt a crimson mess, as I realized what it was. With the manacles shutting down his magic, he wasn't this almighty powerful wizard, he was human. Everything he did to me would heal. He couldn't kill me anymore. I started to laugh, a sick, maniacal laugh that would have made any witch proud.

It just enraged McConnell. With no clue as to why I was laughing, he worked himself into a frenzy. Frothing at the mouth and screaming obscenities, he rained down punches, the chain of the manacles long enough it didn't limit his motion too much.

Blow after blow bounced off my face and skull, streamers of blood trailing in the passage of his hands. After each, I would laugh a little harder, doing my best to smile up at him. This just infuriated him further. Like a whirlwind, he swung his arms and battered me. He showed no signs of stopping until I heard a crack and he reeled back with a shout, clutching at his right hand. Through the blur of blood and swelling, I saw he'd broken it. That made it all so much more amusing. I laughed a little harder.

McConnell snapped and started stomping me, his cowboy boot slamming into my side and bouncing away only to return a second later, as if it were a trampoline. Though I knew none of it was permanent, I started to reconsider my provocation as I felt a couple of my ribs snap inside my chest. I sucked in slow, shallow breaths as he thumped out a double bass rhythm on my side so well any metal band would be glad to have him as their drummer. It hurt so bad I couldn't see any more, my eyes washed out with white. Barely conscious to begin with, I felt the dark creeping back to claim me once more. I wasn't dying, but it sure was starting to feel like it.

Rahim spared me that fortunate release.

Coming up behind McConnell, who was far too worked up to notice, Rahim laid a 2x4 across the back of The Gray's skull. His eyes went wide with surprise before rolling back into his head. He collapsed in a heap, his slack face laying just a few inches from mine.

"You killed Santa Claus," I muttered as Rahim pulled me up, setting my back against the wall. I tried not to whine too much.

"He'll wish he was dead before I'm through with him." Rahim kicked McConnell, more out of spite than for any practical reason, causing him to roll a few feet away from us. He glared down at the man, doing his best to control his raging temper. I could tell he wanted to kill him, but he had something else in mind. I was too tired to care, either way.

I watched the wizard lay on his back like a dead fish with a twinge of satisfaction running through me. I couldn't feel any pity for the guy after all he'd done.

Shit! What he'd done.

Veronica.

"Veronica was here when McConnell attacked. I don't know if she made it out," I blurted out, my voice cracking on the last.

Rahim looked at me like he'd hoped I was joking, having seen the catastrophe of my marriage. When he saw the worry etched across my battered and bruised face, he shook his head, dropped the 2x4 in my lap and started toward the back of the house.

"I'll check for her."

Rahim knew I was playing with fire by letting her back into my life, under my skin. But despite being an all-powerful wizard, he was also a man. He understood. We're weak when it comes to women. It's our nature.

He pointed back at The Gray. "Keep an eye on him. If he moves, thump him. Just don't kill him." With a frustrated shake of his head, he disappeared into the wreckage of my house.

I stared after him until he was gone, then turned back to McConnell. He was out cold. His breath made the whiskers of his beard sway back and forth like a coral bed under the ocean. Mesmerized by the motion, I sat there waiting. It wasn't long. With little left of my house, the remnants blown into a pile in the backyard, Rahim didn't have much to search through. He stomped back into the room, his face humorless.

"She must have gotten away." He ignored my grateful sigh. He looked pensive, as if something weighed on him. It only took a second for him to let it out. He was never the kind of guy who kept his mouth shut. "The residuals in the portal room, which survived by the way, show someone gated out within the last few minutes. I presume that would be Veronica." He held something up, holding it out for me to see. "I did find this in the room though."

I looked up at his hand and saw the glass vial he held. My heart skipped a beat as he handed it to me, my head whirling in circles. I snatched the tube, cradling it in my hands as I examined it. All that was left inside the sealed vial were about two, tiny drops. I knew, without a doubt, what had happened to the rest.

Veronica.

Benedict's Song

The very last of my uncle's blood having run its course through my veins, I stood in front of McConnell as his eyes fluttered open. Tied to a chair in a small interrogation room at DRAC headquarters, the magical bindings of the manacles still in place, he looked up at me in confusion.

"Where—"

"The where isn't as important as the why."

He strained against the restraints as his memory flooded back. His eyes met mine looking me over, disappointment welling up in them. Seeing me in one piece was the last thing he expected. It was certainly the last thing he wanted. He tested his bonds again, but they held. Katon, who stood out of sight behind him, tied them well.

"What do you want?"

"I think you have a pretty good idea of what I want." I leaned in, grinning.

Then I punched him.

The short right caught him on the cheek, knocking his head to the side before he whipped it back to glare at me. "What the hell was that for?"

"That was for not letting me get off before you blew my house down, you big bad wolf you." I raised my fist again and he leaned back in the seat as far as his bonds would allow him. "This little piggy is pissed." I huffed and I puffed.

Katon stepped forward, laying a dark hand on McConnell's shoulder. The wizard flinched.

"I'll take it from here, Frank." His eyes gestured toward the door. "Your interrogation skills are quite impressive, but they lack the subtle dread that produces results." He stepped around the chair and smiled down at The Gray, the sharpened points of his eyeteeth glistening.

Katon was right. I saw McConnell shiver, his eyes moistening against his will.

"Take the pigs to market. I'll find the answers we need here."

I nodded and went wee wee wee, all the way home. Well, more like out into the hall.

Outside, Rahim stood watching the action through a large two-way mirror. His arms were crossed over his chest, his face pensive and dark with bruises. He looked tired. I imagined he was still worn out from his battle with The Gray. It'd been a rough few days for all of us.

"You think he'll give up Asmoday's location?"

"I'm sure he will," Rahim replied. "Betrayal is in his nature."

I sighed. He wasn't the only one apparently. "That's good because my lead ripped me off and slipped away during the chaos." I didn't bother to mention her name. He knew.

Rahim gave me an understanding look. "Maybe it's for the best."

As much as I hated to admit it, he was right. I just wished the timing had been better. You just can't find the equal of succubus love and with so few of them around, you can't replace them. I was gonna miss the lying, stealing, cheating, murderous bitch. Katon came out of the interrogation room and snapped me out of my self-pitying reverie.

"We have the location." He walked up to us, licking a trickle of blood off of his index finger.

"Already?" Even knowing how effective Katon was, I was surprised at how fast he'd broken McConnell. I'd apparently given the wizard too much credit for being a tough guy.

"The nursery rhymes softened him up, no doubt." He winked at me while he passed a hand-drawn map to Rahim. "This is the site of the next power transfer. Asmoday and Glorius are currently there, according to McConnell. He also said Asmoday intends this to be the final ritual. It would appear even angels have an upper limit of power that they can absorb, and Glorius is nearing his. To go beyond that line would kill him with no one being the recipient of his magical energies."

"Is that the reason why the last ritual was so

subdued in comparison to the rest?" Rahim asked.

Katon nodded. "In part, but it was mostly due to Asmoday's concerns we might be closing in on him. He rushed the transfer to take advantage of the distraction provided by his fiends. He also performed it alone, as McConnell had other obligations." He motioned toward me. "I think we've spooked him a bit."

"Now is the time to go after him while he's still weak," I urged.

"We too are weakened and there is yet the matter of Gabriel," Rahim argued, "but I think you're right. Now is the time."

"Don't worry about Gabriel. I've a surprise for him." I smirked like I had it all under control, despite still needing to find a way to meet the terms of Forcalor's agreement. I figured knocking down Asmoday's door would be as good a start as any.

"We'll need as much assistance as we can muster, especially now that Asmoday's fiends have wounded or killed most of our heavy hitters." Katon turned to me. "Can you reach Scarlett? We could use her."

No doubt we could. No doubt at all. The temperature in the room rose ten degrees as I agreed with Katon's words, if not his intended sentiment. "I'll see what I can do."

Katon looked at me with exasperated eyes and shook his head. I imagined he knew what I was thinking. I'm an open book most times. Well, more like an open porno mag, but you get my point. Once you've seen the cover, you know what's going on inside.

"Then we'd best prepare. It won't be long before Asmoday misses McConnell and realizes he's failed in his mission to kill Frank. Our window of opportunity is no doubt closing fast."

I nodded to Rahim. At long last we had some real direction. I ran off to call Scarlett and find some replacement guns.

It was time for war.

Best Laid Plans

Rahim, Katon, and I crouched in the shadows near the location McConnell had drawn on the map. The cowboy lay on the ground behind us, gagged and bound and looking forlorn. I'm not sure what Rahim's plans for him were, but I didn't imagine they were nice. Myself, I was thinking human shield.

In silence, we surveyed the weather-battered barn situated on a small farm a few miles out of town. Out of the way and unassuming, it was the perfect place for an ambush.

At least it wasn't a warehouse.

I couldn't feel the overwhelming residue of magic as I had at the other locations, but I could feel something. More correctly, it was a lack of something. My senses drifted out, encountering nothing. It was a subtle nothingness, like reaching into the void of space. I looked to Rahim to confirm what I felt.

He nodded and whispered, "Dampeners."

I gave the thumbs up sign to McConnell. It seemed he'd given us the right information. He glared back, less than pleased to have been dragged along. I'm sure he thought we'd leave him at DRAC, locked away safe and sound, far from the demon master he betrayed. That'd be getting off too easy.

I smiled and returned my attention to the barn. Though the main doors at the front were closed, a small entrance to the side sat open. A gentle, flickering light shone somewhere inside, creating dancing shadows just outside. I didn't see any security devices, but we stayed out of sight just in case.

I mouthed the word "trap?" as I glanced at Katon.

"Probably, but who knows?" He shrugged, not bothering to lower his voice. "It doesn't really matter. He'll know we're here once we enter the barn so it's not like we can sneak up on him. The dampeners keep him from sensing us the same way they do us from him, but inside past the barrier we'll light up like flares. The only thing we can hope for is that he's not prepared for us to show up."

"Why are we sitting out here?" I gestured to the barn and the field surrounding it. "There's no one out here waiting for us. If he's set something up, it's inside where we're going anyway."

Katon answered, "I was hoping your cousin would make an appearance before we went in. The extra angel power would be nice."

I agreed. I'd tried to get a hold of Scarlett before we left DRAC, but she wasn't answering. I'd even sicced the telepaths on her, but for whatever reason, she couldn't be reached. I wasn't worried so much as I was irritated. Scarlett had her own agenda and it rarely conformed to my own. It wasn't the first time I'd been left in a lurch because she couldn't be bothered. I just hoped it wouldn't be the last.

I shrugged. There was nothing more I could do. "If she was gonna show, she'd have done it by now. I think we're wasting our time waiting on her."

Rahim nodded. "You're most likely right. Let's go." He stood and pulled McConnell to his feet. He dragged the other wizard along as he headed toward the open door.

Katon took the lead and motioned for me to take it up the rear. I debated being offended. I didn't swing that way even for a sweet-talker as smooth as him. It took me a second to realize I'd misunderstood his hand signals. With a flustered smile on my face and my cheeks burning, I dropped behind Rahim and followed the group through the door.

Inside was a short hallway, which led to the main barn, the walls covered in framed photographs of what must have been the farm's prize winning cattle. I had a sudden craving for a T-bone. Rahim nudged my shoulder and motioned for me to follow Katon through the inner door. I wiped the drool from my mouth and did as I was asked. I had a feeling I was gonna regret itWhen didn't I?

As we walked into the barn, all the lights in the room flashed to life, the sudden glare blinding. At least it would have been to a human. Katon and I blinked a few times and our eyes adjusted. It's good to be a devil sometimes. Apparently it's not so bad being a vampire either.

Rahim lingered in the hall for a few seconds, his eyes adjusting slower, before following us in. Katon and I surveyed the room, looking for the trap we expected to be sprung. Turns out, we didn't need to.

In the center of the room, surrounded by a handful of Dread Fiends and the three surviving angels from my earlier encounter, Asmoday stood waiting for us. A broad, white smile appeared above the blackness of his thick beard. Glorius was nowhere to be seen and there were no signs of any ritual preparations.

"Do come in," he called us forward. So much for the element of surprise. He'd known we were coming.

Since it wouldn't change anything in a tactical sense, as we were already inside the killing field of the barn, we obliged him. We did keep back a few extra yards, just to give us breathing room when the shit hit the fan. No point in getting too cozy with a guy who intended to kill us.

"You're turning out to be quite resourceful, Triggaltheron."

And again with that damn name. I shook my head and looked to Katon and Rahim. They were busy taking the lay of the land, so to speak, and preparing themselves for the confrontation to come. That left me to deal with the ass hole. I encouraged Asmoday to continue, giving them time to plot.

"I have my moments."

"That you do. First, you survived my angel companions here." He gestured to the three who stood glaring at me with murder in their eyes. "Oh, and let me introduce you since it appears I was remiss the last time. Silly me." He pointed to each in turn. "Malis, Rafal, and Urtel. You of course knew Israfil, their companion, the one you killed. Quite impressive, I must admit." The angels didn't look impressed. They just looked pissed. "After that, you managed to defeat my Dread Fiends. And to top it all off, you captured my wizard whom I knew couldn't be trusted to carry out his duties alone." He glared at McConnell with fury in his eyes. The Gray stared at the ground, unwilling to meet his master's gaze. There was nothing happy about this particular reunion. "It seems I've underestimated you, Triggaltheron."

"Don't worry about it. It happens all the time." I waved off the underhanded compliment. "It's the combination of charming good looks and my mid-seventy IQ that throws people off. It's hard to cope with a complete package like this." I ran my hands down the length of my body seductively slow, posing while I winked at Asmoday. Gay men everywhere cringed, I imagine.

Asmoday shook his head, not amused. "You should have taken me up on my offer. It was your only chance to escape the coming Armageddon alive."

"I'm not sure what you find so exciting about ruling over a smoldering ruin, but to be honest, I'm not interested in surviving Armageddon. Especially if all that's gonna be left is you and your flunkies. I'd rather be dead."

"Rest assured, you'll get your wish." His dark eyes met mine. Fire danced within them. His servants, apparently feeling the tension ramping up, crept forward a few steps. "You are a disgrace to your uncle's memory. Fortune smiled upon us when you refused the mantle. It would have been a dark day in Hell had you inherited Lucifer's throne."

I could feel the building current of Rahim's power as he readied his defenses. Katon tensed beside him, his hand creeping toward his blade.

Me? I did what I do best. I provoked. "I might not have inherited Hell, but I did inherit Lucifer's trust. He sure didn't offer *you* the job of Anti-Christ, did he?" I could see the anger creasing his face, but surprisingly he remained in control.

"Why would I want to be the Anti-Christ, when I could be God?" A triumphant grin lit up his face. "I will raze the whole of creation and remake it in *my* image. It's too bad you won't be around to witness the glory of my new genesis."

"You still need to contend with us," Rahim told him, stepping forward. "We know your powers have been exhausted by the rituals, and since your accomplice, Gabriel, isn't here to defend you, you might want to put away your delusions of grandeur."

Asmoday reared his head back and laughed. A chill ran down my spine at hearing it.

"It's no wonder Baalth holds your organization in such high regard, you have proven to be worthy adversaries. He gives you too much respect, though." Asmoday signaled to someone out of sight behind him.

Through a door, hidden in the shadows at the rear of the barn, a Dread Fiend ambled out. A long, thick chain, clutched in its claw, ran behind it into the darkness. With an impatient hiss, the creature yanked the leash hard and a figure stumbled into the light. My heart rate spiked.

It was Scarlett.

Bound by the same type of manacles, which held McConnell's power in check, the fiend tugged her along easily. In addition to the magical cuffs, her arms were pinned to her body with thick chains that ensured no movement of her upper body. To add insult to injury, the scabbard at her hip was empty. To top it all off, she was gagged. Her eyes burned like fiery stars above the gag, locking onto mine as she was led toward us.

Under normal circumstances, seeing Scarlett tied up like that would have produced an erection so hard I would have passed out due to the lack of blood to my brain. Today, it just made me angry. If anyone was gonna introduce my cousin to bondage, it was gonna be me, damn it. I growled and started forward.

"Let her go."

Asmoday's bully squad moved to intercept me, forming a wall between us as Scarlett was delivered to his side. The fiend handed her over, then withdrew a narrow, rune-covered blade, passing it along as well. Asmoday wrapped an arm around Scarlett's chest, pulling her into him. He slid the blade under her chin, pressing it hard against her throat.

"I'd say her death would provide me with more than enough power to defend myself, don't you agree, wizard?"

Rahim glowered, his fists clenched into tight balls of fury. But despite his anger, I saw him back down, his shoulders slumping, his hands trembling but opening. I could tell by the look on his face he wasn't happy about it, but he must have felt it best, otherwise he wouldn't have done it.

More than anything, Rahim was a man of conviction. He had vowed to save the world and he intended to keep his promise. It didn't matter to him whether Scarlett lived or died, or any of us really, all that mattered was the cause. He would kill Scarlett himself if it advanced DRAC's agenda. That was the depth of his conviction. His tentativeness meant he understood her death would tip the balance against us. He wasn't willing to risk that when he thought there was still some chance, however slim, we could pull off the win.

"While her death might provide you with enough energy to fend us off, it would also weaken you at the worst possible moment," Rahim countered. He might not have wanted to start a fight, but he wasn't cowed.

Asmoday's eyes narrowed, the blade staying put. He said nothing, but his eyes implored Rahim to go on.

"Do you truly believe your lackeys can hold us off long enough to complete the transfer? Ten seconds is an eternity to place your life in the hands of renegade angels and thick-skulled Dread Fiends." Rahim exuded confidence, taking a half step forward, seizing on Asmoday's hesitation. "Are you willing to wager your life just to find out how resourceful we truly are?"

Asmoday raised his upper lip into a snarl. Rahim had gotten into his head, but the demon hadn't come this far to fail. "What do you propose?"

"A trade." Rahim pointed at McConnell. "The wizard for the angel and you walk away." I wasn't sure what angle Rahim was playing, but I figured he knew what he was doing so I kept my mouth shut.

McConnell, however, didn't seem to care what Rahim was doing, he just knew it wasn't gonna end well for him. His eyes sprung wide as he spewed muffled complaints into the gag, thrashing against the restraints. Asmoday looked him over with cold eyes, as if weighing his value.

Rahim continued his pitch. "Though it's true Scarlett's strength is considerable and her death would provide you with the means to fight us off for a short while, that course of action comes at great risk. Fail and you and all your grand plans end here in an inauspicious grave." He gestured to the ramshackle barn. "What I offer is a way for you to avoid that risk as well as provide you with the opportunity to address the failure of your would-be assassin."

While Asmoday didn't appear to understand Rahim's motivations any more than the rest of us did, he had to know the wizard had some kind of trick up his sleeve. He didn't seem to care though. He must have had one hell of a hand himself.

"I believe I'll accept your offer, wizard. We exchange the angel for my incompetent servant, followed by my departure and nothing more." He didn't bother to wait for Rahim's acknowledgment.

He motioned to his minions. He passed Scarlett over to one of them and it led her past the line. The creature stopped a few feet from us, still holding the leash. Another of Asmoday's fiends stepped forward and grabbed a hold of McConnell, watching us the whole time. The Gray's eyes screamed to us as he was dragged back to his master. He found no sympathy. Once he'd crossed the line of Asmoday's minions, the fiend which held Scarlett released the chain and backed away, its arms raised to show it posed no threat. I jumped and pulled her behind us, fumbling at her binds.

It was all too easy.

Asmoday latched onto McConnell, smiling all the while. "Thank you. I needed the wizard far more than I did your angel, at this point." His grin grew even wider. "Now, as per our arrangement, I shall depart. But let me leave you with this…"

I knew it. Never trust a demon.

"The end is but a dawn away. I go now to prepare Glorius for his final moment." He backed away slowly, pulling the reluctant McConnell along. "His sacrifice shall usher in a new age where the followers of light shall be scoured from existence, the firmament lashed to scarlet shreds. From my sanctum of peace, I will watch as humanity breathes its last and the heavens are burned to blackened ash." He pointed at us as he reached the shadows. "Do what you must to prepare for you have precious few moments left. Farewell."

Darkness welled up beneath them, blurring the forms of Asmoday and McConnell. They were washed away by an obsidian wave, a column of blackness that streaked upward to disappear from sight.

The angels and fiends left behind, smiled in malevolent unison and advanced. I redoubled my effort to free Scarlett as they spread out to encircle us. Katon and Rahim moved to defend while I fidgeted with the chains.

Though I'd thought of Scarlett tied up more

times than I should probably admit, I never pictured a scene quite like this. I cast a quick glance at the approaching minions as my adrenaline-charged hands shook and fumbled with her binds, working way too slow. I sighed and tried to focus.

In even the most wild of my fantasies, I'd never imagined a gang-bang this perverse.

A Tragic Hour

Like fireworks on the fourth of July, sparks of magical energy flashed all around me while I struggled to free Scarlett. I flinched as an explosion erupted right behind me, blocked by Rahim who'd thrown up a hastily crafted shield at the very last possible moment. The heat of the blast filtered through and raised goose bumps along my skin, singeing the hairs on my neck. Determined, now more than ever, to get Scarlett loose and join the fray, I blocked out everything else and focused on the manacles. I traced the silver symbols on the cuffs, hoping my memory worked and I could keep my hands steady enough to get the right order.

I got lucky.

As the symbols lighted up in my finger's wake, a shimmering red glow tracing their outlines, I heard a metallic clank and the cuffs popped open. Scarlett's power flooded back to her, the mystical restraints no longer neutralizing it. Her eyes shined with renewed energy. She howled, though it came out sounding like a strangled cat through the gag, and flexed against the rest of the chains. The links snapped as though they were made of glass. Metal shrapnel hurtled in all directions as the bulk of the chains dropped to the floor at her feet. She tore the gag away and gave me a grateful smile, wicked intentions swirling in her fierce eyes.

Her manner feral, she spun and zeroed in on the closest of the angels, her former brethren. "Traitorous whores!"

Before the words had even cleared her mouth, Scarlett launched herself at Rafal, the closest to her. With her sword missing, presumably still in the hands of Asmoday, she led with her fists. To the accompaniment of thunder, Scarlett crashed into her foe. A flash of blinding light exploded when they collided, the two locked in a streaking comet of whirling limbs. The impact carried them across the room and through the wall of the barn where a cloud of dust and wooden splinters obscured their passage.

Certain Scarlett could take care of herself, I turned back to survey the battle field. Rahim, though weakened by his earlier fight with McConnell, seemed to be holding his own. Like a mythical Gandalf, he had fashioned a sword and shield out of pure energy and stood fast on the front line. Each sweep of his mystical sword carved a deep swath through the ranks of Asmoday's minions. Though it seemed to do little damage, the angels defending against it with their own magic, it seemed to keep them at bay.

It had claimed at least one victim, however. A fiend lay face down on the dusty floor, its stomach gaping wide like the mouth of a carnival fun ride. Its moist intestines bubbled out from underneath it, a never-ending serpent of black and deep red. Wafts of steam and putrid scents drifted from the wound, a gentle serenade of hissing accompanying it.

Katon, skulking behind the wizard, darted out between Rahim's strokes and struck at the minions with his crimson blade. I watched as his enchanted weapon split the ribs of a Dread Fiend, its point piercing the creature's heart. Its eyes rolled back in its head as the vampire pulled his sword free. It shuddered and dropped cold the instant the blade was removed, Katon dancing back to the safety of Rahim's defenses.

Wanting a piece of the action myself, I drew my guns and aimed them at the angels. I figured a couple more souls would look good on my spiritual resume. But before I could fire, I saw a flash of movement at the edge of my vision. My head did the math. Malis and Urtel stood before Rahim and Katon, three fiends with them. A fourth fiend lay dead and Rafal was having his head pounded in by Scarlett outside. That left a fiend unaccounted for.

That was, until right then. I really need to pay more attention.

I growled as I spun, leveling my pistols. The fiend was faster, a trend I was getting real tired of, let me tell you. Its claws sunk into the meat of my side and a split second later, its shoulder rammed into my chest. The wind knocked from me, I sucked in a gasping breath as I was lifted into the air and slammed onto my back.

My left hand struck the ground hard and the pistol in it popped loose, to bounce out of reach. I clutched tighter to the other one as the fiend dropped down on my chest, its taloned hand clutching at my arm to keep me from putting my gun to use.

It leaned in toward me with its snarling mouth just inches from my face, its yellowish quills quivering even closer. I managed to slide my free arm in between us, pressing against its neck to keep it away some. It was too little space to give me much comfort and it was too strong for me to hold it for long. It tore at my defending arm, ripping open bubbling wounds that oozed black blood. I could feel my arm weakening beneath the assault. It wouldn't be long before it failed me altogether.

Its rancid breath curled my nose hairs as it snorted and huffed, trying to bite my face off. Droplets of rank spittle rained down over me. I did my best to not think about what kind of cooties I could catch from it. While the least of my worries at that particular moment, I couldn't help but think about it while gnashing rows of rotten teeth clacked together above me in a rhythmic tattoo, like lines of dark soldiers marching off to war. With every passing second, ravaging and horribly stinky death inched closer.

I struggled beneath the fiend, casting a quick glance to see if my companions had seen my predicament. My heart dropped when I saw they also were close to being overrun. There'd be no help from them.

Desperate, I thrashed from side to side, trying my hardest to delay the seemingly inevitable. The fiend held tight, its claws digging deeper into my arm, the other shredding what remained of my left. Its foul stench struck me like a fist as its gaping mouth pressed closer to my eyes, its bony quills jabbing into my cheeks and forehead. Looking up into the maw of the fiend, its rows of shark-like teeth and dripping putrescence, I knew that wasn't how I wanted to go out.

Give me a good old-fashioned heart attack any day.

Frantic, I bucked my hips up and just managed to get my legs beneath it before it settled its weight back down. Not wasting a second, considering how few I had left, I spread my legs and set my feet on the inside of the fiend's hips. I mustered all my strength and kicked my legs out, pushing as best I could with my wounded arm. Caught off guard, the fiend's lower body was lifted into the air and shoved back about a foot as I yanked my right arm in the opposite direction. It caught its balance and dropped its weight back onto me but not before its restraining hand had slipped free of my arm.

Its oval eyes went wide when it realized what I'd done. I could see the reflection of the gun barrel in them as I brought it to bear. I squeezed my eyes shut and hunkered down as I tapped the trigger repeatedly, the gun hovering just above my nose. I could feel the heat from its report, the smoking hot casings raining down over me. The .45's vicious bark was like music to my deafened ears. The fiend's screeches like a symphony of base satisfaction.

The seven silver deaths struck in rapid succession, each leaving behind a little less of the fiend's ugly face than the last, all wreaking destruction in their wake. Its warm and gooey blood rained down on me, tiny droplets of gross. I could taste the fetid sickness in my mouth and smell its putrid scent in my nose. It was real hard not to vomit.

The screams ended and I felt a moist splash on my chest as the fiend collapsed, the remnants of its head like a shattered pumpkin oozing down my ribs. I shuddered and kicked the thing off of me, wiping at my face to clear my eyes before I opened them. I didn't want any of that vile nastiness in them. I managed to get most of the goop off, but there was nothing I could do about the reeking funk that lingered like an unwelcome house guest.

Knowing I had more important things to worry about, I fumbled at my ammo belt with my one good hand, my left arm hanging lifeless at my side, and looked to see where we stood in the battle.

I should have kept my eyes closed.

Separated from Katon, Rahim was caught between the two angels, both doing their damndest to kill him in close quarters. It was enough apparently. As Rahim spun to deflect the first angel's blow, Urtel slipped behind him and drove his glowing fist into the wizard's back just above the hips. Twenty yards away, I heard the crack of Rahim's spine snapping. My stomach reeled as the wizard cried out and crumpled to the ground in a broken heap.

Rage tunneled my vision as I wriggled the cartridge into the gun with my one good hand and slammed it home against my leg. I chambered the first round with my teeth and ran off after the angels, my .45 leading the way. Distracted by their victory, the two batting Rahim back and forth between them like kittens, adding insult to injury, they didn't see me coming. Big mistake.

I stepped up behind Urtel and rammed my gun hard into his back. "An eye for an eye," I shouted as I squeezed the trigger.

The report was even more satisfying than when I'd shot the fiend. The first bullet ripped into Urtel and shattered his spine in much the same way he had Rahim's, a fountain of golden blood springing up in its wake. The second and third rounds finished the job. He died in silence.

I felt cheated he'd died so quickly. I wanted the bastard to suffer.

Malis would have to suffer for him.

I shouldered the still-standing corpse out of my

way and turned my gun on the remaining angel. There was fear in his eyes.

He had good reason to be afraid.

There are horrors so vile, so blasphemous, lurking in the depths of Hell that even Clive Barker would be hard pressed to imagine. What I intended to do to Malis made those horrors pale in comparison.

But even with the best laid plans, reality has a way of intruding. Once again, in the heat of combat, I'd forgotten about the soul transfer. My hand shook as I raised my pistol, a flood of warmth dancing across my nerves. I moaned as the blood in my veins ignited, my eyes fluttering closed in response to the orgasmic rush.

I heard a shuffle of feet moving toward me and sighed, knowing my involuntary hesitation had cost me my shot at retribution. Still in the throes of the transfer, I waited to get hit.

I wasn't disappointed.

I felt the tell-tale wave of heat an instant before the blast struck. Like a tennis ball smacked by a racket, I was flung backward, my arms and legs trailing out in front of me. My eyes opened to see wisps of black smoke curling away from me as I flew through the air, the room whipping by. The only comfort I had was it didn't hurt. The essence of Urtel's soul was still in flux inside my system. That was a good thing because I didn't feel the barn wall as I smashed through it or the hard ground that rushed up to meet me at the end of my flight. After the impact, I rolled end over end until I came to a stop in the knee-high grass outside, broken pieces of the red wooden wall scattered all around me. A trail of flattened greenery and scarred earth marked my passage from landing point to final destination.

Once the majority of the transfer had subsided, I got to my feet, my body tingling. I was relieved to see my left arm had regained its motion, its strength returned. I was even more thrilled to find I still had my gun. I'd gotten off lucky. That wasn't true for all of us.

Reminded of Rahim and what I'd been doing before being sent on a ride, I gritted my teeth. With vengeance on my mind, I stalked back to the barn. As I neared it, I heard a scrabbling of claws on wood and looked up to see a Dread Fiend crouched in the hole where I'd smashed through the wall. He howled a gravelly challenge to me as I approached. I answered his bark with a bite, four of them, to be precise. Without hesitation I emptied what remained in the clip into the fiend's snarling mouth.

Its challenge died on its hairy lips as the bullets blasted huge holes in the back of its head. A death rattle gurgled deep in its throat and it tumbled from its perch, falling face first into a heap at the base of the barn wall. I smiled wide as it hit. There was something satisfying about the way it laid there, its tongue lolling out of its open mouth, its ass up in the air. It was as if the lack of decency it showed in life was reflected in its death. I felt it fitting.

I pushed aside my armchair psychology and returned to the barn. I dug out another cartridge and cursed as I realized I only had one more left. I slammed it in, hoping I wouldn't need more than that. With a snarl, I leapt through the same hole I'd exited just moments before, wondering what awaited me on the other side. I landed in a crouch, scanning the scene.

I arrived just in time to see Scarlett and Katon dispatch the last of the fiends. Scarlett rode one into the ground, her tiny fists a blur of motion outlined by streams of yellowish blood and bile. The creature crumbled beneath her onslaught.

Katon danced inside of the other's reach and drove his blade deep into its lungs, his arm wrapped tight around the fiend's neck. I could see the fury in his eyes, his face etched with deep lines of murderous rage as he twisted the blade.

Malis lay in moist pieces across the floor like a fleshy puzzle. Not all the king's horses or all the king's men would be putting this Humpty Dumpty back together again. His head, separated from the rest had rolled into a corner where its eyeless sockets stared up at the ceiling. His arms and legs were scattered about, ripped viciously apart at each individual joint. His bloody, battered torso sat in the center of the room, its ribs caved in.

I wasn't sure which of the two had done it, but

I was buying them both a beer once all this was over. They'd earned it.

I took stock of all the bodies, making sure all of Asmoday's minions were accounted for, holstered my gun, and raced to Rahim's side. Katon and Scarlett got there less than a second later.

To my surprise, he was still alive.

He looked up at us as we gathered around him, his eyes reflecting the pain I knew he'd never voice. At seeing him, Katon knelt down and buried his face into the old wizard's chest. Weakly, Rahim draped his arm over Katon's head and pulled him in tighter. He squeezed his eyes shut as a single tear slipped from the corner and ran down his cheek. A quiet sob slipped from Scarlett as she turned away from the pair, hiding her face. For all the rage and violence that festered inside her, she would forever be an agent of the Lord. Her heart would forever be vulnerable to tragedy.

Unable to help, I simply let them be. They stayed there for several minutes, neither speaking nor breaking the embrace. Unwilling to interrupt, I stood and started to back away when I noticed Rahim looking at me.

"How bad?" I asked, knowing full well I wasn't going to like the answer. He, no doubt, hated to admit it even more.

"My spine is shattered," he said as he took a deep, laborious breath. His face winced with the effort.

Katon pulled away to make it easier, settling in beside him. "I can't feel anything below my chest. It's all dead."

My heart sank. In my mind, that was worse than death. "We need to get you back to DRAC." I knew it was the right thing to do, but I wasn't even sure that'd help.

While the members of DRAC had performed many miracles since their inception, healing on the scale Rahim required wasn't one of them. Forget all the stories you've heard about preachers or wizards healing the crippled and bringing the dead back to life, same as they were before. They aren't true. Outside of God and the Devil, no one has the level of power or control necessary to truly resurrect the dead or make a crippled man walk again. Magic doesn't work that way. For all its vaunted reputation, it's rarely useful for anything more than destruction. While somewhat flexible, conforming to the imagination of its specific wielder, its true nature is brute force.

The hammer never cures the anvil.

The soul transfer, the closest thing to a miracle in today's Godless world, would also be useless to him. As a human, Rahim had no ability to partake of a supernatural being's soul. While his suffering could be eased by judicious magical rituals and modern medicine, Rahim's future was in the hands of fate and the surgeons in the employ of DRAC.

He knew this better than any of us.

"There is still much to do, my friends, but I'm afraid I can do little to help." Rahim patted Katon on the leg to motivate him, his moist eyes never leaving mine.

"Take me home."

History Lessons

Back at DRAC, Katon having escorted the doctors who wheeled Rahim into surgery, Scarlett and I were left alone in the small waiting room. Unable to remain still, she paced the room from one end to the other, her leather pants squeaking faintly with every step. So rattled by how fast we'd fallen apart, I sat with my head in my hands and stared at the carpet. I couldn't even bring myself to think something sexual about the sound Scarlett was making.

That alone was a sure sign of Armageddon coming to pass.

With Abraham held captive by Baalth and Rahim broken, perhaps never to walk again, all that was left of the Council was Rachelle. As powerful and as good a person as she was, she would be little help from this point on. Even if she did sense the next ritual, it would be too late to stop it.

Asmoday had done well for himself. In just a few short days, he'd decimated DRAC, clearing the way for the end of the world. Not bad for an underachiever who had been kicked out of Heaven for being the errand boy who delivered the apple to Eve.

Speaking of misguided angels, I glanced up at Scarlett. "Mind if I ask you a question?"

She stopped her pacing and looked at me with baleful eyes, nodding.

"How did Asmoday manage to kidnap you?"

Her face twisted weirdly, as if unsure of what expression to make. "He didn't." She took a deep breath, letting it out slow. "Gabriel did."

I leaned back in the chair, whistling. Scarlett had been drug through the wringer ever since the war broke out and she was forced to take sides. It'd been hard on her having to turn her back on her friends, people she'd known since she came into existence, who had chosen to follow the path of Gabriel. Family one moment, enemies a heartbeat later, she never quite grasped the concept of angels not being the good guys. Her heart belonged to the Angelic Choir of old and she just couldn't understand why it wasn't that way with all of the angels.

Gabriel's betrayal had to have been almost as painful to her as God's disappearance had been. Everything she was, her whole world view, was tied up in the premise that God was on high and he would lead, she would follow. She'd only recently begun to accept the fact things were different these days and they probably would never go back to being the way she remembered. Now, with Gabriel kidnapping her, all that pain had to have come rushing back, the fresh scars torn open and left to bleed.

I felt for her deep down, though I had to admit I

was glad I was on the other side of all that. Demons and betrayal went hand in hand, it went without saying. It was never a matter of if. It was always a matter of when. It's so much easier to deal with that kind of crap when you know to expect it. She hadn't been raised in that environment like I had. This was all new to her.

Though I knew it was eating her up inside, on the surface, she seemed to handle it well enough.

"He's gone insane, you know?"

I'd kinda thought that already. I just nodded, letting her go on.

"Though he didn't say it directly, I think he believes God will come back if he wipes out the world. He blames the humans for so exhausting God's patience He was driven to abandon us." A saw a shiver run through her. "He's not going to stop until we're all gone, Frank."

Hours earlier I might have argued with her, enough of my confidence still alive to make a case for hope. I'd have told her we had a chance of stopping Gabriel and Asmoday and we could still win out. But now, I couldn't even lie to her, let alone to myself. I sank down in my seat, worn out both mentally and physically. Scarlett saw my resignation and went back to pacing.

It seemed to me as though there was little else to do but sit back and wait for the big bang.

It came two seconds later.

Katon burst into the waiting room, kicking the door off its hinges. It flew across the room and landed in a broken heap of splintered wood against the furthest wall. Furious, his fangs glistening under the fluorescent lighting, he screamed epithets that made even me blush. Had I been brave enough to take my eyes off him and spare Scarlett a glance, I'm sure the color of her face would have matched her name.

Rather than do anything to draw his attention to me, I sat back and watched as he gave a row of metal chairs the worst beating of their inanimate lives, thrashing them into tiny pieces and stomping them into the carpeted floor. Even Scarlett took a few steps back, not wanting to get caught up in his tantrum. It was a sight to behold, let me tell you.

Once the chairs succumbed to his rage, he whirled to face me. My heart stopped mid beat. I didn't want to end up like them. I started to sweat.

"I'm going to rip Asmoday's entrails out through his throat and feast on his treacherous heart." He stepped in front of me and leaned in to be sure I heard him, his face a wrinkled mess of ferocity. I sat still, like a cornered rabbit, afraid to move for fear he'd take his anger out on me. "I'm going to tear his testicles off and use his seed to write his epitaph. I'll use his dick as my pen."

I sensed an opening to remind him I was on his side. "Uh...I'm with you, brother," I muttered, nodding like a bobblehead doll.

My heart started up again when he spun around and put his foot through the wall several feet away. I was more than glad it wasn't my head. Not satisfied with that small destruction, he began tearing madly at the plasterboard. Clouds of white dust filled the room, settling thick around us. After a few minutes of frenzied tearing, his shoulders slumped and he leaned against what was left of the ravaged wall for support.

"That was our last chance and we blew it." He turned around and dropped to a seat on the floor, his sad eyes looking up at me. Seems Scarlett and I weren't the only ones feeling doubt. "Armageddon is coming and there's nothing we can do to stop it."

Though unable to cry, Katon's eyes had no problem expressing his overwhelming sadness. It was heart-rending. Scarlett went to his side and knelt down to comfort him. She was braver than me. His head drooped as she wrapped her arms around him and pulled him close.

"We have failed," he whispered, his voice breaking as he said it.

My mind, spurred to life by the adrenaline Katon had stirred up, started clearing the fog of gloom that had stifled its function. I thought back to our encounter with Asmoday as he left to prepare Glorius. Something he'd said rang a bell, but I'd been too distracted, too afraid to recognize it for what it was. It was right there, lurking at the hazy edge of the shadows in my head, but I couldn't remember.

Grumbling to myself, I leaned forward, looking at the embracing pair as I tried to kick-start my brain. My eyes, as they did every opportunity they got, wandered to Scarlett's boobs. Katon's head was nestled between them, safe and secure in the sanctuary of her ample bosom. I watched as her chest rose and fell in steady rhythm, his head drifting along with it, eyes closed. Though I knew he was suffering, Rahim terribly injured, the world about to end, his face had settled into a calm mask. However unlikely it was, he seemed at peace.

A light bulb exploded in my head as I thought that last part. At that moment, I realized something I'd always suspected.

Boobs were the answer for everything.

"There may still be a chance," I whispered, unable to believe even myself we might still be in the fight.

Katon lifted his head to stare up at me. His eyes were narrow and unfocused as though he'd only half-heard what I said. "What was that?"

I took a second to nail down my train of thought before answering, "I think I know where they are."

Both of them sat up straight, twin towers of rigid surprise. "Where?" They asked the question in unison.

I stood up, dredging through the drift of words

to find the right ones. "Back when Lucifer was still around, he and I spent a lot of time together in the Ninth Plane going over things. Intending me to take up the mantle of the Anti-Christ, he had confided in me."

Katon and Scarlett hung on every word.

"After the Fall, when things had settled somewhat, God felt remorse for how he'd handled the situation. He couldn't take it back though because it would make Him look fallible, so He let the war between Heaven and Hell continue, doing nothing to end it."

"Where is all this going?" Katon asked.

"I'm getting there." I waved off any further questions. "Thinking it unfair that He was omnipotent and Lucifer wasn't, the odds forever skewed in His favor, God gifted a sanctuary to my uncle. Within its walls no one, not even God himself, could see or hear what went on."

Scarlett gasped, probably finding it hard to believe any such place could exist, let alone that God would provide it for the Devil.

Katon, more logical than my cousin, simply wanted facts. "What makes you think Asmoday is there?"

"Something he said before he ran off. He mentioned he'd be waiting in his sanctum of peace. I didn't catch it then, but once I had a chance to think, and the proper motivation to get my blood flowing, it all clicked. Thanks, Scarlett."

Oblivious to why I was thanking her, she just looked at me, one eyebrow raised.

"So this sanctum of peace is your uncle's hideaway?"

"Yes, I believe so. Inscribed upon the wall just inside the sanctuary was a poem God had written. He'd had a thing for engraving, like the Ten Commandments thing and all that, so He'd weaved the spell into the poem and carved it into the wall himself. Lucifer showed it to me the first time I was there. It read: *A boon to thee once Morning Star; Where I and eye cast no sight to mar; A sanctum of peace, carved between; Hell and Earth, thy heart unseen.*"

Katon repeated the poem in a whisper, seeming to agree with my logic, however fanciful it all seemed. "How many other people know of this room?"

"Not many. Baalth, Asmoday of course, Duke Forcalor, and maybe another one or two of Lucifer's top lieutenants from the old days. My uncle kept it to himself save for his closest allies...and me."

Katon rubbed his jaw. "What makes you think Asmoday would go there now? It's not much of a hideout if *you* know about it. He'd have to presume you'd find him there. It doesn't make sense."

"That's just it. Asmoday thinks I don't know about it. Lucifer understood I wasn't a popular choice for Anti-Christ amongst most of the lieutenants. As such, he was very careful to keep what he shared with me, between us."

"Wouldn't Baalth realize he'd gone there, making it less attractive to Asmoday?" Scarlett interjected.

"It's possible, but I doubt it. You didn't know Uncle like I did. He was a very private man. No one, and I mean no one, entered his chambers without an invitation. You didn't even cast a glance in their direction without permission. It was second nature in Hell to go out of your way to avoid his quarters. When he left, the lieutenants sealed his chambers out of respect."

"So you expect us to believe they just walked away from an asset as valuable as this sanctuary, leaving it to rot unused?" Scarlett put her hands on her hips and shook her head. Her earlier excitement had been replaced by doubt.

"That's the point you're not getting, its usefulness is limited now. With God gone, it's mostly just another room. While it still defends against magical eavesdropping, that isn't a big deal at the level we're dealing with. All of the lieutenants can shield themselves from even the most talented of psychics with little more than a wave of a hand. To go to the room for such a simple task would be a waste. It's out of the way and inconvenient."

"Why would Asmoday go there?"

"Two reasons. The first is because he believes we don't know it exists. Given that premise, it seriously lowers our odds of finding him. Thus, it makes perfect sense for him to go there." I looked at Scarlett to see if she was following me still. She was, so I continued. "The second reason is the place is a veritable fortress against magic, even more so now it's been sealed off. So when all Hell breaks loose, he's in the safest place to watch it all come down."

"If this sanctum is so well defended, why didn't he just perform the rituals there?" Katon, while wanting nothing more than another opportunity to go after Asmoday, was ever the pragmatist. "And saying they're there now, how do we get inside?"I smiled, having anticipated his questions. "Defensive-minded, Lucifer crafted a magical security system in case his lieutenants ever banded together to overthrow him. This system limits the amount of energy directed into the room from the outside. Though he never could shut the room down entirely, he managed to cap the inflow drastically. As such, Asmoday wouldn't have been able to draw the power needed to charge Glorius. That forced him to do it elsewhere.

"As for how we get there, I have the key." I tapped my temple.

Scarlett sighed deeply. "If we have to rely on what's inside your head that doesn't relate to porn, we're screwed."

I sneered at her. "Fortunately, as far as my mind goes, we only need the coordinates buried inside it.

Beyond that, all that's left is to gate to Hell and mete out some much deserved retribution. That would seem right down your alley, oh destroyer of railyards."

Scarlett grinned, slamming her fist into her palm. She was ready to go. She wanted her sword back and she no doubt wanted to take a couple of heads home with her as well. A nice angel and demon trophy set for the mantle. I was right there with her.

Katon, however, his dark eyes glistening with restrained excitement, only shook his head. "While I agree wholeheartedly with the sentiment, I find us a bit lacking in the follow-through department." He pointed to me, then Scarlett, then to himself. "We three lack the raw power necessary to take on Asmoday and his pet archangel, not even taking into account what minions he might have with him. So even if you're right about all this and they are there, we're woefully outmatched." Ever the realist, Katon reminded us of what we were looking at.

In my excitement, I had forgotten that disappointing fact. With Rahim down and the rest of DRAC scattered or killed by Asmodays' fiends, we were on our own. "I've an equalizer against Gabriel, but the circumstances have to be right. He has to come after me or I lose the ace up my sleeve." I shrugged, picturing how things might work out inside my head. All of the endings were grim. "I don't see we have much of a choice but to do it anyway. What do we have to lose?"

"The whole of creation," Scarlett answered in a quiet voice.

"Seems to me that's already lost," Katon countered. "If we sit here and do nothing, the world ends. If we try to do something about it and fail, at least we die with our boots on." An Iron Maiden song sprang to mind. "I'm not done fighting. Are you with me?"

Scarlett took a deep breath and let it out slow. "I'm in." Both she and Katon turned to look at me.

"I had plans to watch the *CSI* marathon on *Spike* but I *guess* I can put that off. It's not like they don't show the damn program often enough. I'm in too." A cold chill settled over me as I resigned myself to what would probably be the last fight I'd ever get into. I was gonna miss life. "So, what's the plan?"

"Given we don't have a wide range of options, I say we keep it simple. We go after Glorius," Katon answered without hesitation.

I thought about it for a second. While no doubt simple on the surface, the plan held a few twists I don't think he realized—or if he did, he was keeping it to himself. You see, were Katon the one to kill Glorius, everything would be good. However, were Scarlett or I the one to reach the angel, there would be another issue to consider. The soul transfer.

Due to our nature, the killing blow would transfer all of Glorius's power to whichever of us did the deed. While I certainly wouldn't argue the sudden status increase if it were to work out that way, I wasn't sure either of us could handle so much raw power all at once. We could be committing suicide and wouldn't even know it until it was too late. I sighed, unable to think of a way around it, nodding at Katon to let him know I agreed.

Nothing like a good game of Russian Roulette to take your mind off your troubles.

"In theory, it resolves your issue with Gabriel and gives us the best shot at having some small measure of success. If Glorius is gone, Armageddon is off the table, for a little while at least." He turned to face Scarlett. "Are you going to have a problem with this?"

She met his gaze, but I could see her eyes were moist. "I'll do what needs to be done." She was a trooper.

"I guess that's it." He looked to me. "Gather what you need and meet me at the receiving room in twenty minutes." Without another word, he left to prepare.

My eyes met Scarlett's. "You ready for this?"

She shrugged. "As ready as I can be." I shared her sentiment.

I waved her to the door and let her go first. I figured if we were on our way to die, I was gonna get one last good look at her leather-clad ass before I went. It'd be the closest thing to Heaven I would see before Hell came to call.

Into the Mouth of Hell

We arrived in Hell, just inside the cavern of Lucifer's private chambers. Alone in the room, we let loose a collective sigh of relief as our entrance went unnoticed.

Little room for error, I surveyed the scene. With a mixture of trepidation and relief, I noticed the carved archway behind us, which led out into the common area of the Ninth Plane, was open. The massive slabs of stone, which had been used to seal the chambers, were missing, flickering light filtering in from the outside, illuminating the chamber in soft yellows. I gave the thumbs up sign, letting Katon and Scarlett know we were in the right place. Asmoday had to be here.

My guns drawn, I led the way.

I felt the tug of emotion as I crept through my uncle's quarters. Every piece of furniture, every book, even every painting reminded me of the times I'd spent here, listening to Lucifer tell me the way of the world. In my head, I could still hear his deep voice echoing through the rooms as he explained the intricacies of Hell. In his best Pinhead impersonation—he loved the Hellraiser movies—he would tell me of his days in Heaven and of the Fall. He was my own private rock star. I loved spending time with him here.

Now with him gone, the place felt hollow, like a grave that'd been dug up and left open, the corpse long gone. I felt like a thief, sneaking through my uncle's chambers. For the first time in my life, I felt unwanted there. That was hard to cope with.

But with no time to think about the past, its maddening touch both depressive and bleak, I sped my pace and hurried toward the sanctum. As we traveled the long, circuitous route, I glanced back now and again to ensure Scarlett and Katon were still behind me, that they hadn't lost their nerve and dropped off. Resolute, they were always there. Strengthened by their commitment, my own wavering with every step, I continued on.

At last we came to the sanctum God had gifted my uncle. The cavernous entryway was like the mouth of a mythical dragon gaping wide, waiting to swallow us whole. Its upper lip disappeared into the shadows that hovered near the roof. Jagged rocks ran the length of it, each a sharpened tooth, circling down to a point that sunk into the floor. Only a narrow corridor running down the center was clear of the teeth, the flooring stained a deep crimson giving the impression of a lolling tongue. The almost imperceptible scuffling of my companion's feet, which had shadowed me the entire way, ceased suddenly as they looked up in awe at the doorway. I laughed inside. I'd done the exact same thing the first time I saw it.

Taking advantage of the pause, I focused my attention beyond the entryway. From within, a rhythmic thump could be heard, a deep droning beat that was focused by the door and reverberated out toward us. Guttural moans drifted along on the undercurrent of the sound. I could hear the misery and torment in their raw cries, their groans a dirge. I had an idea as to who one of the voices belonged to—Glorius—but I was hard pressed to imagine who the other might be. I figured I'd find out when we got inside.

Seeing no point in delaying the inevitable any further, giving my doubts time to fester and sound the retreat, I crept forward, waving Scarlett and Katon along. At the back end of the tongue, I was glad to see Asmoday had set no guards. I thanked my uncle for having the foresight to keep his lieutenants in the dark as I inched closer.

I reached the edge of the door and peered inside, only a tiny piece of the room visible from where I stood. I was shocked by what I saw.

Embedded halfway into the stone wall was The Gray, Henry McConnell. Upright, spread-eagle, and naked at approximately ten feet from the floor, the entire back half of his body was missing as though he had melted into the rock. His face was contorted in agony, mouth and eyes frozen wide with horror. His bruised face, beard, and body were caked in dried blood, which broke off and fluttered down in dark flakes as he squirmed. Wisps of light drifted up from his eyes, nose, and mouth, to fade away within the obsidian cloud that rumbled just above his head, vibrating the walls. His was the other voice I'd heard as we approached.

I took a closer look, immediately regretting my morbid curiosity. Sickened, I turned away, trying to expunge the image from my mind. The drifting lights came not only from his face, but from every visible orifice of his body. Tendrils of illumination also leaked from his ears, his nose, and even oozed from the tip of his dick as though he were orgasming a sunbeam in slow motion. Even worse, it was obvious the light had substance, his flesh shifting and stretching painfully to accommodate its passage.

As much as it would upset me to see anyone suffer such horrific torture, I couldn't find in it in me to feel sorry for McConnell. He'd known this was coming and if he'd had his way, it would be Rahim buried in the wall, in his place. Sad as it was to admit, that thought made it just a little easier to stomach what I'd seen. I still didn't like it, but it couldn't have happened to a nicer guy.

Scarlett, anxious to get on with it, went to look around me. I stepped in her way.

"You don't want to see it. Trust me," I whispered.

The look in my eyes must have been convincing. She stared at me for a second, backing down without argument. Katon didn't even bother to try.

After I steeled myself, I moved even closer to the edge of the door so I could see further into the room. I purposely avoided looking at McConnell, my eyes half closed as they swung past, ignoring the nearby shelves with my uncle's belongings piled atop them. Once all that had moved to my peripheral vision, McConnell out of sight, I peeked once more.

What I saw was even worse.

Stretched out inside a silvered pentagram etched onto the floor was a man who I could only presume to be Glorius. Like McConnell, he was also naked. His muscular arms and legs were bound to the rock floor with the magic-nullifying manacles, the cuffs glowing bright white like they'd just been removed from a blacksmith's forge. I could see tiny drops of something leaking out from inside the cuffs, dripping slowly to the floor. A small puddle of the waxy substance coalesced on the rock beneath him. I remembered the other sites and a shudder ran down my spine as I realized it was his flesh that was being melted away from his wrists. Unable to bear the sight, I examined the rest of his body. I immediately wished I hadn't.

One of these days I'll learn to keep my curiosity in check.

Pustulant boils sprung up all along his skin, each easily the size of a quarter. They rippled like a churning storm-driven ocean, bubbling up with vile, blackened pus that seeped from their bursting heads. For each which spewed its repugnant load, tiny volcanoes of sickness and rot, another rose up to take its place in an endless parade of gurgling putrescence.

Unable to stomach any more, I looked to his face. Though hard to see beneath the wild mass of his blond hair, I spied the misery carved there in deep lines. Yellowish-gold tears streamed from his narrow eyes. They trailed down his cheeks in waves, staining his flesh in bright streaks. His face was scrunched as he fought against what must have been excruciating pain. His teeth were bared, snapping together in a frenzied staccato. Though he seemed to be screaming, little sound came from his throat. I had no doubt he'd screeched it raw, the vocal chords so damaged they could only produce a senseless groan.

His head thrashed about, swaying from side to side without rhythm, squirming to be free. The muscles beneath his boiling flesh rippled with strength as he fought against his binds. I didn't care what Gabriel had claimed, one look at Glorius's tortured face made it clear to me he wasn't accepting his fate peacefully. He was fighting his bondage with all of his might. There was no way Glorius was a willing accomplice in Asmoday's plans, he was a victim.

I sighed. That was a twist I hadn't foreseen coming into this.

As if to reinforce my presumption, I heard Gabriel's voice call out to the angel.

"Be still, Glorius. Put aside your anger and accept your fate. Your struggling changes nothing. The end is at hand. Let us finish the ritual without distraction so you may find your peace."

A shimmering white light settled over Glorius, the manacle cuffs flaring up. The angel's head snapped back and slammed into the stone floor with a dull crack and lay there as though being held by some unseen force. His squirming arms and legs struggled against the light, yet they too succumbed, sinking to the floor to twitch helplessly. Though pressed down, Glorius still fought. Every muscle in his body surged as he strained against the restraining magic. For several seconds it looked as though he might win out, his limbs lifting away from the floor, battling the pressure to stay down. Then, I heard a muffled snap and saw his arm bend back at an awkward angle. Mouthing a scream, his resistance crumbled. His body slammed once more to the floor and he lay shivering, writhing.

Behind me, Scarlett gasped. Having snuck up alongside me while I was distracted, she had seen Glorius's arm break. Her agonized voice carried out into the room.

Any chance we had of catching Asmoday and Gabriel off guard died on the vine. All eyes in the room turned to us.

Gabriel sneered, rage burning in his cheeks. "I should have known you'd fail me, Asmoday." His hands glowed with shimmering white light, yet he didn't move to attack. He did, however, throw up a spell.

The air around Glorius twisted and warped, vomiting color like a demented kaleidoscope. The space between him and us was instantly distorted, so much so I could make little out of the entire back half of the room. My stomach tightened into hard knots as I recognized what he'd cast, its magic altering the very nature of the affected part of the room. So much for my guns.

I'd hoped to take Glorius out from a distance, avoiding a close brawl with his captors, but Gabriel had ruined that idea with his spell. Anything that struck the whirling shield, which was smaller than a man and faster than a turtle, would be reflected away uselessly by the colorful maelstrom. With that, Gabriel had effectively cut our options in half. If we were gonna kill Glorius, we'd have to do it up close and personal, and that was really gonna suck. The last thing I wanted to do was murder the guy while he watched it happen.

It was a good thing I'm part devil, because this was the kind of shit that gets you sent to Hell.

Asmoday just stood there oblivious to what his partner was doing, his eyes wide with surprise. He stared at us, saying nothing as I imagine he tried to figure out how we knew where to find him. I saw sudden realization dawn on his face. Appearing crestfallen, I watched as he struggled with the fact Lucifer had betrayed him, favoring me over his own lieutenant.

The look on his face warmed my heart, but I didn't get the chance to enjoy it. Scarlett, enraged, shoved me out the way and leapt at Gabriel, her arms outstretched, hands balled into fists. Stumbled, I couldn't stop her.

She streaked through the air like a missile, ramming her fists into Gabriel's face. Judging by the offended look on it, he seemed more galled she'd actually gone and done it than he was hurt by it. The two tumbled into a ball of wailing limbs, rolling about on the ground in a flurry of sparkling energy. Thunderous booms echoed throughout the room as they battled.

Katon stepped out from behind me, his crimson sword held tight in his hand. "Like we planned, Trigg. Nothing changes, do you hear me?" His voice was like steel, tempered only by his professionalism.

"Yeah," I muttered, as I tore my eyes from Scarlett's suicide mission. Angry she'd screwed up our plan, there was nothing we could do but go on and hope for the best. She didn't stand a chance at beating Gabriel so we needed to get on it fast before we had the archangel up our asses.

Katon understood the same. In a blur of movement, he launched himself toward Glorius, weaving back and forth to avoid being struck by Asmoday's magic. I took off after him, tracing my own winding path toward the bound angel, making sure there was plenty of room between us so the demon couldn't target us both.

Asmoday, his disappointment having turned to rage, was raring to fight. Firelight leapt to life at his fingertips. Clearly not interested in trying to snipe Katon, his lateral movement random and unpredictable, Asmoday settled for an area effect. He tossed two flaming balls of fury into the air, which took off of their own volition. They streaked above the running assassin and as they neared, rather than try to strike him directly, they exploded in the air above him. Fire rained down like a volcanic storm. Katon did his best to avoid the burning fall, but there was too much of it.

One projectile struck him in the thigh, the sizzle of his flesh drowned out by his growling complaint. He stumbled, the burning flesh of his leg slowing him just long enough to be caught up in the storm. A second seared down the length of his back, melting through his leather jacket and leaving a trail of blackened, scorched skin behind. I could smell charred meat thick in the air.

His rhythm interrupted, he could do little but endure. A third and fourth ball of flame tore into him, one setting his chest on fire, the second burning his arm as he frantically tried to put the first fire out.

I gritted my teeth and forced myself to continue on without going to his aid. It took all of my willpower to not stop, but I knew we'd only get one chance at taking out Glorius and I was gonna have a hard enough time pulling that off without getting caught up in heroics.

So, leaving Katon to take care of himself, I cast a glance at Scarlett as I continued to run. I was amazed she was still holding her own against Gabriel. Flashes of light sparked all around them as they slugged it out. Gabriel, his hands still glowing, seemed out of sorts. He looked tired, distracted perhaps. Whatever it was, I hoped it lasted.

Turns out, it didn't really matter.

Asmoday, confident he had Katon delayed, turned his fury on me. Distracted as I was by Scarlett's success, I'd failed to notice the demon charging at me. I heard him an instant before he reached my back. With a hiss, I spun about to fire, but Asmoday was already on top of me.

He threw a right hook that would make Mike Tyson proud. Reinforced with magical energy, his fist slammed into my face like a high speed train wreck. Brilliant lights flashed in front of my eyes as my head snapped almost horizontal to my neck. Through the cluttered haze of my head, I heard several pops as I stumbled back and fell to the ground. The pain yet to penetrate the fog of impact, I didn't want to think about what kind of damage had been done. Not that thinking in general was all that easy at the moment anyway.

I tried to open my eyes and see where Asmoday was only to realize he was standing right in front of me.

Though it was hard to see him, his image wavering back and forth like a bad acid trip, I could see the murder in his eyes. I moaned as I noticed his hand extended toward me, his palm glowing with flame. Not a big fan of being charbroiled, I curled into a ball just as he released it.Like a flame thrower, his magic tore into me. I screamed, but my breath was sucked from my lungs by the heat while the fire lapped at my flesh. All of my nerve endings picked up the pain signal at once and roared to life in a cacophony of searing agony. My face covered, I felt my scalp boiling up, blisters springing to life beneath the torrent of flame. The backs of my hands were the same.

Frantic, I fumbled with my gun belt with one hand, hurling it away before the shells could go off. Once it was clear, I threw myself at the ground, ignoring the violent collision as I rolled to put the fires out. My lungs tightened, the blast burning up all the oxygen in the surrounding air. Unable to see, I flopped against the hard stone, rolling back and forth. I could feel the heat melting my clothes, adding their scent to the bitter conflagration of burned flesh. After what seemed an eternity, the heat backed off, though I wasn't sure if it was due to the fire going out or if my nerves had just been seared insensate.

I pulled my arms away from my face, daring to hope, and drew in a deep, pained breath. I could breathe again, however much it hurt. The fires were gone and I was still alive. For what that was worth. I opened my eyes, dried out from the blast, and blinked to focus. Once I could see again, the tear ducts reluctant to engage, I looked to see how bad off I was.

Nearly naked, my clothes having been burnt away, the skin beneath was black as coal. Much of it was the same consistency. The only parts of me that didn't look like a charcoal briquette were my face and my backside where the flame hadn't managed to reach. Overall, it could have been much worse. Given the level of power Asmoday wielded, I'd gotten lucky. Under any other circumstances, he'd have killed me outright. I guess our theory as to his having spent most of his energy performing the rituals was a good one. Though it gave me little comfort, it did conjure up some small inkling of hope we might survive long enough to pull off our plan.

As a living representation of fire safety, I pulled my crispy ass to my feet while looking for Katon. The assassin, having overcome his own encounter with Asmoday's flames, was in the midst of engaging the demon. Though slowed by the damage he'd taken, he was still quite nimble. He dodged and weaved in close to Asmoday, taking him on up close.

Across Asmoday's flank were several long wounds, evidence Katon had been having some success in his assault. However, Katon looked far worse for wear. His face was blooded and marred with scorch marks. He ducked and stepped inside over and over, catching glancing blows as he did, yet landing no strikes of his own. He was tiring and his accuracy was suffering for it.

Hoping to help, I looked for my guns. They lay on the floor a short distance away, the outside of the holsters singed black. Agony accompanied every step as I raced to retrieve them. Though warm to the touch, they'd sustained no damage. I almost cried. I would have if my eyes hadn't been seared dry. At least something had worked out in the cluster fuck of our assault.

I settled my pistols in my scorched hands and leveled them to fire, squeezing tight to keep them steady. In the time it took me to focus my eyes to aim, Asmoday had gained the advantage.

With a vicious backhanded sweep, the demon struck Katon across the side of his face. Oblivious to me, he stumbled into my line of fire holding his head and blocking my shot. I went to shout, but that's when I realized what one of the snapping sounds I'd heard earlier was. It had been my jaw.

Sharp spikes of pain shot up my cheeks and down through my teeth as I tried to open my mouth. My eyes shrugged off the fire damage and sprung to life, moistening and blurring my vision. Before I could clear them and shake the pain off, Asmoday got in a lucky shot.

Katon slipped left when he should have slipped right. Asmoday launched a hook and the assassin moved directly into it. I saw his head snap back as blood sprayed into the air from his shattered nose. While Katon would normally take a blow like that in stride, backed by magic, there was no way to describe the punch as normal. His legs wobbled and buckled beneath him, sending him crashing to the floor, a look of shock on his face. Asmoday wasted no time. Like he had with me, he raised his hand, firelights springing to life. He was gonna cook Katon. I couldn't let that happen.

The assassin out of my way, I raised my gun and pulled the trigger. Asmoday's blast went off at the same time.

Before I could act, Katon was engulfed in licking flames. My shot, way off its mark, struck the demon in the meat of his shoulder, miles from being a fight-ending blow. He growled and ducked for cover as he felt the sting of the demon-slaying bullet, leaving Katon behind to burn.

I popped off a few more shots to keep Asmoday at bay as I tried to orient on the obscuring spell and was surprised when I actually saw Glorius instead. Through the rapidly shifting web of Gabriel's spell, a handful of holes the size of fifty cent pieces had begun to appear. The colors had faded, many settling into a dull gray while the distorting effects had lessened.

Through the swirling holes, I saw Glorius straining once more against his restraints, his functional limbs tugging against the manacles. He was determined to break loose and seemed to be gaining ground.

I cast a glance at Gabriel and saw his hands had also lost a measure of the glow that had been a constant since we'd arrived. Though in trade, he seemed less weary. He also seemed to be winning his fight with Scarlett.

My brain clicked into high gear.

The reason Scarlett had been doing so well was because Gabriel had been expending all his energy restraining the supercharged Glorius. Now that he'd let his hold slip somewhat, the angel was fighting free. His strength was more than the manacles alone could contain, and Gabriel was gaining the upper hand over Scarlett. I looked back toward Glorius, firing a few more shots to keep Asmoday away, and made up my mind. If ever there was time to try for the angel, this was it.

Though it hurt me to once more to turn my back on a companion, a fellow soldier in the war against Armageddon, sacrifices must be made. I didn't like the choice I was faced with, but considering the consequences if I failed, we were all dead anyway. It wasn't hard to make up my mind. I'd worry about the morality of it later.

Unable to get a clear shot at Glorius, the remnants of the spell moving randomly and at a sufficient speed to muddle my aim, I fired another shot at Asmoday, who'd begun to creep closer, and bolted toward the angel. At a full sprint, I felt like I was moving in slow motion. I could hear Asmoday bellowing behind me, anxiety and frustration thick in his voice. That only spurred me on. I took the last few steps in a single bound, readying myself for the disorientation that would strike me as I passed through the barrier.

But just before I reached the edge of the spell, its colors suddenly dropped away, the obscuring magic dissipating only to be replaced by a shimmering shield wall. Unable to stop my momentum, I slammed hard into the shield, face first. White flashes of pain reverberated through my jaw as I bounced back, barely managing to retain my balance. My brain rattled inside my head as stars danced in front of my eyes. I cried out in frustration and anger and no small amount of agony.

As my pain receptors eased off the pedal a bit, I looked through the translucent wall and saw the blurred image of Glorius, once more fully restrained by the glow. My heart dropped in my chest.

I'd failed.

Defeated, I turned around slowly and saw Gabriel bearing down on me, waving Asmoday off. Past him, Scarlett lay in a bloodstained, battered heap. She wasn't moving. I glanced around the room for Katon. He was nowhere to be seen. I looked back to Gabriel.

"Valiant effort, Triggaltheron. I applaud you."

Gabriel stalked toward me, stopping about twenty feet away. Wary, his left hand shimmered with a small shield, crafted by magic.

"You can take your praise and shove it." I spoke through clenched teeth. I wasn't feeling up to being witty and my jaw hurt.

"Come now. It's over. Put away the guns and act civilized and I'll let you live to see the start of Armageddon."

I took a deep breath and let it out slow, calming my nerves. "Front row seats to the end of the world, how generous of you."

"I thought so." He shrugged, looking magnanimous. "What say you, Triggaltheron? Will you put away the hostility to see the most majestic sight to ever grace your mongrel eyes, or will you die like your companions, unheralded and alone?"

It really didn't matter how I answered, the end result would be the same. I'd die and so would the world. My decision here would only alter the order of those two certainties by a matter of minutes. Did it really matter which happened first? I felt the weight of failure settle heavy on my shoulders. I pictured Abraham, held at gunpoint by Baalth, looking up at the darkening sky as Armageddon rolled in. I could imagine the disappointment in his eyes. It was heart-breaking. I thought of Rahim, lying in his bed, the use of his legs given up in the hopes of staving off the end. He would earn nothing for it but cold, unrelenting death.

I'd failed them all. Scarlett had believed in me. She'd followed me to the depths of Hell and she'd died there, far from the bright lights of Heaven where she belonged. The saddest part was she wouldn't even know her sacrifice had been in vain.

Katon had done the same. Burned to ash while giving me a chance to save the world, he too died for nothing. I felt tears coming to my eyes. I didn't bother to hold them back. If ever there was a time to cry now had to be it. Cold hard reality shivered down my spine as I clenched my guns tight. Ready for it all to be over, I looked up at Gabriel.

If this was the end, I was going out in a blaze of glory.

As our eyes met, I caught a glimpse of a shadowy form at the edge of my peripheral vision, just beyond Asmoday. I did my best to hide my reaction lest it show on my face. "Is it too late to join the winning team?" I asked, looking to keep the archangel's focus on me.

Gabriel's eyes narrowed, sensing something afoot in my sudden change of attitude. A cry from Asmoday drew his attention before he could form a reply. He spun carefully, keeping his shield between us, his attention split.

From behind the demon, a scorched and beaten Katon leapt at Asmoday. Exhausted and near death, his attack carried little threat behind it. His trembling thrust just grazed Asmoday's side as the demon sidestepped, leaving behind a shallow cut along his ribs. Asmoday's response was far more damaging. He grabbed Katon's wrist and bent it back, bones snapping as the assassin's sword tumbled away. The last of his strength fell away as well, his defeat accompanied by a soundtrack of silence. He had nothing left to give.

Katon hung limp in Asmoday's grip as the demon raised his free hand, magical energy building around his fist as he readied to end the assassin's life. Though ready to race to my death just moments before, now thanks to Katon, I saw a chance to inflict at least one casualty on the enemy before I went.

I jumped to the side, angling so Gabriel couldn't block my shots, and fired my pistols as quick as my barbecued fingers could hit the triggers. Gabriel snarled and Asmoday shrieked as they heard the guns go off.

Asmoday, like a skittish rabbit looking for a hole, released Katon and dove for cover. I didn't get to see whether my shots hit or not. The instant I fired, Gabriel's shield slammed into me, exploding as it did. The concussive force blew me back into the wall. Shards of stone flew in all directions as the rock wall cracked and shattered against my back. I felt nothing as my head collided with the wall, a cold blackness threatening to overtake me. I slid to the ground in a rubbery pile, a heap of broken bones. Numb, I felt ready to pass out but a quiet voice nagged in my ear for me to remain conscious.

I told it to fuck off, but the damn thing wouldn't be quiet.

After what seemed like an eternity, me and the voice going round and round, I gave in and opened my eyes. At my feet, a tiny blue gem glistened. I couldn't help but laugh when I saw it, needle sharp pains lancing through my jaw as I did. I didn't care.

Gabriel came to stand in front of me, his face taught with suspicion, ready to kill. He glared down at me as Asmoday limped toward Glorius, my shots having apparently only struck him in the leg. Though his pain was evident, he had a smug look on his face as he passed knowing I'd failed to stop him. It just made me laugh harder.

"You're a strange one, Triggaltheron. Moments from death and yet you laugh in its face. You have courage, I'll give you that."

I grinned as wide as my broken jaw would allow. "That's me, all balls no brains." I winked at Gabriel. "Have you met my friend?"

He leaned back wary, his eyes casting about. Seeing no one and probably thinking I was more nuts than he'd surmised, he asked, "What friend?"

I gestured with my eyes for him to come closer, my arms too weak to direct him. "My little blue friend on the floor there."

His gaze followed mine, spying the gem for the

first time. He stared at it for a moment, recognition gleaming in his eyes.

"I think I'll call him Duke Forcalor. Sound good to you?"

Gabriel stumbled back, his mouth gaping as the gem sparked to life like a magnesium flare, casting off rays of light that illuminated the dark cavern.

"Asmoday!" Gabriel shouted for his ally, his panicked voice echoing through the room.

Asmoday turned just in time to see the explosion of light that burst from the gem, obliterating all the color in the room in a whitewash of energy. He fell to his knees, his hands covering his eyes.

A moment later, the light faded, returning the room to its natural, dim shades. Wisps of black smoke wafted about, and in their midst, Duke Forcalor stood.

The duke, no longer the epitome of comfort he'd been when I'd last seen him, was dressed in full battle regalia. He wore reddened plate armor covered in twisted, sharpened spikes. In a scabbard at his side, a dark sword hung, its pommel embedded with blood red stones that seemed to pulse. His long white hair hung loose, blowing gently back, though I could feel no wind. A satisfied grin held fast on his face as he pointed a metal gauntleted finger at Gabriel.

"Unprovoked, you have struck a blow against my servant. To do so is an act of war. I demand satisfaction."

Gabriel trembled, the glow of his hands becoming dimmer. He said nothing, but his eyes went to Asmoday. They looked almost pleading. Asmoday hauled himself to his feet, but he looked no more courageous than Gabriel. He stayed where he stood, leaving Gabriel to face his fate alone.

The glow around Gabriel's hands extinguished as he turned away from his cowardly ally and met Forcalor's gaze. He drew up his chin and straightened his shoulders. "If this is how it must be. So be it, traitor."

I had to give him credit. Weakened by his efforts to control the supercharged Glorius for nearly a week, he had to have known he couldn't win, yet he still stood his ground. There was a lot of brass still left in his sack.

The lines drawn, he got to it. He leapt at the duke. Forcalor met him halfway. They clashed together like two wrecking balls colliding in midair. A resounding boom accompanied their battle, flashes of light and dark exploded intermittently. The chamber rumbled as the two went at it, paintings falling to the floor, Lucifer's books and personal items falling from their perches. Gusts of wind were whipped up in their wake, their lashing tongues battering everything and everyone in the room.

I looked to Asmoday and saw he'd gathered his courage at last, using Gabriel's fight as cover. Headed toward Glorius, he fought the gale-force winds that slowed his progress while the angel continued his struggle against the neutralizing manacles. From where I sat, he wouldn't be free in time to escape Asmoday. That was a shame.

I sighed, though difficult to draw breath through the windstorm, and looked back to the battle content to watch at least one of the bastards die for what they'd done. Covered in yellowish-gold blood, Gabriel was being manhandled, his expended state no match for the duke who'd come to the fight fresh and prepared. It was clear Gabriel had little time left. That didn't stop him from going all out. He held nothing back as he let loose blast after blast, only to have Forcalor bat each aside and return a dozen of his own, which crashed through the archangel's defenses.

At last, Gabriel fell beneath the onslaught. As he crumpled to the floor, the hurricane winds died off and the room descended into silence. Much to Asmoday's obvious relief, the duke ignored him and strode to Gabriel's side. He lifted the limp archangel, cradling him in his arms, then turned to face me.

"Our deal is done, young Trigg. Make the best of it." Without waiting for a reply, a shimmering shadow engulfed him. When it faded, both the duke and Gabriel were gone.

With nothing left to do but watch Asmoday bring about the start of Armageddon, I rolled my head his direction. He'd just reached Glorius, still casting furtive glances over his shoulder, the wind no longer impeding his progress. The angel growled and hissed at him, the chains still just enough to hold him in place. Asmoday smiled wide in satisfaction of that fact as he turned back to smirk at me, confidence etched on his face.

"Your hand was well played, Triggaltheron, but as you can see, it wasn't enough. You should have joined me. It would have saved you all this needless grief." He gestured about the room, to Katon and Scarlett. "You could have been a king in the new world, but you chose to fight the inevitable. So now, there's nothing left but for you to sit back and watch as it all comes to an end."

Asmoday clenched his hands together as what power he had left gathered about them, his fists glowing with white hot light. His eyes sparkled with energy and malevolence.

Exhausted in body and spirit, I did as he suggested and leaned back as comfortably as I could. If the world was gonna end, at least I had a backstage pass. What more could I ask for?

Fait Accompli

"Never were there more ironic words spoken, old friend."

Asmoday frantically spun about to see Baalth standing behind him. I'm not sure who was more shocked, him or me. I'm gonna have to go with Asmoday as he was the one facing down the deep barrels of my two stolen weapons.

Marcus and Poe stood at Baalth's side, guns leveled at Asmoday. They didn't wait for him to recover. Merciless, both guns roared to life, driving Asmoday back under a hail of deadly fire. The demon screeched, the bullets ripping into his flesh as he did his damndest to avoid them. After being pressed back about thirty feet, Poe and Marcus stopped firing just as Asmoday managed to conjure a shield. His face and chest were covered in boiling, black blood that poured from his wounds. He glared at Baalth and his cronies, unable to do more. If looks could kill, Asmoday wouldn't have needed Glorius to destroy the world.

Baalth only smiled in return, his cultured face looking as though this were just another day at the office. To him, I guess it was.

Too battered to do anything else, I watched as

Baalth strolled forward and stood over Glorius.

"It seems a pity to let all this time and effort go to waste."

He tinkered with the manacles while Glorius stared up at him in wary rigidness. Asmoday looked much the same. The collective breaths in the room were stilled, silent.

"What's that saying? Waste not, want not?"

Baalth's smile grew wider as his hand burst into reddish-orange flame. Without hesitation he drove his burning fist into Glorius's chest, smashing his way through the angel's ribs, golden blood spraying up like a busted fountainhead.Glorius bucked against the chains, unable to fight back. His eyes were filled with pain and terror in equal amounts. His voice squawked, unable to do much else, his throat far too ravaged to scream as Baalth dug around inside his chest cavity. After an agonizing moment, he stilled as Baalth must have seized his heart. I saw the muscles of Baalth's forearm tightened as he bore down. Under the pressure, Glorius twitched his last and died. His head dropped, his sightless eyes gazing up toward Heaven. He wouldn't find any peace there.

Asmoday went white, his legs wobbling, nearly failing. He inched backward, but Poe waggled a finger at him, pushing his gun out slightly. Marcus reinforced the threat by taking a step forward, making a show of aiming his gun at Asmoday's head. The demon froze.

He knew the jig was up.

Behind his gun-toting goons, Baalth pulled his dripping hand from Glorius's chest and looked up at Asmoday. A subtle grin played across his lips. A second later, I saw his eyes roll back and a wave of pleasure washed across his face. He dropped to his knees in the throes of a soul transfer so fierce none of the rest of us could ever hope to fathom its depth.

If I'd had the energy to cry, I'd have let loose like a bawling baby. Despite all the suffering and sacrifices we'd endured to stop Asmoday from gathering enough power to bring about Armageddon, I never once imagined Baalth would arrive at the last minute and steal victory out from underneath all of our noses. In but a few seconds, he had altered the status quo of existence. And all in his favor, go figure.

Uncertain of what it all meant in the grand scheme of things, Baalth a far cry from the kind of demon Asmoday was, I could only wait and see where things went. It's not like I could stop him. In the end, I guess it didn't matter all that much anymore. No matter what happened, I was still bent over the barrel like all the rest of the grunts. I was out of this fight. Resigned to being a helpless voyeur, I turned my focus back to Baalth as the transfer neared its end.

Baalth rose to his feet, his tanned face flush with excitement. I didn't even need to extend my senses to feel the power that emanated from him. It wafted off in thick waves. I could feel it almost like a physical presence. I watched his eyes glisten as he glanced around the room, perhaps seeing it in a way none of the rest could. He exuded a confidence I'd never seen in anyone, save for Lucifer. In one fell swoop, Baalth had realized his dreams. There was no doubt he'd become the new Satan. Only now, there was no God to rein him in. We were in for a wild ride.

Baalth smiled at me with surprising warmth before turning to confront Asmoday, his face cold. He stepped past his flunkies and moved to within feet of his once fellow lieutenant.

"I have to hand it to you, Asmoday, this was quite a scheme." He gestured to the room with his hand still stained in Glorius's blood. "Did you truly think you'd get away with it?"

Asmoday shivered. His confidence had broken rank and fled. His head drooped to his chest, eyes locked on the floor. "I had to try," he replied, his voice shaky.

Baalth nodded. "I suppose you did. I can't fault you for playing to your nature, now can I?"

Asmoday raised his eyes, a glimmer of hope shining in them. "I am what I have been made to be. Forgive me?"

Baalth raised his chin, his eyes narrowing as he looked Asmoday over. "In time, perhaps." He managed to sound magnanimous despite the hint of condescension in his voice. "Though I imagine, in doing so I would be showing you far more kindness than you would have shown me had you succeeded with your plan."

Asmoday swallowed loud. He hung his head in a show of staged humility. He knew his fate rested in appeasing Baalth. "I am your humble servant. Do with me as you will."

"Brownnoser," I muttered, my jibe coming out between clenched teeth.

Asmoday kept his cool and ignored me, though Baalth broke out in an amused smile.

"I'll spare you for now, old friend, but you've much to atone for."

Asmoday loosed a sigh of relief and dropped to his knees, kissing Baalth's hand. Baalth shooed him off, taking a step back.

"I'll deal with you later. Begone from my sight."

With a wave of his hand, Asmoday was engulfed in a billowing cloud of darkness. It whirled up around him, drifted up through the roof, disappearing a moment later. Asmoday was gone with it. Wiping his moist hand on his suit, Baalth turned to stare at McConnell. After a few silent moments, he waved his hand once more and The Gray disappeared in a similar manner.

Done with the wizard, Baalth walked over to me. Poe and Marcus followed on his heels. The mentalist's face was a mask of neutrality, but Marcus couldn't help but grin at my predicament, chuckling as he stared down at me. He had to be loving this.

"I have to thank you, Frank. None of this would be possible without you." Baalth knelt down beside me. I tried to feel honored.

"Make the check out to the emergency room." I met his cool gaze. "You'll have to forgive me for not groveling at your feet like your pal, Asmoday, but I'm really not feeling up to it."

He smiled at me and winked. "I'll let it go, this time."

I rolled my eyes. "There's only room down here for one smart-ass and I was here first." I pulled myself up straighter so I could look him in the eyes with a semblance of confidence. "How'd you find us?"

He gestured toward the entrance. "It seems we have a friend in common, you and me."

I followed his gaze and my heart sank. Veronica stood at the doorway, Abraham by her side. The joy at seeing Abraham alive did nothing to temper the heartbreak I felt at learning just how much my ex-wife had betrayed me. I turned back to Baalth, unable to look at her.

"She tracked you to the Ninth where you disappeared. It didn't take much to figure out where you'd gotten off to from there." He shrugged. There was an unexpected compassion in his expression. "Sorry,

Frank. Never trust a succubus."

My eyes drifted around the devastated room, everywhere but at Baalth. I didn't want to look at his face for fear he'd see just how hurt I was. "So what now?"

"For the most part, life goes on," he answered with no trace of deception.

"No big bang, no end of the world?"

Baalth shook his head. "That doesn't serve my purpose, at this time. Maybe one day, but not now." He got to his feet, dusting his suit pants off. "Before he disappeared, your uncle left you something knowing you'd manage to find your way back down here one day."

I tried my best not to look surprised Baalth had known about mine and Lucifer's secret meetings. "I— I—"

He waved off my sputtering response. "You'll find it hidden beneath the altar." He motioned to the back of the room and made a face when he noticed the state of the sanctum, his focus having been elsewhere. "It's buried somewhere under that mess." He called for Veronica to release Abraham. "I'll see you soon."

His goons in tow, he headed for the exit, nodding to Abraham as they passed. At the archway where Veronica stood waiting, he called back to me. "Don't forget, Frank, you still owe me a favor." With that, he left, Poe and Marcus at his heels.

Veronica lingered for a moment and our eyes met. Even as angry as I was, I couldn't bring myself to look away. Though I probably imagined it, I thought I saw a trace of regret flicker across her face. She looked at me and raised her hand in a tentative wave, a half-assed attempt at a smile creeping to her lips. Unable to bear it, I turned away. I heard her footsteps a second later, scuffling off into the distance as Abraham arrived at my side. Hurt, I focused my attention on him.

"How you doing, Abe?"

He dropped down beside me, looking me over. "I'd have to say a slight bit better than you." He glanced around the room. "Katon, Scarlett?"

I shook my head, my eyes beginning to tear up. "They didn't make it. I'm sorry." I hung my head as Abraham placed a comforting hand on my shoulder, holding back his own tears.

"Don't be so quick to count us out, Trigg," a quiet voice spoke from nearby.

We both popped our heads up and looked to the wreckage. There, about twenty feet away, Katon lifted his scorched head from out of the detritus and looked at us with mild amusement. "It takes more than a little fire to put me in my casket for good." He climbed to his feet and though he spoke with confidence, his movement didn't reflect the same. He limped unsteadily over to us. His dark skin was ash black in places while rosy pink in others where the flames had gouged deep and new flesh was forming, his vampiric regeneration already kicking in. Though motley in appearance, with only a few strips of cloth keeping him from being naked, he looked as though he'd pull through okay.

"Have you seen Scarlett?"

He nodded. "She's back that way a bit." He thumbed over his shoulder. "I checked on her as I circled around to get to you. She's unconscious and hurt pretty bad, but she'll make it if we get her help soon."

Relief flooded my face. Abraham sighed, as obviously relieved as I was. His fears of our deaths allayed, he stood up, taking charge. "You have enough energy left to trigger the gate?"

I shrugged. "I'll find it."

Abraham smiled as warmly as I'd ever seen him. After a brief moment, he turned to Katon. "Gather Scarlett. We can take stock of things once we've returned to DRAC." He bent down and slipped beneath my shoulder, wrestling me to my feet.

He impressed me. Wounded as I was, I was dead weight, but he managed to get me up and support me without hurting himself. I smiled at him. I guess there was still some life left in the old guy after all.

Once Katon returned with Scarlett, hanging limp over the shoulder of his battered arm, we started toward the gate. Dragged along, I peered back behind us, saddened by the destruction of my uncle's sanctum.

"What about—"

Abraham cut me off. "It's not going anywhere, Frank." He said it with such certainty I couldn't help but let it go. "I'll send Katon back once I've got you two safely back at headquarters."

I was too tired to argue. I let him pull me along, my eyes fluttering with exhaustion over the slow haul. With all my adrenaline burnt off, I was crashing fast. At the gate, I could barely keep my eyes open. How I managed to trigger the portal is beyond me, but the next thing I knew I was being dumped into an uncomfortable bed in the emergency room at DRAC. Abraham stayed at my side until unconsciousness welled up to claim me. Dosed with painkillers, I drifted off on a cloud of flickering darkness.

Under the influence of the PK cocktail, I remember dreaming of my uncle. He stood upon a grassy hill as the sun rose majestically behind him. The beautiful reds and oranges shimmered above his head like a fiery halo. He smiled at me, its warmth brighter than the sun, before he turned and walked away to disappear from sight behind the rise.

I'd never seen him happier.

The Aftermath

A couple of weeks after Asmoday's bid to bring about Armageddon had gone south, things were just starting to get back to normal. Well, as normal as they could in a world full of wizards, demons, and angels.

The media had latched onto the destruction caused by Asmoday's fiends and McConnell's attempt on my life, but with the timely intervention of DRAC's Public Relations branch, a squad of aggressive mentalists, what had been front page news turned into fodder for the tabloids. Dismissed by all but the most dedicated of conspiracy theorists, the near end of the world went pretty much unreported.

I'd moved into DRAC headquarters for the time being as I waited for my house to be rebuilt. Thanks to the rampage of Asmoday's pets, I wasn't alone. The place was seriously overcrowded. Many of the DRAC families whose homes were also destroyed had been squeezed in wherever they'd fit, spread out across all of the locations. Though there were a handful of headquarters, they really weren't built to accommodate that many people. I'd taken to sleeping on the couch in Abraham's office. While roomy and surprisingly comfortable, the old geezer was an early riser and I'd always been more of a get up at noon kinda guy. He was cramping what little style I had.

This morning, he strolled in at about six a.m., whistling happily, Rachelle bouncing along at his side. Knowing my sleep was at an end, I muttered a few unkind words under my breath and sat up to see what had gotten the old boy so worked up.

"Viagra prescription come in, Abe?"

He chuckled as Rachelle blushed while she went about flicking on the lights and powering up the computer.

"Something better has happened, Frank, something *much* better." He dropped down into his chair, a contented smile plastered on his face.

Rachelle sat beside him, quite closely I might add, an air of happiness about her. Abraham looked pleased with himself as well, but neither said anything.

"So, are you gonna tell me what's got you two pissing rainbows, or what?"

"It'd be easier to show you." He gestured to the office door.

Right then, as if on cue, it swung open. I glanced over and my jaw dropped as Rahim walked into the room, Katon at his elbow. Well, more like he limped slowly while leaning heavily on a cane, but you could call that walking. Either way, he was up and about, something none of us ever thought we'd see again.

After we'd returned to DRAC and Scarlett and I had been dropped off, Katon returned to Lucifer's sanctum. He'd dug through the mess around the altar and found what Baalth had said my uncle left for me. It was a letter as well as a small package. Katon brought them both to me.

He'd also managed to find Scarlett's sword, which he returned to her through a flurry of grateful kisses. She was beyond ecstatic. Her trusty demon slayer, Everto Trucido back in her hands, she took off in a flash to put it to use. She'd missed it so much.

Inside the package were two small vials of my uncle's blood. I think I cried when I saw them. In his letter, Lucifer wrote he'd figured I'd need more of it one day, given my penchant for getting into trouble, so he thought he'd provide a backup for the vials he'd already given me. And though I'd rejected the mantle of Anti-Christ, he knew one day I'd return to where I belonged. Hell.

I guess, in a way, he was right.

After Scarlett and I had ingested a few drops, we were as good as new. Rahim was another story though. Human, I had no idea if the blood would cure him or kill him. I left that choice up to him. A fighter to the core, he took a chance.

At first, we'd thought it had failed. Nothing had changed. The outlook remained bleak. But a week later, the doctors saw sudden improvement overnight. Out of nowhere, his shattered spine had begun to heal. Piece by piece it was reconstructing itself while the nerves sparked back to life with a vengeance. Despite the agonizing process, his body ravaged with pain, Rahim never once voiced a complaint. Through all the suffering, his smile never left his face.

Now, only two weeks after he'd been crippled, he came into Abraham's office under his own power. The smile was still there.

I pulled myself off the couch and went over to him, giving him a gentle hug. "Good to see you up and about. You had us worried there for a bit."

He hugged me back fiercely. "I was worried myself." He broke the embrace and patted me gently on the cheek, his eyes bright. "Thank you." He limped his way to a chair near Abraham and Rachelle and dropped into it with caution.

Katon and I sat in the chairs in front of the desk, giving each other tired looks; he was ready to go to bed, I was ready to go back.

Down to business, Abraham ignored our grumbling as he read through a stack of files, his face serious. After going through a couple, he paused on one, his eyes narrowing. He took a deep breath and passed the folder to the wizard. No rest for the weary, apparently.

Rahim cracked it open and looked inside. After a moment, the ever-present smile dropped from his lips. He looked up at us, loosing a quiet sigh, his face grave.

"It seems we have a problem."

I groaned, slumping down in my chair. "When don't we?"

About the Author:
Tim Marquitz

Raised in far West Texas, Tim Marquitz has always been drawn to the perverse and terrifying. The words of Clive Barker, Stephen King, Jim Butcher, and Anne McCaffrey are what inspired Tim to write. Like his inspirations, he feels the need to find his own road, preferably a dark alley littered with the weird and unexpected, the violent and tragic, all tempered with the occasional laugh. Care to come along?

Myspace: www.myspace.com/mercylessfate
Facebook: http://www.facebook.com/profile.php?id=10000
0003603833&ref=profile
Twitter: www.twitter.com/marquitz
Web Page: www.tmarquitz.com

Also from Damnation Books:

Blanket of White
by Amy Grech
Horror short story collection

ISBN: 978-1-61572-018-7 ebook
ISBN: 978-1-61572-017-0 print

*Blanket of White*_True love knows no bounds.

Crosshairs A young boy learns the perils of hunting fare game firsthand.

*Prevention*_Murderous twins help their dear mother into and out of trouble.

*Perishables*_A nuclear fallout survivor finds sustenance in an unlikely place.

Plus two brand new stories by Amy Grech.

www.dAmnAtionBooks.com

DAMNATION
BOOKS

HORROR
DARK FANTASY
PARANORMALS
SCIENCE FICTION
THRILLERS
EROTICA

EBOOK
digital
tRAde PAPERBACK

LaVergne, TN USA
12 October 2009
160677LV00001B/15/P